HOLY WAR
BOOK TEN OF
ABNER FORTIS, ISMC

P. A. Piatt

Theogony Books
Coinjock, NC

Copyright © 2024 by P. A. Piatt.

All rights reserved. No part of this publication may be reproduced, distributed or transmitted in any form or by any means, including photocopying, recording, or other electronic or mechanical methods, without the prior written permission of the publisher, except in the case of brief quotations embodied in critical reviews and certain other noncommercial uses permitted by copyright law. For permission requests, write to the publisher, addressed "Attention: Permissions Coordinator," at the address below.

Chris Kennedy/Theogony Books
1097 Waterlily Rd.
Coinjock, NC 27923
https://chriskennedypublishing.com/

Publisher's Note: This is a work of fiction. Names, characters, places, and incidents are a product of the author's imagination. Locales and public names are sometimes used for atmospheric purposes. Any resemblance to actual people, living or dead, or to businesses, companies, events, institutions, or locales is completely coincidental.

Cover Design by Elartwyne Estole.

Ordering Information:
Quantity sales. Special discounts are available on quantity purchases by corporations, associations, and others. For details, contact the "Special Sales Department" at the address above.

Holy War/P. A. Piatt -- 1st ed.
ISBN: 979-8893190434

"It is impossible to fully comprehend the evil that would have conjured up such a cowardly and depraved assault upon thousands of innocent people."
Joseph Jacques Jean Chrétien, Canadian Prime Minister 1993-2003

"The wars of Israel were the only 'holy wars' in history... there can be no more wars of faith. The only way to overcome our enemy is by loving him."
Dietrich Bonhoeffer, *The Cost of Discipleship*

"Vengeance is a human right."
Gaspar Noé, *Irreversible*

* * * * *

DINLI

DINLI has many meanings to a Space Marine. It's the unofficial motto of the International Space Marine Corps, and it stands for "Do It, Not Like It."

Every Space Marine recruit has DINLI drilled into their head from the moment they arrive at Basic Training. Whatever they're ordered to do, they don't have to like it, they just have to do it. Crawl through stinking tidal mud? DINLI. Run countless miles with heavy packs? DINLI. Endure brutal punishment for minor mistakes? DINLI.

DINLI also refers to the illicit hootch the Space Marines brew wherever they deploy. From jungle planets like Pada-Pada, to the water-covered planets of the Felder Reach, and even on the barren, boulder-strewn deserts of Balfan-48. It might be a violation of Fleet Regulations to brew it, but every Marine drinks DINLI, from the lowest private to the most senior general.

DINLI is also the name of the ISMC mascot, a scowling bulldog with a cigar clamped between its massive jaws.

Finally, DINLI is a general-purpose expression about the grunt life. From announcing the birth of a new child to expressing disgust at receiving a freeze-dried ham and lima bean ration pack again, a Space Marine can expect one response from his comrades.

DINLI.

* * * * *

Prologue

The Master lay prostrate on the floor of his private chapel at Sanctuary, the spiritual center of the Kuiper Knighthood in the Free Sector. He murmured into the cool stone floor and was deep in thrall to the voices that whispered back. There was no time or place, no past or future. Only the voices.

Brother San Fehoko, dressed in a black smock with red piping denoting his position as aide to The Master, entered the chapel noiselessly. Although he hadn't made a sound, his presence changed the atmosphere in the small space. The Master remained still for a long moment as he adjusted to his return to the present. He had left strict instructions that he wasn't to be disturbed during his devotions, so he knew, whatever the reason, it was of critical importance.

"Why do you come, Brother?"

Fehoko approached and knelt next to The Master so he could speak in a whisper, as was the custom of the Knights.

"Most Holy One, I bring bad news. The Terrans destroyed *Colossus* at the Upper Hebrides."

The Master breathed deeply as the news pierced his soul. *Colossus*, former ISMC flagship and arsenal ship for weapons decommissioned during the force drawdown, had a key role in his plans for the rise of the Knighthood in the Free Sector. He'd intended her to be an important part of their continued growth.

"What of our brothers?"

"Destroyed, with the ship. Brother Nicaro…" Fehoko sobbed. He and Nicaro had grown close while they traveled to Sanctuary on the same ship, and Fehoko felt his loss deeply.

The Master didn't react, but the news wounded him. Several thousand brothers had been aboard *Colossus* as she sought to spread the True Faith throughout the system, and now they were gone.

"And the weapons?"

"We brought many weapons here before *Colossus* departed, and the slaver collected his before the Terran ship arrived."

"Then our business with the slaver is concluded."

The Master paused for so long that Fehoko thought he might have fallen asleep. Finally, he continued.

"Activate the travelers."

"Master, are you sure?"

The Master rolled over and stared at Fehoko. "Are you questioning me, Brother?"

Fehoko gasped and covered his face with his hands. "Never, Master."

"The UNT drove us from our homes and attacked us here in the Free Sector. We must punish them for their arrogance. They will never leave us in peace unless we teach them that they are not invulnerable."

"Yes, Master."

The Master rolled back over and put his cheek to the floor. "Go and do as I command."

* * * * *

Chapter One

"Praise to The Master. Praise to The Master."

Tom Julian repeated the phrase over and over as he drove his truck to the rest stop, and it comforted him. "Praise to The Master."

Julian's heart skipped a beat when he saw a tactical police vehicle parked on the highway shoulder ahead, but the vehicle was empty. He kept an eye on it until it disappeared from his rear view mirror, and he let the tension drain away with a deep breath.

"Praise to The Master."

The Master's word was law to a fervent devotee and knight errant like Julian, and he found comfort in it. Some of the other Knights privately questioned The Master's teachings, but Julian hung onto every word.

Julian had discovered an envelope inside his door that morning, as he had several times in the past. Inside, he found the usual sheet of instructions and a key to a truck parked down the street from his apartment. He figured it was another test of his devotion to the Knighthood.

His task was always the same: drive the truck to the designated destination, park it exactly as instructed, and leave the key inside. He always found the vehicle parked where the instructions indicated, and the destination was always a deserted rest stop on the beltway that bypassed crowded city streets. After he parked the truck, another

Kuiper Knight would bring him home. Julian didn't know what was beneath the tarp on the back of the truck, nor did he understand the purpose of his task, but the process never varied.

Julian downshifted as he approached the off ramp and rolled into the rest stop. It surprised him to see a row of identical trucks lined up where he normally parked. A man waved him to a stop.

"Welcome, Brother. Back it in at the end of the row, exactly within the lines."

Julian did as he was directed, and the man signaled him to stop. Julian shut off the truck and climbed out.

"Praise to The Master!" the man exclaimed with a big smile. He opened his arms wide, and the two men embraced. "Today is a glorious day."

"Praise to The Master," Julian said, still mystified about what was happening.

"Your ride is waiting, Brother." The man pointed to a bus parked near the entrance to the rest stop. "The others are waiting for you."

Others?

Julian boarded the bus and counted eleven other men.

"Praise to The Master!" they shouted in greeting.

Their enthusiasm was infectious, and Julian grinned. "Praise to The Master!" Something big was happening, and he couldn't contain his excitement.

Julian slid into an empty seat and watched as a group of men pulled the tarps off the backs of each truck. Each truck bed held four large pipes, and he stared as a rack on the first truck elevated the back ends of the pipes.

"What are they doing?" he asked.

Before they could figure it out, the men had elevated all the pipes. They all ran for a van parked near the rest stop exit.

Suddenly, plumes of smoke billowed from the backs of the tubes. Thick clouds of smoke blanketed the rest stop and engulfed the bus, and Julian heard rockets *whoosh* from the tubes.

Rockets!

"Praise to The Master!"

A brisk breeze blew the smoke away, and Julian saw the blackened remains of the launcher trucks. Some of them smoldered, lit by the backblast of the rockets. He saw a man standing by the van. The man raised his hand as if to wave farewell, and the bus exploded in a flash of fire and pain.

* * *

The excitement in the valley was palpable as nearly two hundred and fifty thousand children and adults gathered for day three of the Children's Global Peace Rally. The first two days had been a dizzying array of pop stars, celebrity guests, and child performers from every region of the United Nations of Terra. The Big Four was also represented, and it seemed that the animosity between the two major powers on Terra Earth had disappeared under the surge of goodwill generated by the rally.

The first musical act of the day was performing final sound checks when all eyes turned skyward at an odd buzzing sound that seemed to come from all directions. A sharp-eyed youngster pointed as a mass of black objects appeared above the mountains to the south. While the people stared, the objects grew larger, and the buzzing sound increased. One of the objects made a sharp dive and detonated on the valley floor several kilometers away. The ground trembled from the explosion, and the people realized something was very wrong. Some lucky few on the edges of the massive crowd escaped, but for those deep in the valley nearest the stage, there was no escape.

The objects, now easily recognizable as rockets, rained down on the valley. Explosions tore through the throngs of people and left gaping holes filled with the dead and dying. Thunderclaps echoed across the valley as plumes of black smoke rose into the clear blue sky.

To the people trapped in the valley, it felt like the attack went on for hours, but post-attack analysis showed that the last rocket landed 37 seconds after the first. Panicked crowds raced for the exits, and hundreds were crushed under the ensuing stampede.

A trio of tanker trucks parked along the main exit road erupted, and thousands of gallons of burning fuel washed across the area like a tidal wave from Hell. Dozens of vehicles erupted in flames and added to the panic as they exploded.

The screams of injured and terrified people drowned out the sirens of emergency vehicles, and it took thirty minutes for first responders to fight their way to the scene.

The Terra News Network (TNN) had 26 cameras spread throughout the valley to capture the sights and sounds of the Children's Global Peace Rally and beam them around the planet and to distant colonies. Instead, all of humankind watched the horror unfold in real time for eighteen minutes until TNN executives terminated the satellite feed.

No one would ever forget where they were on that horrific day.

* * *

Major Abner Fortis sat at his desk in the Intelligence, Surveillance, and Reconnaissance branch building and stared at his computer screen. Even though regulations specified the format and language to use in the letter, he'd struggled to write it.

I, MAJOR ABNER FORTIS, DO HEREBY RESIGN MY INTERNATIONAL SPACE MARINE CORPS COMMISSION, EFFECTIVE...

He leaned back in his chair and folded his hands behind his head. A surge of emotion welled up in his chest, and he blinked as the wave broke inside his mind.

When he joined the ISMC, the deal was simple: Serve for four years, and the ISMC would pay off his student loans. What he hadn't factored in was the price he would pay for that service. His osseointegrated right leg, along with his many other scars, was a physical testament to the dangers he'd faced. The emotional scars were another matter.

There was a quick tap at the door, and Corporal Edward Mathis stuck his head in.

"Major, quick! Turn on the news!"

Fortis switched his computer from word processing to the news broadcast, and a holographic newscaster appeared over his desk.

"To recap, an apparent rocket attack at the Children's Global Peace Rally in North America earlier this morning killed thousands of rally-goers and caused massive damage..."

Fortis and Mathis exchanged shocked glances as the newscaster went through what was known so far about the attack. The gut-wrenching images of rockets slamming into the crowd, and the dazed and wounded survivors stumbling away from the carnage, bloodied and torn, burned into Fortis' mind.

"Who would do this, sir?"

Fortis could only shake his head in shock and disbelief.

* * *

"One hundred and ten thousand."

UNT President Kofi Okoye hammered his fists on the conference table as he jumped to his feet.

"ONE HUNDRED AND TEN THOUSAND!"

He kicked his chair away, and it tumbled into the corner.

"Who did this?"

The cabinet ministers gathered around the table in the UNT Grand Council Building in Lviv kept their eyes down on the papers in front of them. Most were idealistic policy wonks, adept at crunching numbers and nuancing political positions. They'd faced many administrative crises together since Okoye's election, but the terrorist attack on the Children's Global Peace Rally three days earlier was beyond anything they could comprehend, much less deal with.

Minister of Defense Marjorie Brooks-Green, known as MBG to friends and foes alike, waited in silence with the rest of the cabinet. She knew none of them had the answers that Okoye needed.

Okoye pointed to one of the men near the head of the table. "Minister Herbig, you're the Interior minister. Who's responsible for this attack?"

Finian Herbig, a sallow-faced man with a long neck and copper-colored hair that stuck to his head like a pile of rusty steel wool, let out a nervous squeak and fumbled with the stack of folders in front of him.

"Uh, Mr. President, at this time, uh, we haven't reached any conclusions. The tac police, uh, well…" His voice faded away under Okoye's withering glare.

Everyone present knew Herbig had been foisted on the Okoye government because of his father's influence. The Interior Ministry seemed like the safest place for someone with his lack of abilities—until terrorists committed mass murder.

"So you don't know?"

Herbig's face flushed an unnatural shade of yellowish red as his mouth opened and closed like a newly landed fish. For a long moment, MBG thought he might vomit on the conference table. He swallowed hard and managed to find his voice.

"Sir, the obvious perpetrators are the Kuiper Knights, but we haven't confirmed that yet."

"Mr. President, if I may?" MBG waved her hand and fluttered her fingers.

"Yes, Minister, go ahead."

"As you know, my ministry has been working with Minister Herbig's people to process the launch site. They've identified twelve vehicles, with four launchers per vehicle, for a total of forty-eight rockets. This total coincides with the thirty-five explosions recorded at the rally, and thirteen other impacts that we believe were weapon failures. One of them didn't detonate, and we've analyzed the weapon.

"It has a simple pulsejet engine and a crude navigation system. The warhead is two hundred kilos of commercial-grade explosives and a contact fuse. The technology is hundreds of years old, and it's not a precision strike weapon. An average high school student could have designed and built them."

"Thank you for that information, but it doesn't answer my question. Who's responsible for this attack?"

"Almost anyone could be, Mr. President. Angry divvies. African separatists. I even heard a theory that a cabal within the Big Four did it as a false flag operation. There are many actors who *could* be involved, but if I were a gambler, I'd put my credits on the Kuiper Knights. They have a presence here on Terra Earth, they're fanatical enough to commit a horror like this, and they've made statements about seeking vengeance for *Colossus*.

"In addition to assisting Minister Herbig, I've directed my people to focus on the Kuiper Knights until their involvement is proven or disproven."

"On this side of the Freedom Jump Gate, I hope."

Brooks-Green blinked but didn't otherwise react to Okoye's pointed barb.

Bastard.

"Of course, Mr. President."

Okoye sat down. "Unless anyone has anything to add, that's it for now. We'll reconvene in six hours, and somebody better have something for me at that time. Thank you."

As the cabinet ministers filed out the door, Herbig grabbed Brooks-Green by the sleeve.

"What the hell, Marjorie? I had all that information. I was going to give it to the president."

MBG gave Herbig a cool look. "Then why didn't you, Fin? You had his attention, and you fumble-fucked around with your papers instead."

"Minister Brooks-Green, would you stay behind?" President Okoye called.

She winked at Herbig and turned back to the president.

"Of course, sir. My pleasure."

After another minute, the only cabinet members in the conference room were MBG, Vice President Deshan Bhatt, and Eryk Cruz, Okoye's chief of staff. They gathered at the end of the table next to Okoye.

"You seem very certain about the Kuiper Knights," Okoye said. "That's unlike you. What do you know that you haven't shared?"

MBG smiled. "You don't miss much, do you?" She looked at each man in turn. "What I'm about to tell you must remain within this room. The source is so sensitive that if it's revealed that we're aware of its existence, it will disappear."

The three men nodded.

"Agreed, Minister," Okoye said. "Please continue."

"Two days ago, the Special Signals Service discovered a secret communications channel between Terra Earth and the Freedom Jump Gate. They haven't managed to decrypt all the traffic yet, but indications are that it belongs to the Kuiper Knights. Thus far, we haven't observed any specific references to the attack, but there's been a lot of traffic back and forth, with congratulatory messages about someone called 'the travelers.' It's no great leap of logic to conclude that they were involved in the attack."

"Where does the channel originate?"

"Regretfully, MoD has no assets to track it beyond the jump gate."

It was Okoye's turn to blink.

Take that, you prick.

"Touché, Minister."

They traded smiles, and the tension that existed between the two evaporated.

"I appreciate you working with Minister Herbig. He's without a doubt the least capable Interior minister the UNT has ever had, and the task of investigating this disaster is well beyond his limited abilities. That said, we must use all available resources to identify the perpetrators and bring them to justice."

"I'm happy to help in any way I can, Mr. President."

"Good. Forget about Herbig. Find the Kuiper Knights and kill them all."

MBG's eyes widened in surprise. "Sir?"

"You heard me. Bring me a plan for how we can find them and kill them. Every single one of them. A hundred and ten thousand Terrans deserve justice."

Okoye's aide slid a folder across the table to MBG.

"That's an Executive Directive that gives MoD full authority to pursue the Kuiper Knights wherever they go, including the Free Sector."

"What about the Big Four, sir?"

"The Big Four are party to this directive. The terrorists murdered many of their citizens, too, and they've agreed to suspend NUMFA until the Knights are eradicated."

NUMFA, the Non-Use of Military Force Agreement, was an agreement between the UNT and the Big Four that gave UNT citizens unfettered access to the Free Sector in exchange for a promise by the UNT to never send military forces through the Freedom Jump Gate. Both sides had honored NUMFA until the former director of operations for the UNT General Staff had ordered Fleet destroyer *Comte de Barras* to jump through the gate and destroy the former flagship *Colossus*, which the Kuiper Knights had hijacked. The resulting tensions had pushed UNT/Big Four relations to the breaking point.

"If NUMFA is suspended, does that mean we'll drop the charges against Generals Boudreaux and Anders?"

The president shook his head. "They violated the agreement before it was suspended."

"For the same reason it's now suspended. To destroy the Kuiper Knights."

"Regardless of what happened afterward, they could have triggered a war with their actions. A message must be sent that orders are to be obeyed, Minister. I think we're too far down that road to turn back now. I'm inclined to leave it to the military legal system to decide their fate, and I promise I'll abide by whatever the tribunal decides."

Okoye and MBG locked eyes, and he gave a slight nod.

Nothing's going to happen to them.

MBG returned the nod. "As you wish, Mr. President."

"I'd like to hear your thoughts regarding how best to proceed against the Kuiper Knights as soon as possible. At the next update in six hours?"

"I'll be happy to bring you something by then, sir."

* * * * *

Chapter Two

The conference room was crowded as the cabinet reconvened six hours after the last meeting. Most of the attendees had nothing to contribute to the meeting, but word of Minister Herbig's embarrassing breakdown in front of the president had spread throughout the capital, and they wanted to see if Herbig would collapse again. Ladder-climbing was a blood sport in the UNT government, and there was nothing more satisfying than watching a competitor fail in spectacular fashion.

Eryk Cruz, the president's chief of staff, finally ordered all the ministers to identify one important aide to remain in the room and ordered the rest to wait outside. There was grumbling among the early arrivals who'd jockeyed for the best positions near the head of the table, but none dared protest too loud. Eryk Cruz was a skilled political assassin who wouldn't hesitate to ruin the career of anyone who earned his displeasure.

Fleet Admiral Albert Schein, chief of the UNT General Staff and commander of all UNT armed forces, had accompanied MBG. She'd waved him into a chair along the wall behind her and smiled inwardly at his apparent discomfort at being relegated to a back seat. In her opinion, it was good to remind the highest-ranking military officer that he was subordinate to the most junior minister in government.

All attendees rose as the door opened, and President Okoye entered. He took his place at the head of the table and waved everyone into their seats.

"I don't expect most of you to have anything significant to contribute," Okoye said as he fired a pointed look at Minister Herbig. "So, let's start with Minister Brooks-Green. Minister?"

MBG thought she saw a flicker of disappointment on Okoye's face as she smoothly reacted to his clumsy maneuver to catch her off-balance.

"Thank you, Mr. President. Since our last meeting, Admiral Schein and his staff have developed a plan to pursue and punish the perpetrators of the Peace Rally attack. Shall I go into the details here or wait for a more limited session?"

"All the details, please, considering sources and methods, Minister."

"We believe the Kuiper Knights are behind the attack. We know the Knights have a presence here on Terra Earth, and we've learned the location of and details about their headquarters in the Free Sector.

"The first phase of the plan involves using Minister Herbig's tac police to raid every known Kuiper Knight location here on Terra Earth, focused on the areas surrounding the Peace Rally and the ISMC headquarters in Kinshasa. My people will provide the intel and assist as required."

MBG saw Herbig's eyes widen with confusion. It was bad form to commit his ministry without consulting him beforehand, but she knew Herbig wasn't in a position to do anything but agree.

"Why Kinshasa?" Okoye asked.

"Many of the former Space Marines who joined the Kuiper Knights did so from Kinshasa, and there was a well-established organization that transported them to the Free Sector. We also believe this hub serves as a conduit of information to the Free Sector. It's imperative that we impede the flow of intelligence to the Knights before we enter the second phase of the plan."

"Which is?"

MBG motioned to Admiral Schein, who stood.

"Mr. President, in three days, we'll deploy 2nd Division to the Free Sector to seek and destroy known Kuiper Knighthood strongholds. The division is currently at 90 percent combat effectiveness and will achieve 95 percent before deploying."

"Do you believe one division will suffice? I heard the number of Kuiper Knights was upward of thirty thousand."

"Yes, sir, I've heard that number, but they're scattered across several planets in the Leavitt Peripheral and beyond, and they're armed with castoff weapons stolen from *Colossus*. My ordnance folks believe the failure rate of those weapons may be as high as 50 percent. Most of their colonies are incapable of accommodating large numbers of people, so we'll strike the population centers first and mop up the smaller colonies afterward."

Okoye looked from Schein to MBG. "2nd Division is capable to undertake this mission? Minister, only last month you testified in front of the Budget Committee, bemoaning military spending in the budget and the severe impact on military readiness." He held up a sheet of paper. "Here's a transcript of your testimony. 'If military spending isn't increased by 70 percent, Fleet readiness will decline to dangerous levels, and the ISMC will be reduced to one combat-ready division.' Military spending hasn't increased, yet it seems your opinion has changed. Minister, can you explain why?"

MBG's ears grew warm as blood flushed her face, and she fought the urge to fire back at the president. She didn't look around the table, but she sensed the smirks of the other cabinet ministers. Okoye may have scored points in a petty game, but she was an expert at the long game. She nodded.

"That was my testimony then, and that's my opinion now, Mr. President. However, in the face of an inadequate budget, the Defense Ministry realigned funding from lower priority requirements to readiness. Thanks to the tireless efforts of Admiral Schein and his people, 2nd Division was reconstituted in record time. Just in time, as it turns out."

"Where's 1st Division?"

MBG turned to Schein.

"Mr. President, 1st Division is scattered piecemeal throughout several sectors in response to requests for assistance by various colonies to deal with bugs, pirates, and other hazards. Given the time necessary for those elements to disengage from their current tasking and form up, Minister Brooks-Green ordered the rapid reconstitution of 2nd Division."

The president, either satisfied with their answers or bored with the game of tripping MBG up, turned to Minister Herbig.

"Minister Herbig, is the Interior Ministry ready to execute your phase of the plan? Are you able to meet your responsibilities within the three-day window as briefed by Defense?"

MBG almost laughed aloud at Herbig's response. He must have decided that Okoye wouldn't address him, because he and his aide looked completely surprised by the sudden pivot. They fumbled and muttered for a full minute before Herbig answered.

"Sir, uh, yes, we can achieve those goals within three days." He shot a narrow-eyed look at MBG. "Provided the Defense Ministry is ready to deliver the promised support."

"My people are standing by to provide whatever assistance you need, Minister," MBG replied.

"That settles it. Commence Phase One immediately, and three days from now, deploy 2nd Division." Okoye stood up, and everyone followed suit. "I don't need to remind all of you that what we've discussed here must not become public knowledge. This plan requires absolute secrecy to achieve surprise, and it's incumbent on all of us to keep it confidential."

MBG watched as meeting attendees filtered out of the room, and she scowled when she saw Herbig in the lead.

Probably looking for the first microphone to make a statement.

Admiral Schein stepped up next to her.

"Ma'am, Fleet Intelligence has been in contact with the tac police, and they're standing by to execute the raids as soon as Minister Herbig gives the order."

MBG turned and smiled. "Let's not waste any time, Admiral. Conduct the raids as soon as possible, and then let's focus on getting 2nd Division into space."

* * *

The next day, Fortis paged through the messages in his queue, looking for anything new on the Global Peace Rally attack. With General Anders incommunicado after his arrest for the *Comte de Barras* incident, Fortis was in an information vacuum. He thought about scanning open-source news programming, but it was less accurate than even the occasional update through official ISMC channels.

Fleet Admiral Albert Schein, chief of the UNT General Staff, had issued an alert to all UNT military forces to prepare for action on short notice, and speculation about what that meant was rampant. He'd also issued a deployment warning order to the newly reestablished 2nd Division, which set the entire ISMC base in Kinshasa buzzing with excitement. When he'd first heard the news, Fortis placed a call to Schein's office, looking for guidance for the ISR branch, but he hadn't made it past the receptionist. He'd been waiting ever since.

Just as he logged out, someone rapped on his office door, and a familiar face peeked in.

"Major Abner Fortis?"

Major Holly Markovsky from ISMC Manpower entered. Since his return to Kinshasa, Fortis and Markovsky had developed a casually intimate relationship.

"Hi, Holly." Fortis flashed a sheepish grin and gestured at his desk. "I wasn't expecting company, or I would have cleaned up."

"That's not necessary, Major." The door swung wide open, and he saw she was accompanied by two burly ISMC sergeants wearing military police armbands. "This isn't a social visit."

Markovsky's formal manner and the presence of the MPs surprised Fortis. Before he could speak, she opened a folder and began to read.

"By order of the chief of the UNT General Staff, the ISR branch is hereby disbanded, effective immediately. All personnel are to vacate the headquarters, taking with them only those items deemed personal property. Signed, Fleet Admiral Albert Schein."

She passed the paper to Fortis, and his eyebrows knotted as he read it.

Disbanded?

"I don't understand. What am I supposed to do with all this stuff?"

Major Markovsky shrugged.

"The sergeants are here to ensure that all government property remains in the building. I understand you're living in the other wing?"

Fortis nodded. She knew where he lived, since she'd been there two nights ago.

"At this time, we'll accompany you to your quarters. You'll be allowed to pack only your personal property. Make sure you get everything, because once you leave the building, you won't be permitted reentry."

Fortis wobbled on wooden legs as he followed Markovsky across the quarterdeck and into the berthing wing. He struggled to remain calm and tried to ignore the looming presence of the MPs close behind him as he unlocked his door.

"Do you need help packing, Major?" Markovsky asked.

"No, I don't have much. Uniforms, mostly."

"Sergeants, that'll be all. Stand by on the quarterdeck."

"Yes, ma'am."

The MPs left the room, and Fortis had the sudden feeling that he could breathe again.

"Can you tell me what's going on?" Fortis asked as he stuffed his things into his duffel. As usual, the majority of his stuff was uniforms and other ISMC gear.

"Have you seen the news this morning?"

"No." Fortis clipped the shoulder strap on his duffel and retrieved his dress uniform bag from the closet. "I try not to watch the news on an empty stomach. It ruins my appetite."

"Charges have been filed against Generals Boudreaux and Anders, and they decided to shut down the ISR permanently."

"That's why you brought the MPs? I'm under arrest?"

"No, of course not. I brought them in case you… well… *disagreed* with this."

Fortis shrugged. "DINLI."

He checked all the drawers and shelves, but they were empty. "I'm ready. What now?"

"Now we go outside."

When they were on the front sidewalk, Markovsky handed Fortis an envelope.

"These are your orders, signed by the head of Manpower. Tomorrow morning, you'll report to 2nd Division, 1st Regiment, for duty as commanding officer, 2nd Battalion. Congratulations."

The orders stunned Fortis. "Battalion command? I don't, I mean, how? Why me?"

"2nd Battalion is scheduled to deploy in two days as part of 2nd Division. They need a CO, you're an infantry officer, and you meet all the requirements of command. Most importantly, you're available."

Fortis couldn't keep the surprise from his face.

"Don't look so disappointed, Abner. You've been pushing for an infantry command for a long time, and now you have it."

"I'm not disappointed, I'm astounded. An infantry command is the last thing I expected."

"Needs of the service. First thing tomorrow morning. Don't be late."

Fortis looked around and saw the MPs were out of earshot.

"Are you busy tonight?"

Markovsky shook her head.

"Sorry, lover. It's been fun, but I'm not looking to be the girl back home. Go to war, and we'll pick it up again when you get back."

Fortis stared as Markovsky and the MPs climbed into a waiting vehicle. He shouldered his duffel, and with the uniform bag in the other hand, started for the main gate to catch a taxi to Ystremski's apartment.

* * * * *

Chapter Three

As part of Gunnery Sergeant Petr Ystremski's clandestine mission to infiltrate the Kuiper Knights and locate *Colossus*, General Anders had arranged for the ISMC to discharge, or divvie, Ystremski as part of his cover story. His family moved to North America, and Ystremski had moved into a run-down apartment in downtown Kinshasa.

Since Ystremski's return to Terra Earth, he'd been living in the apartment as he struggled with the ISMC to reinstate him. Without Anders to confirm the mission, Manpower refused to believe his story, and Ystremski had made little headway in his struggle.

Ystremski greeted Fortis when he knocked on the door. "Hey, stranger." He looked at Fortis's bags. "You moving in?"

"Just for tonight." Fortis gestured to the lumpy sofa. "Where's Sam?"

"He's out somewhere. Probably scouting Gunny Pete's again."

Sam Hart was the retired ISMC corpsman Ystremski had adopted to look after the apartment while he was gone. Since Ystremski's return, he and Hart had come up with a plan to purchase and reopen Gunny Pete's, an old-school dive bar and epicenter of off-base ISMC social life that had closed following the military drawdown.

"Still dreaming about that place, eh?"

"Yeah, but it's okay. It keeps him sober most of the day, so that's a good thing. What's your story?"

Fortis told Ystremski about his morning. "I'm supposed to report to 2nd Division first thing tomorrow morning to command a battalion."

"You're such a lucky asshole," Ystremski said, and then he smiled. "Congratulations. I'm happy for you."

"Thank you. What about you? Any progress?"

"Hurry up and wait. I'm sure some numbnuts colonel in Manpower has my file sitting on his desk. I guess he's waiting for divine inspiration to get off his fat ass and deal with it."

"They filed charges against Boudreaux and Anders. I don't have any details, but it looks like they'll be out of the fight for a while."

Ystremski groaned. "That figures. Punish the best guys for having the balls to do what needed to be done and leave me in limbo. Do you think they're going to charge you with anything?"

"I doubt it. If they were going to, they would've arrested me instead of giving me a command."

"What's the latest on the attack? Have they figured out who did it?"

"2nd Division is deploying in two days, so somebody knows. They're not sharing the information, but I think it was the Kuiper Knights."

"Wouldn't surprise me. Crazy fuckers. Speaking of the Kuiper Knights, the tacs have been rounding them up all over the place. Shipping them off to a prison in the Canary Islands, I hear."

"Maybe I should turn you in?" Fortis said with a smile.

"Don't even joke like that, dickhead. I'll be lucky not to get scooped up by an overzealous tac squad before Manpower gets their shit together."

Just then, the apartment door opened, and Sam Hart entered.

"What the hell's going on in here?"

"We were just discussing how corpsmen are as worthless as a screen door on an airlock," Ystremski said. "What are you up to?"

"I went by Gunny Pete's again this morning," Hart said. "It's still for sale." He winked at Fortis. "Whaddya say, Major?"

Fortis and Ystremski traded amused looks.

"What would you do to the place if you owned it, Sam?"

"Not a fucking thing. Sweep the floors, change the sheets on the beds upstairs, and start slinging drinks."

"Do you think there are enough Space Marines left in Kinshasa to keep the place running?"

"Only one that matters. Me."

The trio had discussed reopening the iconic Space Marine watering hole several times. Hart calculated that it would only take five hundred thousand credits to purchase the building and get it up and running. Fortis was the obvious money man, since he'd had precious little time to spend any of his Space Marine salary or the pension he received as a winner of the *L'ordre de la Galanterie* on his cherry drop. The longer they talked about it, the more appealing the idea became to Fortis, especially since he'd planned to resign his ISMC commission and needed a job.

The attack on the Children's Global Peace Rally had changed everything.

* * *

Deep in a cave in the jungle-covered mountains that surrounded the Kuiper Knights' headquarters, known as Sanctuary, Bender stopped digging and leaned on his shovel to wipe the sweat out of his eyes.

"Bloody hell."

The humidity outside was stifling, but down here, it was almost unbearable. All around him, Kuiper Knights swung picks and shovels by the dim light of sputtering lanterns, burrowing deeper into the mountain in accordance with Brother Zerec's directions.

Bender was one of the first former Space Marines to join the Kuiper Knights after the ISMC divvied him. It was widely suspected that the Knights were involved in the Free Sector slave trade, and he'd figured joining would be a good chance to continue the search for his goddaughter. Instead, he'd been posted to the Knighthood's headquarters, where he'd been assigned to various construction projects.

"Who told you to stop digging, Brother?"

Bender turned and saw the red smock of a knight errant. The knights errant were the fanatical followers of The Master who received the most important assignments, like overseeing the excavation of the bunker complex. He straightened to his full height and towered over the smaller man.

"Just catching a breather, mate. It's hot work, y'know."

The knight errant's reaction to Bender was almost laughable. He was used to the submissive deference shown toward the knights errant, and Bender's response seemed to unnerve him.

"Yes, well, don't dally too long. We must keep to Brother Zerec's schedule."

The knight errant disappeared into the gloomy depths of the cave, and Bender sighed as he plunged his shovel deep into the dirt.

Wanker.

* * *

Aboard the converted crew transport vessel *Sun City No. 12*, orbiting on the far edge of the Leavitt Peripheral, Theo Leishman waited impatiently for the video call to synch and the encryption light to turn green. When the connection was made, The Leader appeared on his screen.

"Which one of you damned fools authorized the attack?"

The Leader blinked in surprise at the vehemence of Leishman's assault, and it took a long second for him to respond.

"That's a matter for the Knighthood, Mr. Leishman."

"We had an agreement!"

"Our agreement concluded when you took possession of the weapon. Our mutual obligation ended at that point."

"Do you understand what you've done?"

"The UNT destroyed our ship in the Free Sector, in contravention of the Non-Use of Military Force Agreement. We reminded them that they're not invulnerable."

"'Reminded them?' Are you insane? You murdered a hundred thousand people, including citizens of the Big Four. If they weren't angry before, they are now. Do you understand what's about to happen?"

"I didn't know divination was one of your abilities, Mr. Leishman. That seems a bit mystical for a slaver."

Leishman ignored the barb.

"My sources report that the Big Four have suspended the NUMFA, and the UNT plans to deploy a division of Space Marines through the Freedom Gate."

The Leader scoffed. "We have many Knights who were former Space Marines—more than a mere division—and we have their weapons, too."

Leishman fought back the anger rising in his chest. "They aren't just coming for you. They're coming after anyone who had anything to do with the attack, including me."

"You worry too much, Mr. Leishman. We're protected by the True Faith, as we always have been. The soulless minions of the UNT will fall under our swords, as they have so many times in the past."

"We'll see about that."

Leishman stabbed the disconnect button, and The Leader's face disappeared from his screen. He swiveled to face Mark Bowen, his assistant, who was seated just off camera next to him.

"That crazy old bastard doesn't understand the danger he's put us all in."

Bowen shrugged. "He's a fanatic. Fanatics view the world differently than we do. We seek to maximize profits while minimizing risk. For him and his followers, it's about self-actualization, achieving inner peace, or whatever the fuck they're seeking, and the risks be damned. What kind of maniac attacks innocent civilians?"

Leishman glared at Bowen. Leishman's criminal empire was built on the slave trade, which he fed by attacking colonies and transport ships.

Bowen blushed and laughed nervously. "I didn't mean it like that."

Leishman waited an extra second before he spoke.

"The Leader is delusional if he thinks all his former Space Marines will remain loyal to him when the fighting begins. It was one thing for them to recite some mumbo-jumbo in order to get a job. It's quite another when their leader's committed mass murder, and the weight of a division of Space Marines is about to drop on them. I wouldn't be surprised if some of them grab the crazy bastard and try to work out a deal with the UNT.

"If we're lucky, the Space Marines will kill The Leader and all the Knights who know about our transaction before they get a chance to rat us out. It won't look good if they discover we're hauling around proof positive that we were involved with *Colossus*."

"What of the Space Marines?"

"The last report I received said deployment was 'imminent,' meaning days, not weeks. They're sending 2nd Division."

"Do we have anyone in 2nd Division?"

Leishman shook his head. "Not yet. They divvied all our reliable people, and they've been shuffling the rest around to fill up 2nd Division. Our source in Kinshasa will inform us when they deploy, but that's the best we're going to get."

He leaned back in his chair and considered the options. Leishman had no use for the Mark-654 High Yield Ground Penetrating Munition, or HYGPM, the Kuiper Knights had given him in exchange for the intelligence that enabled them to hijack *Colossus*. However, in the shadowy world where he did business, someone would pay him dearly for a weapon so powerful it had earned the nickname Planet Killer.

The biggest challenge was where to store such a weapon. As a slaver, he didn't maintain a main operating base, and it would've been foolish to hide the weapon there if he did. Somebody would try to steal it, or the UNT would show up to take it back by force.

He didn't want to carry the weapon, either. *Sun City No. 12* was well armed to repel pirate attacks, but even Leishman's fearsome reputation couldn't deter them all. Pirates willingly took insane risks, and someday a band of them might decide that attacking Leishman to steal the weapon was worth it.

The most important consideration for not carrying the HYGPM was that it could serve as a bargaining chip if the UNT managed to capture Leishman. They might hate him and how he made a living, but he doubted the government could resist the temptation to recover the weapon in exchange for his freedom.

He sat up.

"Let's find a place to stash the bomb and get the hell out of this sector. When 2nd Division blows the shit out of the Kuiper Knights, I don't want to be collateral damage."

* * * * *

Chapter Four

Major Abner Fortis drew more than the usual looks warranted by a major as he walked across the base to the 2nd Division headquarters area. The war bond tour years earlier had made him a minor celebrity in the Corps, but his involvement in the recent Free Sector mission had put him on the Space Marine map. He got plenty of stares and doubletakes, but he ignored it all.

Fortis got a strange, almost unsettled feeling as he approached the headquarters. The buildings were as he remembered, but he noticed a marked difference in the vibe of the area as he returned the salutes of those who crossed his path. The Space Marines he encountered actually looked like they were headed somewhere instead of the usual skylarking. A division of five thousand Space Marines, many of them still teenagers, should've had the NCOs busy riding herd on them, but there was none of that.

He presented himself to the 1st Regiment desk watch, and the corporal escorted him to the deputy commander's office. COL J. WEISS read the hand-lettered sign taped to the door. The watch tapped on the door and opened it.

"Colonel, Major Fortis is here."

Fortis entered, stopped the prescribed two paces from the colonel's desk, and saluted.

"Major Abner Fortis, reporting as ordered, sir."

Weiss returned his salute. "Thank you, Corporal. That's all." He stuck out his hand, and Fortis shook it.

"Have a seat, Major." Weiss gestured to the piles of paper spread across his desk. "I apologize for the mess, but the Corps hasn't seen fit to fill my clerk billet yet."

Weiss was a nondescript officer of medium build, plain faced, with wispy brown hair trimmed tight on the sides and combed carefully on top. Fortis' first impression was of a manager who would've been more at home in a Terran accounting firm.

Fortis nodded but said nothing.

"We're certainly glad to have you aboard. The drawdown and rebuilding of 2nd Division has created a lot of turmoil, and the addition of experienced officers will help alleviate some of it. Anyway—" Weiss stood, and Fortis followed suit "—let's go meet the boss."

The colonel led Fortis across the hall to a door marked 1ST REGIMENT COMMANDING OFFICER.

"Colonel Feliz only just took command," Weiss said in a low voice. "We haven't even had time to make a sign for his door." He tapped and entered. "Major Fortis is here, sir."

Fortis repeated his report, and Feliz broke into a wide grin as he stood and offered his hand.

"Welcome aboard, Major. Please, sit down. General Anders speaks highly of you."

Feliz was a head taller than Fortis, with a spare frame and a gleaming bald head. The skin on his face was drawn tight over his cheekbones and chin, which gave him a skeletal appearance. A pencil-thin moustache hovered between a narrow nose and thin upper lip.

"I've had the pleasure of serving with the general several times over my career," Fortis said.

"I was two years behind him at Fleet Academy, and we've stayed in touch. Do you keep in touch with your classmates, Major?"

Weiss cleared his throat.

"I didn't attend Fleet Academy, sir. I was a direct accession after *Imperio* disappeared."

"Ah, shit." Feliz fumbled with a folder on his desk as his ears reddened. "Of course. I saw that in your record."

Before Fortis could respond, Weiss spoke up.

"Colonel, we should leave soon if we want to make the briefing on time."

"You're right." Feliz stood and ushered Fortis to the door. "You got here just in time for the all-officer briefing with General Moreno. Maybe we'll finally be told where we're going and what we'll be doing."

* * *

"Attention on deck!"

The officers of ISMC 2nd Division rose as one and stood at attention as Major General Nola Moreno strode across the briefing theater stage to the waiting podium. She looked out over the group for a long second before she waved them into their seats.

"Carry on, Marines."

A holograph of a large smear of stars in a spiral formation appeared above the stage behind the general.

"This is Libertas Centralis, the primary galaxy in the Free Sector. As you can see, it's a spiral galaxy, much like our own Milky Way, except it lacks the band of stars across the center. I don't know what that means, and I don't give a shit, either. What I do know is, I command a division of killers, and there are some fuckers in the Free Sector that need killing."

Mild laughter rippled across the theater. Fortis smiled and nodded, but the tough talk didn't impress him. He'd heard enough of it in his career to know that boasting usually showed either overconfidence or uncertainty. Either one usually led to a lot of dead Space Marines.

"There are a lot of new faces here today, mine included. Many of you are combat veterans, and all of you are here because you're the best. Every one of you lost someone or knows somebody who lost someone in the Peace Rally attack. President Okoye has given us the task—no, the honor—of seeking out and destroying the evildoers responsible for this atrocity. Let me be clear. We're going to the Free Sector to kill them.

"One final point before I turn this over to Colonel Kim and the division operations staff. I'm aware that there are former comrades of ours among the Kuiper Knights. They won't receive any special consideration from us. They chose to join the terrorists, and we'll make them pay for that decision. If there's any officer here who doesn't think she or he can carry out their assigned duties, this is your chance to opt out of this mission. If you leave now, you'll be separated from the Corps without consequence. If you stay, I expect your complete loyalty and adherence to the plan. Are there any questions?"

Many of the officers looked around to see if anyone accepted the general's offer. Fortis stared straight ahead; if there were officers unwilling to do their duty, they weren't his concern.

After a pregnant pause, Moreno gestured to a colonel who stood beside her. "This is Colonel Kim, 2nd Division operations officer. He's here to cover the strategic plan. Individual regiment and company missions will be briefed by their respective chains of command."

Kim stepped up to the podium. "Thank you, General." He opened his arms wide as if welcoming the audience. "Welcome to Operation Grand Slam."

The holo zoomed in on a small section of the galaxy.

"This is the Leavitt Peripheral, a cluster of habitable planets on the edge of Libertas Centralis. We've conducted extensive intelligence collection in and around the Peripheral, and we've identified twelve main Kuiper Knight settlements."

A scattering of red dots appeared on the holo.

"We estimate that there are between twenty-five and thirty thousand Kuiper Knights spread unevenly across those twelve settlements."

There was some throat clearing and shifting in seats. Kim nodded.

"Thirty thousand is a daunting number, but they're dispersed over a wide area. They're armed with pulse weapons plundered from *Colossus*. We have intelligence reports that indicate many of those weapons are inoperable or functioning far below design specifications. They lack mech support and don't have aviation assets, either.

"Our plan is simple: Find them, fix them, and destroy them, using a series of near simultaneous attacks. Wreck their centers of power and don't give them a chance to breathe. Cut off their escape routes and pursue them until they're all dead or captured.

"Their headquarters, which they call Sanctuary, is located here, indicated by a red star. Sanctuary and two other settlements have spaceports capable of operating heavy lift spacecraft. The rest can only handle smaller passenger and cargo shuttles."

Three geometric shapes appeared on the holo over the red dots.

"We divided the Leavitt Peripheral into three sections, one for each of the three regiments. Since 2nd Regiment is the largest and has an aviation battalion, they're assigned to the center section, which includes six settlements. 1st Regiment has the section to the far left, and 3rd Regiment has the section to the far right.

"When ordered, 2nd Division will embark the flagship *Mammoth* and proceed through the Freedom Jump Gate to our mission jump-off position near the Leavitt Peripheral. Upon receipt of the final go order, *Mammoth* will follow a predetermined track through the Peripheral, dropping battalions and companies as planned. This will be a bump and dump; there's no time for fancy landing maneuvers. Speed and surprise are the keys to the operation.

"After all Space Marines are inserted, *Mammoth* will loiter in the vicinity and stand by for exfil." Kim looked out over the crowd. "Are there any questions?"

An officer seated in the second row stood up. Fortis couldn't see his face, but he could tell by his neat but faded utilities and gray crewcut that he was an experienced Space Marine.

"Colonel Dag Rolf, commander 2nd Regiment. How long do you expect this operation to last? Will we receive logistical support?"

"We're still working out some of the details, Colonel, but you should plan on being self-sufficient for two weeks."

"*Two weeks?* That's a helluva long time to operate without a log hit."

General Moreno stood up.

"Colonel Rolf, my staff is doing everything possible to reconstitute capabilities that were lost due to the recent drawdown. We've necessarily focused on warfighting, but I can assure you that logistics are of a critical concern. If you'd like, I'll be happy to discuss this further with you offline."

"Yes, ma'am. Thank you."

When Rolf sat down, Fortis felt a palpable change in the atmosphere of the briefing theater. Even the greenest officers knew the importance of logistics. Individual Space Marines could carry two weeks-worth of pig squares and enough pulse weapon batteries for a few days of intense fighting, but everything else they might need had to be provided by the supply system. A division-sized operation required a massive logistics chain, and a dispersed operation like the one Colonel Kim had briefed would add extra strain on the system.

"If there are no further questions or comments, that concludes our brief. Regiment commanders, take charge and prepare your troops for embarkation. I signed the embarkation order just before we assembled here. You have twenty-four hours before the first shuttles depart from the spaceport."

* * *

Fortis followed Feliz, Weiss, and another two dozen officers to a meeting room back at 1st Regiment's headquarters building.

"You all heard the same thing I did," Colonel Feliz said. "Is there anything that'll prevent this regiment from meeting the twenty-four-hour deadline?"

No one spoke up.

"Good. Deputy, take charge and get them moving. I want a readiness report every six hours."

"Yes, sir," Weiss said as Feliz turned and left the room.

Weiss gestured to Fortis. "This is Major Abner Fortis. He's taking over 2nd Battalion. We don't have time for the usual getting-to-know-you festivities, but I'm sure you'll have plenty of time on our way to the Leavitt Peripheral for that. Battalion commanders, you have your deployment checklists. The CO wants a report from me in six hours, so I want a report from you in five. Get it done."

Some of the officers gathered around Fortis as the others headed for their battalion buildings. A broad-shouldered black captain with a tired look in his eyes stuck his hand out.

"I'm Captain Tindal Stone, Bravo Company CO, and acting 2nd Battalion XO, and I'm damned glad to see you."

The rest of the officers smiled and nodded.

"Why are you dual-hatted as XO? Where's the officer who's supposed to be the XO?"

"That's a good question, Major. The next time you talk to the general, ask her."

Stone's response puzzled Fortis. Another captain stepped forward.

"Captain Ivan Litvinenko, Battalion Ops/Intel. The former XO was reassigned to serve on the general's staff. It made more sense for the division to have an assistant logistics officer than for 2nd Battalion to have an XO. DINLI."

"Yeah, DINLI indeed." Fortis surveyed the group. "Where's the first sergeant? In fact, where are all the sergeants? Don't tell me the general took them, too."

Stone smiled. "No, sir, sergeants we have." He looked over his shoulder. "Colonel Weiss has some old-fashioned ideas about relations between officers and enlisted Space Marines. He doesn't like them to come to these things."

"Who's the first sergeant?"

"That's another of those dual-hatted situations," said a female warrant officer in mech crew coveralls. "I'm Warrant Sandra Loren, CO of Charlie Company. Master Sergeant Dominguez, my XO and maintenance chief, has been doing his job and riding herd on the battalion as first sergeant at the same time."

"So no first sergeant?"

"No, sir. We were told there was one on the way almost a year ago, but nothing yet."

"Huh. Well, I love sergeants. They've been saving my ass since my cherry drop, and they're going to be part of everything we do, whether the colonel likes it or not." He looked around the group. "I owe Colonel Weiss a readiness report in five hours. What's our status?"

"We're short a couple bodies in the battalion staff, but Alpha and Bravo deployment checklists are complete," Stone said. "Charlie Company is another story."

Fortis looked at Loren. "What's up with the mechs?"

Loren threw up her hands in disgust. "Parts. It's always fucking parts. Daisy Two's been down for three months with a major fault in the main pulse cannon power generator. The same goddamn problem we've been having since they upgraded the power plant four years ago. We order the replacement part, it gets put on backorder, and then the requisition disappears."

A ruddy faced, ginger-haired first lieutenant raised his hand.

"Sir, Lieutenant Aiden Fuller, Logistics officer. The warrant's right. I've been chasing the power generator through the system since the issue came up and have gotten nowhere. I've kicked it up to Regiment, but so far, nothing."

"How many mechs do we have?"

"Seven total, sir," Loren said. "One command, two recon, and four main battle. Daisy Two is one of the main battle mechs."

"That's it? Just four? I thought a mech company had ten main battle mechs."

Loren shrugged. "When they rebuilt this division, they originally designated 2nd Battalion as the regimental recon battalion, with no main battle mechs. 1st Battalion was a mechanized infantry battalion with all the mechs. Then somebody changed their mind, spread the mechs out across the regiment, and designated all three as mechanized infantry battalions. That changed again, and we became regular infantry battalions with a light mech company. 1st Battalion also has four main battle mechs, we have four, and 3rd has six main and three light battle mechs. It's way out of balance, brought to you by pencil pushers playing around on an org chart."

"All right. It's too late to change that now. At the brief, they said it would be two weeks before we could expect a log hit, so tell your Marines to plan on two months. Lieutenant Fuller, that's beans, bullets, and boots for four hundred. For the rest of you, go back over your checklists and look for the last-minute 'oh shits.' Talk to your troops and make sure they're ready. Most of them have probably deployed before, so they should know what's expected. Big or small, the only problems we can't solve are the ones we don't know about. Don't be afraid to bring them up if need be. Does anyone have any questions?"

Heads shook around the group.

"Good. Let's link up in the battalion office in four and a half hours so I can give Colonel Weiss his report."

The group broke up. The whole time they'd been gathered, a vaguely familiar female first lieutenant had stood at the back of the group, beaming at Fortis. She approached, and he gave her a puzzled look.

"Do I know you?"

Her face broke into a wide smile. "I'm First Lieutenant Ludana Vidic."

Fortis still couldn't place her.

"Ludana Vidic. I was on *Imperio*."

Realization dawned on Fortis, and he laughed aloud as they shook hands.

"Vidic! Of course. Now I remember you. What are you doing here? I mean, how?" He gestured at her Space Marine utilities. "The last time I saw you, you were a Fleet mechanic."

Vidic had been an enlisted crewmember aboard *Imperio*, the Fleet Academy training ship captured by slavers several years earlier. Fortis had led the rescue operation that ultimately freed the cadets and crew.

Vidic blushed. "When we got home, Colonel Anders recommended me for an appointment to Fleet Academy. It took a lot of work, but I graduated."

"That's fantastic. I'm glad to hear it. Are you in 2nd Battalion?"

Vidic nodded. "I'm your personnel and acting admin officer, sir."

"Well, we'll have plenty of time to talk, then. I don't mean to cut you off, but I have a lot to do." He chuckled. "We're deploying in less than twenty-four hours, in case you haven't heard. Are you ready?"

"Yes, sir. Personnel and Admin are good to go."

Just then, Captain Stone returned.

"Excuse me, Major. Do you have a few minutes?"

* * * * *

Chapter Five

Stone followed Fortis to the battalion commanding officer's office and closed the door behind them.

Fortis waved the captain into a chair. "What's on your mind, XO?" he asked with a smile.

"I want to get you up to speed on the battalion, sir."

"Okay, shoot."

"I don't know how much you know, so I'll start at the top. Our former CO, Seth McNeely, was a hovercopter pilot with 3rd Division at Maltaan. The Corps divvied him, but he appealed and won."

"No shit? I didn't think that was possible."

"McNeely found an obscure appendix to the Budget Realignment Act that allowed for appeals. He said they weren't happy when he was approved for reinstatement, but they had to let him back in. Of course, they got theirs in the end. He thought they'd assign him to a flying billet, but they reassigned him to command an infantry battalion instead."

"That figures. A pilot assigned to the infantry."

"McNeely was a good officer, but he wasn't cut out for infantry command. Weiss rode his ass all the time with the usual administrative nitpicking. It didn't help that the XO and first sergeant billets are vacant. I did what I could, but I have a company to lead, you know?"

"I'm sure you did your best."

"I—we did what we could to support him, but McNeely didn't do himself any favors. He butted heads with Weiss and made some public comments, too. I don't know how they do things in the aviation world, but you know how it is in the infantry. Shut up and DINLI."

"When did they fire McNeely?"

Stone scoffed. "They didn't. He got himself fired, and divvied, too. He went back into the BRA and found a section that gave division commanders the discretion to divvie personnel as they saw fit. He went to see General Moreno, and the next day he was gone."

"Damn."

"Anyway, I got formally dual-hatted as the XO, and we've been lurching along, with Weiss giving us extra attention."

"Why didn't Litvinenko get the XO hat? That would make more sense, since he's the operations officer, and he's already on battalion staff."

"Captain Litvinenko is a cherry, sir. No combat drops, and no combat experience, either."

"How do you make captain in the ISMC without any combat experience? He hasn't even been on a bug hunt?"

"I don't know the whole story, but he was with 7th Division orbiting Maltaan during the invasion before everyone went home."

All nine active ISMC divisions deployed for the invasion of Maltaan, but only 1st, 2nd, and 3rd Divisions dropped and saw combat. Maltaan resistance crumbled after less than a week of fighting, so the other six divisions of Space Marines returned to Terra Earth without seeing any action.

"Hmm. Okay. Anything else I should know?"

"Ace Williams, Alpha Company CO, is a stone-cold killer. He dropped on Maltaan with 1st Division as a sergeant and won a battlefield commission by shredding a bunch of Maltaani with his kukri. Ace eats, breathes, and sleeps the Corps, and he's not afraid of anything."

"I don't recall meeting him," Fortis said.

"He wasn't at the brief." Stone chuckled. "Weiss forbids him from attending anything General Moreno will be at because he has a way of asking awkward questions. Remember how Moreno responded to Colonel Rolf's question? Imagine that question coming from a captain. That's okay, though. He's got a capable XO in Lieutenant Orndorff."

"Good."

"In case you're ever in need of coffee, Orndorff is your gal. I don't think I've ever seen her without a mug in her hand, and it's real coffee, too. None of that ersatz shit from the chow hall."

"I like her already."

"Warrant Loren and Master Sergeant Dominguez have Charlie Company running like a machine, no pun intended. She likes to bitch about things and beat up on Lieutenant Fuller for her parts, but she's a solid mech commander."

"What about this part for Daisy Two? What's the real story?"

"Loren has a legit gripe about that one. I've personally submitted a requisition and carried it to regimental supply. New policy dictates that parts requisitions can only sit in the system for ninety days before they're closed, one way or another, and we have to resubmit. Apparently, the power generator she needs is manufactured on an as-needed basis with a six-month lead time."

Fortis shook his head. "The manufacturer probably has a warehouse full of half-built power generators they started to build and put on the shelf when the requisition was cancelled."

The pair laughed at the absurdity of the idea, but Fortis knew it probably wasn't far from the truth.

"I'll make the power generator a top priority," Fortis told Stone. "We don't have much time, but I'll do what I can. What about the rest of the staff?"

"I overhead that you know Vidic, sir?"

"Yeah, I do. I know her from *Imperio*."

Although the mission that had resulted in the rescue of the Fleet Academy cadets and crew aboard *Imperio* was an open secret, Fortis didn't elaborate on his role.

"She's young, but she's eager," Stone said. "Between her and Gunny Porter, the battalion communications NCO, they keep the staff running."

"What about Bravo Company? How are things there?"

Stone smiled. "The CO is a shameless tattletale, but he has a good XO in Lieutenant Tate. 2nd Battalion might have a couple personnel holes that need plugged, but we're in decent shape. I feel a lot better now that you're here. The whole division is that way, really. We've been thrown together without much planning, but I think one good field training exercise would work out all the kinks. Maybe Operation Grand Slam will do just that."

"Based on the brief we just had, we're in for more than a field training exercise. The people with knowledge of the Kuiper Knights think they're a pretty capable force, so we better work out the kinks most rikki-tik, or we might end up in trouble."

* * *

Fortis spent the next few hours looking into the status of the battalion staff. The two areas that most concerned him were Logistics and Medical.

Lieutenant Fuller and his supply sergeants scrambled to amass the two months of supplies Fortis directed, and it seemed to Fortis that the issue of the faulty main pulse cannon power generator had been forgotten.

Staff Sergeant Ezra Pope, the lead corpsman, was the polar opposite of the frantic lieutenant. He and the two corporals assigned to him were swapping stories when Fortis entered the Medical office. When Fortis questioned Pope about medical supplies and trauma kits, the sergeant seemed nonchalant.

"We're expecting to be in action," Fortis told him. "Perhaps as long as two months."

"Ah, no, sir. I heard two weeks," Pope replied.

"The general said that to 2nd Regiment. This is 2nd Battalion, 1st Regiment, and I said prepare for two months."

Pope got a hurt look on his face. "Where are we supposed to put all that stuff, sir? We can only carry so much."

"Just get it. Let me worry about how to move it."

As Fortis made his way through the staff, the absence of a full-time XO to oversee the administrivia of making the staff function was obvious everywhere he looked. He'd have to follow up on any direction he gave, which would take time away from his responsibilities as battalion commander.

The company commanders and battalion staff gathered at the appointed time and updated Fortis on their deployment preparations. There were no major changes, so Fortis told them to stand by while he went over to Regiment and reported to Colonel Weiss. He found Weiss at his desk, still surrounded by stacks of paper.

"Sir, 2nd Battalion is ready to deploy, with one major material issue, and two major personnel issues."

"What are your issues, Major?"

"One of four main battle mechs is combat ineffective due to a faulty main pulse cannon power generator. It's a long-standing supply issue."

Weiss sighed and pinched his nose between thumb and forefinger.

"Major Fortis, that issue has been up and down the chain many times over the past several weeks. I've told Captain Stone there simply aren't any spare parts available. What doesn't he understand about that?"

"Don't blame Stone, sir. I'm bringing it up again because my mechs are at 75 percent strength before we even drop."

"Okay, fine. It's noted. What other issues do you have?"

"The 2nd Battalion XO billet is vacant, which requires me to divert attention from my command responsibilities. It wouldn't be a major problem, except that I also don't have a full-time first sergeant, which further diverts my attention."

Weiss got a sour look on his face. "Are you telling me battalion command is too much for you, Major?"

"No, sir, that's not what I'm saying at all. Every command has billets that need to be filled, and 2nd Battalion is no different. I'm merely notifying you of critical manpower needs. We can deploy and fight without them."

"Very well, Major. Is there anything else?"

"What's the regimental policy toward liberty tonight? I need to go pack my duffle bag, and I'm sure there are other Space Marines in the same position. I'd like to knock them off until first thing tomorrow morning."

Weiss raised an eyebrow. "You're certain they'll be back in time?"

"No, sir, I'm not certain, but I know if I don't give them a chance to get their stuff in order and see their families, the temptation to go AWOL for a few hours tonight might be too much."

"They're your responsibility, Major. Do what you think is best, but make sure they understand there will be zero tolerance for stragglers in the morning. 1st Regiment is scheduled to depart for the spaceport at 1600 hours tomorrow. Keep that time to yourself for now, understand?"

"Yes, sir, will do."

Fortis returned to 2nd Battalion and his waiting officers.

"I briefed Colonel Weiss on our status. Unless you have an urgent need to keep people here, I'm putting down liberty call to expire at 0600 hours tomorrow. Remind them that our deployment isn't public knowledge, and stress to them that they need to be here and ready to go no later than 0600." He looked at Warrant Loren. "We'll revisit the part issue first thing in the morning and see what we can do about it. Does anyone have any questions?"

Nobody spoke up.

"Carry on."

* * *

When Fortis returned to Ystremski's apartment, he found Sam Hart snoring in his usual place on the couch, and Ystremski at the kitchen table with a drink in front of him.

"How was your first day at school, dear?" Ystremski raised his glass. "Did you make a lot of new friends?"

"Pretty much what you'd expect. We're deploying tomorrow, so it's a clusterfuck."

"Tomorrow?"

"I can neither confirm nor deny, but the rumor is that we're going to mete out justice to some fuckers who badly need it."

Ystremski scoffed. "Figures. Look what came for me today."

He pushed a letter over to Fortis. It was from ISMC Manpower, notifying Ystremski that his case was still pending appeal, and giving themselves another ninety days to complete their evaluation.

"What the fuck? How hard is it to call General Anders and get the story?"

Ystremski tossed back the last of his drink and reached for the bottle. "DINLI." He poured a healthy slug and pushed the glass over to Fortis. "You know the worst part of it? I'm going to miss the show in the Free Sector. Even if they reinstated me tomorrow, it would take too long to get orders before 2nd Division deploys."

Fortis tossed back the drink and winced as he slid the glass back across the table.

"So come with me."

Ystremski stopped in mid pour.

"What?"

"Yeah, come with me. I need a first sergeant, and you're the perfect guy for the job."

"Did you hit your head? I'm a fucking civilian. I can't just show up and be your first sergeant."

"Why not? They're going to reinstate you eventually, so let's get ahead of the problem. We'll fake our way through the paperwork until we're too far away for the Corps to do anything but go along with it. If they get pissed off, I'll tell them it was my idea. What's the worst that could happen, they divvie us?"

Ystremski laughed at Fortis' sincerity and tossed back his shot. "I've seen you pull some bullshit before, but this is borderline fuckery."

"Don't worry about it. Nobody's going to blame you for wanting to kill those mass-murdering bastards." He took another shot. "You said it yourself. If you don't come along tomorrow, you'll miss your chance. If you stick around here, you'll probably be grabbed by the tacs."

Ystremski said nothing for a long moment as he stared at Fortis. Fortis opened his mouth to speak, but Ystremski raised a finger to silence him.

"Fuck it, I'm in." He threw a dish towel and hit the sleeping Hart in the face. The old-timer sputtered and rolled over. "Wake up, you old bastard. I'm deploying tomorrow."

Fortis and Ystremski huddled over the kitchen table and plotted out how they'd get Ystremski aboard 2nd Battalion. When they were done, Ystremski was almost sober, and Fortis was almost drunk.

"I thought mud-sucking Boudreaux was nuts, but this?" Ystremski shook his head. "That was child's play compared to this."

Ystremski was referring to the time Fortis had maneuvered General Boudreaux into promoting Ystremski and assigning him to Fortis' Tango Company prior to the Maltaan invasion.

"Sometimes it's easier to ask forgiveness than permission," Fortis said. "I remember a certain gunnery sergeant saying something like that."

Ystremski set about packing his duffel with everything he'd need as they talked about their plan. They paused periodically to chuckle, and by the time he finished, their spirits were high.

"I'm really glad you agreed to come with me," Fortis said.

"Kill 'em all, right?" Ystremski dumped his duffel by the door.

"Indeed."

* * *

"Hey, Abner."

A kick to his feet woke Fortis, and he peeled his eyes open to see Ystremski standing next to him, dressed in his uniform.

"Time to wake up, sleepyhead."

The room was still dark as Fortis rubbed his face and unfolded himself from the lumpy spare bed. His body ached, but his mind was surprisingly clear, considering where he'd slept.

He pulled on his boots and laced them up as the aroma of fresh coffee teased his nose. Ystremski pushed a mug into his hands, and they drank in silence.

"It's 0500," Ystremski said as he rinsed out their mugs. "Plenty of time." He went to the couch and poked Hart.

"Hey, Sam. Sam."

"What the fuck do you want?" Hart groaned and sat up. "Let an old man sleep, would you?"

"I'm going on deployment, you prick. My card is on the table. Pay the rent when it's due, and make sure you eat. Don't blow it all on booze."

"Fuck off." Hart rolled over. "Do the deed, dickheads," he said before he buried his face in the couch cushions.

"If you're sober when we get back, we're gonna buy Gunny Pete's, Sam," Fortis said.

Hart jolted upright with a surprised look on his face.

"No shit?"

"No shit, but only if you're sober. I'm not gonna bankroll a bar run by a drunk."

Hart jumped to his feet and threw up a wobbly salute. "Color me sober, Major."

Fortis and Ystremski laughed as they returned the salute.

* * *

The sky was just beginning to lighten as Fortis and Ystremski arrived at the battalion building. They mounted the steps and went inside.

"This is Gunnery Sergeant Ystremski," Fortis told the desk watch. "He's our new first sergeant."

He led Ystremski down the hall to the door marked COMMANDING OFFICER.

"This is me." He pointed to the door across the hall marked FIRST SERGEANT. "That's you."

Fortis put his duffel on the deck in his office. Before he could turn around, Lieutenant Vidic appeared in the doorway.

"We have a new first sergeant?"

"Yeah. He just reported."

Vidic fumbled with a stack of papers she carried in a folder. "Sir, I don't see anything in the morning message traffic about a new first sergeant. Are you sure he's in the right place?"

Ystremski joined them and closed the door.

"I'm sure," Fortis said. "This is Gunnery Sergeant Petr Ystremski. He was out of the Corps for a little while, but he's back, and he's joining 2nd Battalion. We're just waiting on Manpower to make it official."

"I don't understand. We don't have orders on him."

"You won't have orders on him yet, but you will. Just trust me. Process him in like you normally would. If anyone asks, he reported this morning. If they insist, refer them to me."

Ystremski smiled at the lieutenant's confusion and discomfort, and he winked at Vidic.

"Don't worry, LT. The major knows what he's doing."

"Yes, sir. I mean, yes, First Sergeant. Welcome aboard, and if there's anything you need, please ask."

Fortis and Ystremski shared a chuckle when Vidic was gone.

"Vidic is the personnel officer. That was the hard part," Fortis said. He checked the time. "Let's go meet the rest of the battalion."

2nd Battalion was drawn up in ranks by company on the battalion parade ground. Captain Stone stood at the front and saluted when Fortis and Ystremski approached.

"2nd Battalion, all present or accounted for, sir."

"Very well. Put them at ease."

Stone faced the formation.

"2nd Battalion! At… ease!"

All eyes were on Fortis as he walked across the formation.

"Good morning. I'm Major Abner Fortis, your new commanding officer." He pointed to Ystremski. "That's Gunnery Sergeant Ystremski. He just reported as our first sergeant.

"It's no secret that we're going to deploy this afternoon. I don't know exactly where or for how long, but we're going. I don't have any special words of wisdom for you except this: Any problems you have right now won't get better after we leave. Your squad leaders, platoon commanders, company commanders, and I can solve a lot of problems except the ones we don't know about.

"Your fellow Space Marines need a hundred percent of your effort and attention when we're on task. That means everything back here needs to be sorted out before we leave." Fortis looked at Ystremski. "First Sergeant, do you have anything to add?"

"No, sir."

"All right then. 2nd Battalion, atten…hut! Company commanders, take charge of your companies and carry out the orders of the day."

The battalion staff joined Fortis and Ystremski and made their introductions.

"Unless there've been any changes overnight, my number one priority this morning is logistics. Specifically, a replacement for the main pulse cannon power generator in Daisy Two, followed by rations and water for two months, and medical supplies for the same. First Sergeant, I'd like you to touch base with Lieutenant Fuller and Warrant Loren to run down the pulse cannon part. I brought it up with Colonel Weiss yesterday evening, and I don't think we're going to get any help through the chain of command. Do what you can and let me know where we are no later than 1100 hours."

The meeting broke up, and Fortis returned to his office. For him, the worst part about having command was not having anything to do when everyone around him was busy. He looked over the company deployment checklists, but they were complete, and nothing new had shown up since the previous day. He spent some time reading through the 2nd Division and 1st Regiment standing orders, but they were the standard stuff he'd seen many times before.

Bored, Fortis went for a walk through the company spaces. Space Marines were hard at work, cleaning weapons and preparing their gear. Fortis greeted them with smiles and nods of approval, but he knew he was only getting in the way. On his way back to his office, a strange voice behind him called his name. He turned and saw a lanky captain approaching.

"I'm Ace Williams," the captain said as he extended his hand. "CO, Alpha Company."

"Ah, yes. Good to meet you."

"The pleasure is all mine, sir." Williams had a deep sunburn on his forehead and cheeks, and his voice was a hundred percent southeastern North America. "Sorry I missed you at the brief yesterday."

"Captain Stone told me you weren't permitted to attend."

Williams chuckled. "Yeah, ol' Colonel Weiss doesn't much like me."

"Why's that?"

"Officially, it's because I asked a question that embarrassed him in front of the commander."

"And unofficially?"

"He was my company commander when I was a lance corporal. He turned a routine bug hunt into a shit show and got tossed out of the infantry. I guess I remind him of that."

"Colonel Weiss isn't infantry?"

"I dunno, Major. I guess they brought him back when they needed bodies to fill out the 2nd Division org chart. That's above my paygrade."

"Huh. Well, how are things in Alpha Company? Are you good to go?"

Williams' eyes narrowed, and his voice took on a menacing tone. "Yes, sir. I lost two cousins at the Peace Rally. We're ready to kill those fuckers."

Fortis nodded. "I'm sorry to hear it, but save some of that for the battlefield. We'll get our chance soon enough."

"Aye, aye, sir."

After his encounter with Williams, Fortis returned to his office and busied himself with make-work. At 1100, Ystremski and a master sergeant appeared at Fortis' office. Both men were dressed in greasy coveralls, and both wore big smiles.

"Major, this is Master Sergeant Dominguez, Charlie Company XO and maintenance chief of the battalion mechs. We found a replacement power generator for Daisy Two, and a whole lot more."

* * * * *

Chapter Six

"The supply squirrels at Division gave us the same runaround we got from Regiment," Ystremski said. "No parts, no availability, blah blah blah. I got to thinking about where we could get one, and it occurred to me that I didn't see any mechs on *Colossus*. The question is, where did they go?"

Dominguez jumped in. "I was in 5th Division when we transferred all our weapons from *Herculean* to *Colossus*. We deorbited all our mechs before she went to salvage orbit. I heard the Corps was going to put them into storage in the desert up north. It's a good thing they didn't."

Ystremski laughed. "Damn right. We tracked them down to a giant field outside the other side of the city. A whole fucking boneyard of mechs. Fifty square kilometers, at least. And not just mechs, either. Artillery, mobile command posts, and trailers, too. You know, the kind a command mech can tow? Anyway, they were all there for the taking."

"So you stole the parts?"

"No, sir, no stealing involved. There's a little shack with an old guy inside watching over the mechs and playing holos. He was hired to oversee the boneyard until the Corps came back for the vehicles. One day the colonel in charge of the mechs stopped coming around. After a couple weeks, the old-timer tried to call the colonel, and his office told him the colonel had been divvied. Nobody there knew anything about the mechs, so he's been waiting and watching ever since."

"Gunny Ystremski talked him into letting us pull power generators from three of the mechs."

"Fantastic! Well done, gents."

"It gets better." Ystremski gave Fortis a mischievous smile. "Dom says he can weld tow bars onto the main battle mechs, so we got six trailers, too. One for each main battle mech, and one for each recon mech.

"And if that wasn't enough, he told us about a warehouse complex on the far side of the spaceport where they stored all the other supplies. We found pallets of pig squares and hydration packs stacked to the roof, and enough medical supplies to outfit an entire hospital many times over. It cost Dom ten gallons of DINLI, but the trailers will be loaded and delivered to the Charlie Company mech lot no later than 1300 hours."

"Good, because we're heading for the spaceport at 1600 hours."

Ystremski slapped Dominguez on the shoulder. "You better get to welding, unless you want to tow those trailers to the spaceport by hand."

Fortis laughed so loud that Vidic poked her head into his office.

"Are you okay, Major?"

He wiped the tears from his eyes and gestured to Ystremski and Dominguez.

"If you want to see how to get things done in the Corps, watch these two."

* * *

Word of the vehicle boneyard and the supply warehouses spread quickly through 1st Regiment, and then the rest of the division. Fortis was gratified to learn that several other mech companies in the regiment had parts issues that were resolved by a quick trip to the boneyard. Several other battalion commanders stopped by to thank Fortis, and he referred all of them to Ystremski and Dominguez.

Dominguez and his Space Marines worked through lunch and finished welding tow bars onto all the mechs just in time to meet the trailers. They stuffed the trailers full of rations and medical supplies and had the mechs waiting in column as the rest of the battalion fell into ranks with the regiment to board the shuttles to the spaceport.

Colonels Feliz and Weiss drove along the formation atop the regimental command mech in an impromptu inspection. Space Marines engaged in last-minute preparations stopped to render salutes, which the colonels returned with great relish. When they passed 2nd Battalion, a puzzled expression crossed Weiss' face.

"Quite the dog and pony show," Ystremski muttered after the mech rolled past.

"Be glad the regimental commander rides with 3rd Battalion," Stone replied. "Otherwise, we'd have that bullshit all the time."

The Charlie Company mechs joined the convoy of vehicles headed for the spaceport just as the shuttles arrived to load the troops. Fortis and Ystremski watched with satisfaction as 2nd Battalion crowded aboard their assigned vehicles.

Ystremski shook his head and climbed into the last shuttle.

"Unbelievable. Not one Space Marine in the entire battalion came running up, hitching up his utilities after one last quickie in the bushes with Miss Right Now. What's the Corps coming to?"

At the spaceport, the Space Marines boarded the shuttles that would take them to *Mammoth*, waiting in orbit. After each company reported readiness to blast off, Fortis gave the order and strapped into his seat. He nudged Ystremski with his elbow.

"This is gonna work," he said as the engines wound up and the G-forces shoved him back into his seat.

* * *

It took nine hours to complete the transfer of troops from the surface to *Mammoth*. Fortis listened in on the various communications nets as delays mounted, and frustration turned to anger. From what he could gather, there was nobody in charge of the overall evolution.

Everyone, from the shuttle pilots to the deck crews on *Mammoth*, knew what to do. What they lacked was coordination from a unified command. Typically, the assistant division operations officer served as embarkation coordinator, but that individual, a major, had never done a full divisional embarkation before. Colonel Kim, the division operations officer, got involved, as did Colonel Weiss. Between them, they issued confusing, and at times contradictory, orders.

Finally, a Fleet master chief petty officer aboard *Mammoth* took over. She ignored the orders of everyone but the flagship commanding officer, who seemed content to allow her to run the show. The flagship recovered the heavy-lift shuttles bearing the mechs, offloaded them, and relaunched them. The shuttles carrying the Space Marines came alongside and connected flexible tubes called umbilicals to the flagship. The umbilicals allowed the troops to transfer without requiring the shuttle to recover aboard *Mammoth*, which saved a great deal of time.

When it was 2nd Battalion's turn, Fortis led the way through the umbilical into an empty cargo bay. The rest of the Space Marines followed, and after a quick muster, *Mammoth* crewmembers hustled them out of the cargo bay and dispersed them to their assigned troop berthing. A petty officer led Fortis and the other 1st Regiment officers to their quarters, and Fortis saw he was assigned to a four-man stateroom with Major Perkins, CO of 1st Battalion, and Major Bishop, XO of 3rd Battalion.

"Who's the fourth?" Perkins asked as he dumped his duffel on a vacant bunk.

"Probably some idiot from division staff," a German-accented voice at the door responded. Fortis turned and recognized the speaker as Steve Vogel, with whom he'd deployed to Maltaan with Lima Company before the invasion.

"Steve!"

"Abner!"

The two Space Marines embraced, and Fortis introduced him to the others.

"This is Steve Vogel, the best damned hovercopter pilot in the Corps."

Vogel laughed and thumped Fortis on the shoulder. "I thought I saw your name on the division roster." He pointed to Fortis' major tabs. "A major already. Very impressive."

Fortis waved his hand. "I've been busy. What are you doing here, Steve?"

"I'm the 2nd Division air operations officer."

"Be nice to this guy," Fortis told Perkins and Bishop. "He might be the difference between hot chow and no chow."

"There won't be any chow flights on this trip," Vogel said. "I've got a whopping ten birds for the entire division, so delivering chow won't be a priority."

"Ten birds? What the hell? Are we out of pilots?"

"Pilots we have; it's maintainers that we need. The drawdown hit the squadrons hard, since most ground crew and mechanics are a bunch of hellraising drunks. After they flushed everyone with a discipline record, we didn't have enough guys to maintain a single squadron of hovercopters. It doesn't help that the transition to fast movers for tactical air support is draining hovercopter resources, either."

"That's the Corps for you," Bishop said.

"DINLI," Vogel replied.

After Fortis and Vogel agreed to link up later, the four officers went their separate ways. Fortis found the 2nd Battalion office, where he discovered Vidic set up and ready to support the battalion. The rich aroma of coffee filled the space.

"What's that delicious smell?" Fortis asked. "Is that real coffee?"

"Yes, sir. Compliments of Lieutenant Orndorff. She called it a housewarming present."

"Oh, man." Fortis reveled in the steam as he poured himself a mug. "Remind me to give her an award. A lifesaving medal, or something like that."

"Sir, while we're on the topic of lifesaving, Captain Thoms came by and asked about Gunny Ystremski's orders. I told her I'd get back to her later, but she wasn't very happy."

"Who's Captain Thoms?"

"Regina Thoms. She's the regimental personnel officer. I guess Colonel Weiss has been riding her pretty hard over Gunny Ystremski. When do you think we'll get his orders?"

Fortis smiled and sipped his coffee. "Any day now, LT. Don't worry about Captain Thoms, or the colonel. Just make sure you're carrying the gunny on the battalion muster sheet."

"Will do, sir."

* * *

It was 0200 by the time 2nd Division completed their embarkation of *Mammoth*, and Ystremski and Dominguez were able to sit down and rest for a moment. The mass movement of troops required their attention to a thousand details and ten thousand things that could go wrong. Foresight and patience were essential, and it helped to have an experienced leader like Major Fortis overseeing the evolution.

Dominguez slid a mug of coffee across the table in the goat locker, the berthing compartment traditionally reserved for senior enlisted.

"Here's to a good day, Petr."

"Damn right it was. Long, but good."

"I can't thank you enough for getting that power generator, and the spares. That was a life saver."

Ystremski shrugged. "Just took a little out-of-the-box thinking."

"When all that stuff rolled into the mech yard, and everybody stopped and stared, it was like the good old days, you know?"

"Dom, there's something I want to ask you. I've been away from the regular Corps for a long time, pretty much since the Maltaan invasion. I got locked down on Maltaan the whole time while the drawdown happened, so I missed all that, too. Now that I'm back, it sure feels like there's something different about the Corps, you know?"

"I'm not sure I understand what you mean."

"It's hard to explain but let me give you an example. I saw zero grab-assing today. This is an infantry battalion full of young fire eaters, and I didn't hear a single wisecrack. I didn't hear a single nickname, either. I'm sure they're all good kids, but it feels… I dunno, different.

They just don't have the same spirit I remember, if that makes any sense."

Dominguez nodded. "It does. The French call it *joie de vivre*. Basically, enjoyment of life. And you're right, it's missing in the Corps today."

"Why do you think that is?"

"The drawdown. They divvied almost everyone with a disciplinary record, so all those personalities are gone. You know, the 10 percent we spent 90 percent of our time on. Some of them were a pain in the ass, but they were also the ones who could make a bad day bearable just by cracking a joke. The Marines that remain are good kids, like you say, but they're timid. Back in our day, a joke aimed at the wrong sergeant might earn some shitty extra duty or wall-to-wall counseling. Now, they could find themselves at the main gate in civilian clothes. That takes the starch right out of them.

"I'll tell you another thing. These guys have seen a lot of their friends get divvied, which makes them reluctant to form bonds with anyone. They work well enough together, but the comradery isn't there anymore. When I was a pup, we'd stand shoulder to shoulder against a bar full of Fleet pukes and take on all comers. We learned who we could count on pretty damned quick. These days, I can't remember the last time I heard some of them getting together off-duty for anything, much less drinking. It's a shame."

"Are they going to be okay in a fight? We don't have a lot of time to fix any of this, you know."

"They'll be fine. We did some training before the old CO left, and it went okay. They're Space Marines; they'll find a way to win."

After a few more minutes, they decided to turn in and grab a couple hours of sleep before reveille.

* * * * *

Chapter Seven

The next morning at 0615, Fortis stepped out of his stateroom and found Ystremski waiting for him in the passageway.

"Good morning, sir."

"Good morning, First Sergeant. Another fine day in the Corps."

"Every day is a holiday, sir. The battalion is formed up in our drop ship bay."

"Outstanding. What's the plan for today?"

"Well, sir, after you get done mollycoddling them, I'd like to do some team building exercises with them."

Fortis blinked in surprise. "Really? 'Team building?' That doesn't sound like you. I'm curious to see what you have in mind."

"With all due respect, I'd like to keep it just enlisted folks, sir."

"Okay. You're the first sergeant, after all. I'll honor that request. Still, I have to know, what sort of team building are you going to do?"

Ystremski opened the hatch to the cargo bay and motioned Fortis through.

"Pain, sir."

All three companies and the battalion staff were drawn up in formation. Captain Stone rendered a crisp salute when Fortis approached.

"2nd Battalion, all present or accounted for, sir."

"Very well. Put them at ease."

All eyes were on Fortis as he addressed the group.

"Yesterday was a long day, but all of you worked hard and got the job done. We solved some nagging issues, and I'm proud to say that 2nd Battalion is battle ready. Take a moment to congratulate yourselves but understand that the hard work is just beginning. In a few days, we'll make a combat drop onto an unfamiliar planet, and every single one of you must be ready to fight. Prepare yourselves and prepare your gear. Any problems need to get up the chain; I want no surprises when we get where we're going. Now, the first sergeant has an announcement to make."

"When the company commanders dismiss their companies, all enlisted Space Marines remain here, including the enlisted battalion staff."

The company commanders turned and looked at Fortis, and he nodded.

"That's all I have, sir."

"Very well, First Sergeant. Company commanders, take charge of your companies. When you're finished, all battalion officers muster with me in the main weight room."

Twenty minutes later, all the officers were gathered in the weight room.

"It's important that officers lead by example, and that includes physical fitness," Fortis told them. "All of you are strength-enhanced to some level, and it's my responsibility as your commanding officer to ensure you build on that enhancement. I want all of you to pair up with an officer you don't normally work with on a day-to-day basis. Enhancement levels don't matter; teamwork does."

The officers broke up into pairs, and Fortis moved around the weight room, slipping in for a set of reps here and there. It pleased him to see the infantry officers paired up with the staff officers. The infantry were more likely to be strength enhanced to higher levels and would challenge the staff.

He'd just finished a set of bench presses when Colonel Weiss called to him from the hatch.

"Major Fortis, a word please."

Fortis followed the colonel out into the passageway. "Yes, sir."

"You have a new first sergeant?"

"Yes, sir. Gunnery Sergeant Ystremski reported yesterday morning."

"It's strange that I didn't see any orders on him come through the system. Do you have his orders?"

Fortis knew he was dancing on the knife edge of lying to a superior officer, and he chose his answer carefully.

"I don't have his orders, sir. I'll check with my administrative officer when we're finished here."

"Hmm. Okay." Weiss looked through the open hatch. "What are you doing, anyway?"

"Working out, sir. A little team building with my officers. We're going into battle in a few days, and I need to learn as much about them as possible. I think the gym is a good place to do that. Would you care to join us?"

Weiss rolled his eyes and shook his head. "No can do, Major. I've got an invasion to plan. Speaking of that, 2nd Battalion is scheduled for an intel briefing with Colonel Price and his staff at 1300 hours in the division briefing room."

"Roger that, sir. I'll have my folks there."

"Good." Weiss turned to leave but stopped. "Hey, Major, one more question. What's this about two months' worth of rations? It was made clear at the briefing that the plan called for a log hit after two weeks, and that's only if the mission lasts that long."

"Yes, sir, that's what was put out, but it's been my experience that plans sometimes go awry. The enemy has a say in how things go, as do the weather and terrain. Carrying extra rations shouldn't affect our combat effectiveness, and if they do, we'll dump them."

"Okay, Major, it's your battalion. I appreciate you hitting the ground running, but I'd like you to keep me in the loop. Perhaps I can offer you some advice."

"Yes, sir. Your advice would be welcome."

When Fortis rejoined the group, he moved to spot Captain Williams with Lieutenant Vidic.

"What was that all about, sir? If you don't mind me asking," Vidic said.

"Colonel Weiss, checking up on things. Asked about Ystremski."

Her eyes widened. "What did you tell him?"

"The truth. He reported yesterday, and I don't have his orders."

"Don't you think he's going to be angry when he finds out what's going on?"

"Maybe, but we'll be too far along for him to do anything about it. What's he going to do, take command of 2nd Battalion himself, or give it to one of his staff guys? I think we'll be just fine."

* * *

Three hours later, Ystremski rapped on the battalion commander's office door and poked his head in.

"How'd it go this morning?" Fortis asked as he poured the gunny a mug of coffee from an urn on the desk.

"Some of those kids can do a lot of fucking pushups, but I think I got the point across to them." He recoiled when he sipped the mug. "Is this *real* coffee?"

"Courtesy of Alpha Company. Hey, I didn't get a chance to ask earlier. What prompted your 'team building' this morning?"

Ystremski described his late-night conversation with Dominguez.

"They're all good Space Marines, sir, not a shitbird among them, but they lack cohesion. To focus them on 'we,' not 'me,' I made them compete as squads, platoons, and companies in a series of physical challenges. I reminded them that winning is a conscious decision, and they win or lose as a team. By the time we were done, there were challenges issued and accepted for tomorrow. How did it go with the officers?"

"I split up the infantry officers to make sure the staff types got some work. There's going to be some sore bodies tomorrow, I think. The big news is Colonel Weiss is aware that you're here. He asked about your orders, and I gave him an answer that he might consider lying by omission. He's got the regimental personnel folks looking into it, and I'm sure he's brought it up to Division, too. Even so, I'm pretty sure we'll be through the jump gate before they get an answer."

"Do you think he'll be angry when he figures it out?"

"Lieutenant Vidic asked me the same thing. He might be, but we'll be a day or two from a combat drop. What's he going to do, replace us with people from his staff? I think he'll threaten to do something when this is all over, and then hope neither one of us makes it back alive."

"Great. Another deployment where the chain of command is rooting for us to fail."

"Bah, no worries. Once he hears that you're the reason the division got all those rations and medical supplies, he'll forget about being mad. Besides, he's not the commanding general."

* * *

Fortis stood at the briefing room door and checked the time.

1243.

Ystremski appeared and nodded a greeting. Litvinenko was next, two minutes later, followed immediately by the company COs and XOs. He checked the time again.

1245. Excellent.

He led the way into the briefing room and saw a colonel and a handful of junior officers and enlisted Space Marines fussing with the holographic projection system.

"You're early," the colonel told Fortis.

"Yes, sir."

The 2nd Battalion leaders slid into a row of seats to wait for the brief to start. 1300 hours came and went, and then 1305 and 1310. Finally, the door burst open, and Colonel Weiss bustled inside.

"My apologies, I lost track of time. Please begin, Colonel Price."

A holo of the Leavitt Peripheral appeared briefly before it zoomed in on the section assigned to 1st Regiment.

"This area is designated Leavitt Alpha, assigned to 1st Regiment." The holo zoomed in further to a single planet. "We named this planet Leavitt Alpha Minor, or LAM for short. Based on the level of Kuiper Knight activity observed on LAM, the regimental commander assigned LAM to 2nd Battalion.

"LAM is approximately the same size as Terra Earth, and the gravity and atmosphere of LAM are consistent with Terra Earth's. We didn't observe any surface water, and frankly, we haven't had time to collect much more data than that."

Price highlighted a dot on the holo, and the image zoomed in. Fortis saw a rudimentary spaceport with a long runway, large, flat spots with scorch marks indicating drop ship activity, and clusters of biodomes and hangars. Lush, green jungle bordered the spaceport on three sides, and steep hills climbed away behind it on the fourth.

"We've detected one area of human colonization, located here. Intelligence sources indicate this might be the settlement known to the Kuiper Knights as Sanctuary."

Ystremski nudged Fortis with his elbow and nodded.

"We assess this colony can support no more than one thousand humans. Given the apparent lack of activity at the spaceport, the population is probably five hundred or less."

Price paused as if he expected a reaction to the number, but the 2nd Battalion officers remained quiet.

"Are there any questions?"

Fortis rose to his feet. "Major Fortis, commander of 2nd Battalion. Sir, you said a thousand Kuiper Knights. How are they armed?"

"Closer to five hundred, but we don't have specifics, Major. Assume they were armed from the weapons hijacked from *Colossus*. Pulse rifles and grenades."

"Do we know if they have routine logistics support and from where?"

"Again, Major, we don't have specifics. LAM is a recent discovery, and we haven't had the time or assets to do a full target analysis. There was no activity observed at the spaceport."

Fortis considered asking more questions, but he knew the colonel wouldn't have the answers. Instead, he nodded.

"Thank you, Colonel."

"If there are no further questions, that's all I have. Colonel Weiss, I'll provide a full target package to your staff to support mission planning. Thank you for your attention."

As everyone got to their feet, Fortis consulted the time.

1326. Fastest battalion intel brief in history.

He looked at the officers gathered around him.

"Meet me at 1500 in the battalion office so we can start planning our mission. Captain Litvinenko, that gives you ninety minutes to digest both paragraphs of the intel brief and be ready with some useful information. Can you handle it?"

Litvinenko grinned. "Yes, sir, I'll do my best."

* * *

A short while later, Fortis was on his way to the battalion office when a group of officers caught up with him in the passageway. A tall major with tight blond curls and an upturned nose stuck out his hand.

"Major Fortis, I'm Lance Perkins, CO 1st Battalion," the major said as they shook. He gestured to the other officers in the group. "This is Elisa Moore, my XO. Sheila Fitzhugh is CO 3rd Battalion, and that's Selwyn Bishop, her XO. Welcome aboard."

"Thank you. Please, call me Abner."

"How are you getting on?"

"All good so far. I'm anxious to see what regiment comes up with for an assault plan."

"It would have been nice to delay the deployment until Colonel Vogel could round up a few hovercopters," Fitzhugh said.

"Woulda, coulda, shoulda, Fitz. I don't know what you're worried about, anyway. You'll be snuggled up with Regiment. Hot chow and plenty of rest."

"Wanna trade?"

Perkins held up his hands in mock surrender. "Not a chance. I'd rather hump in the jungle."

Fitzhugh shook her head. "DINLI."

"DINLI," echoed the group.

"We're usually not so doom and gloom," Perkins told Fortis. "It's been a little crazy since the Corps reorganized the division, but it's getting better. Plenty of combat experience up and down the chain. Especially since you got here."

"Well, I like what I've seen so far of 2nd Battalion," Fortis said. "It's easy to spot the difference between combat ready and headquarters spit and polish."

Perkins extended his hand again. "Thank you for finding that mech park, and the rations, too. Spare parts and supplies have been a bitch to get."

"I'll take the credit, but that was all Master Sergeant Dominguez and Gunny Ystremski. I turned them loose, and they found all that stuff on their own. I'm just glad they didn't steal it. Or maybe they did. Either way, I don't want to know."

The group laughed.

"We'll leave you to it, Abner," Perkins said. "We figured it was time to get the 'getting to know you festivities,' as Colonel Weiss calls them, out of the way. If there's anything you need, don't hesitate to ask." It was obvious from his tone that he didn't think much of the colonel.

Fortis shook hands all around again.

"I appreciate the welcome, and I'm looking forward to working with all of you. And if not, DINLI."

The group laughed again and disappeared down the passageway.

*****

Chapter Eight

Ystremski caught up to Fortis in the battalion commander's office. He was silent until he closed the door. "What kind of half-assed intel brief was that?"

"I'm not surprised. There are a lot of things around here that—"

The door opened, and Colonel Weiss stuck his head in.

"Ah, good. I hoped to catch you here." He stuck out his hand to Ystremski. "You're Gunnery Sergeant Ystremski."

"Yes, sir."

"Tell me, Gunny, how did you end up with 2nd Division and this battalion?"

"Well, sir, you see, I showed up, and Major Fortis said he had a job for me."

"You 'showed up.' When did you receive your orders?"

Ystremski seemed to struggle for an answer, so Fortis jumped in.

"I recruited the gunny, sir. I told him to report, and I'd take care of the rest."

"So you're here without orders?"

"Sir, it's my—"

Weiss cut Fortis off with a raised hand. "I asked the gunnery sergeant, Major."

"That's correct, sir. The Corps divvied me as part of a mission I conducted on behalf of the General Staff. When the mission ended, there was a delay in Manpower reinstating me. I didn't want to miss this fight, so the major told me to come with him and sort it out later."

An incredulous look crossed Weiss' face. "You're not a Space Marine?"

Ystremski shook his head. "Not exactly, sir. I was, and I will be again, but right now, I'm caught up in a paperwork churn."

Weiss stared for a second. "Gunny, you've been in the Corps long enough to know that this isn't the proper way to do things. Why would you do something like this?"

"I heard 2nd Division was deploying, and I didn't want to miss the opportunity to kill Kuiper Knights, sir. If I'd sat on my ass waiting for Manpower to unfuck themselves, I'd have ended up as a staff pogue somewhere, driving a desk and hassling the troops. That's not where I belong."

Fortis resisted the urge to laugh, but Weiss didn't seem to register the insult. The colonel touched his chest where Fortis and Ystremski had the crimson number 9 sewn onto their utilities.

"You knew the major from before, with the Bloody 9th?"

"Yes, sir. We fought side by side on Balfan-48."

Weiss got a distant look in his eyes. "Hmm. I lost a lot of friends and Fleet Academy classmates on Balfan-48." He blinked and returned to the present. "Anyway, Gunny, I appreciate your candor. Please note that in the future, it's much easier to seek my permission than my forgiveness." He stepped aside. "Now, if you don't mind, I'd like to speak to the major in private."

Weiss closed the door behind Ystremski. When he turned back around, Fortis saw fire in his eyes.

"Major Fortis, what the actual fuck are you trying to do here?" The colonel's face flushed, and spittle flew from his mouth. "You're making a mockery of me and the ISMC. You lied to me, and I have half a mind to bring you up on charges. There's absolutely no excuse for this. What have you to say to that?"

"I don't have an excuse, sir. I took command of a battalion missing two thirds of the command triumvirate, that being an XO and a first sergeant. I saw the opportunity to solve a big part of that problem, so I took it."

Weiss stabbed the air between them with a finger. "Instead of coming to me, you chose to lie."

"I acknowledge that what I did isn't the right way to get it done, but the results speak for themselves. Since his arrival, Gunnery Sergeant Ystremski played a big role in obtaining the spare part to get Daisy Two repaired. He also located enough rations for the entire division to sustain themselves well beyond the two-week log window."

"I should have you two confined until a court martial can be convened."

"Do what you will to me, Colonel. Relieve me, arrest me, and replace me with an officer from your staff. Ystremski had nothing to do with the decision to come aboard like he did, and he deserves much of the credit for improving the combat readiness of 2nd Battalion in the short time he's been here."

The colonel's eyes narrowed, and Fortis could almost hear the wheels in his head turning. Weiss's face began to return to its normal color.

"I might just do that, Major. Unlike you, I recognize that there is a right way and a wrong way to approach problems such as this, and I'm going to consult with the chain of command before I decide what to do with you."

You lose, colonel.

"I'd be happy to explain myself to Colonel Feliz or General Moreno, if necessary."

"The colonel and general are too busy planning the invasion to get involved in an administrative matter like this."

"I'm standing by to turn this battalion over to whomever you choose until the colonel or general have the time, sir."

Weiss shook his head. "No, Major Fortis, I'm not going to do that. I'm not going to reward your underhandedness by keeping you safe here on the flagship while your battalion's fighting on LAM. No, sir, you're going to where the fight is."

Fortis smiled inwardly, but he kept his face expressionless. "Roger that, sir."

"And another thing. Colonel Feliz and Colonel Kim will present the regimental operations plan at 1900 hours tonight. I expect you and your officers to be there, ready to fully participate. Let me warn you, if you think I'm tough, wait until Colonel Feliz gets ahold of you."

Weiss spun on his heel and exited the space. Fortis sat down and started to count. When he got to eight, Ystremski stuck his head in the door.

"Is the coast clear?"

Fortis waved him into a chair. "We're good. He's mad, but he's not crazy." He told Ystremski about his conversation with Weiss.

"He's not going to 'reward' you by leaving you here. Some reward."

"That's the difference between pogues and field Space Marines."

There was a soft rap on the door, and Lieutenant Vidic entered.

"Is everything okay, Major? I just saw Colonel Weiss storm out, and he didn't look happy."

"Speaking of pogues," Ystremski quipped, and he and Fortis laughed.

Vidic's eyes grew wide. "What? What did I do?"

"Nothing, LT. We're just having a little fun at your expense. And yes, everything's okay." He gave her a quick rundown of Ystremski's situation. "Colonel Weiss is aware that Gunnery Sergeant Ystremski is a stowaway, so it's all good now."

"What are we going to do?"

"We're going to review the intel and see what the group comes up with. Feliz and Kim are presenting the operations plan at 1900 hours, so we'll see what their plan is. If there's fallout from this, it'll land on me when we get back from LAM."

"It won't be much of a plan, since we don't know shit about the place," Ystremski said.

"That's because we have terrible intel sources."

"Blow me, dickhead."

Vidic watched this exchange with a confused look.

"Don't worry about it, LT. If we're lucky, we'll get the benefit of their years of tactical experience."

Fortis and Ystremski laughed again while Vidic stood there and shook her head.

* * *

At 1500, Litvinenko led off the planning session with everything he'd been able to glean from the targeting package he'd received from Colonel Price.

"The spaceport on LAM is an afterthought to the General Staff planners," he told the 2nd Battalion officers. "It wasn't on the target list until four days ago, when they intercepted an unknown signal from there, which explains why there hasn't been any dedicated collection. They diverted a single drone for a fly-by, and that's it."

"Are there plans to do more collection before we drop?" Fortis asked.

"No, sir. Colonel Rolf of 2nd Regiment has been making a lot of noise with the division staff, so they're throwing everything his way. Intel, logistics, you name it."

"The squeaky wheel," Ystremski said.

"It would seem so, Gunny. I tried to work my contacts in the division intel shop, but there's nothing they can do."

"If there's nothing we can do about it, let's move on," Fortis said. "Have you learned anything new about LAM?"

Litvinenko put up a holo of the target area. "The intel techs ran the imagery through every filter and algorithm they could think of, but they couldn't squeeze anything more out of it. The topography looks flat enough, but the jungle canopy is too thick to tell for sure. For all the contrast and definition they were able to develop, a canyon might appear as flat."

"They could fit a lot more than a thousand people in those buildings," Captain Stone said.

Fortis looked at Ystremski. "You've been there. What do you think?"

The group looked at Ystremski in surprise.

"You've *been* there?" Litvinenko asked with incredulity in his voice.

Ystremski waved off their looks. "It was a long time ago." He pointed to the holo. "I don't know why Sanctuary was an afterthought. It was their headquarters when I was there, and it's big enough for more than a thousand troops, too. A lot more."

"Maybe we should pass that intel up the chain," Litvinenko said.

"It was all in my report. I guess they got better information from somewhere else."

"What do you think, Major? Is the entire regiment going to drop onto the spaceport?" Lieutenant Tate asked.

Fortis frowned. "I don't know. If we do, we'll have to drop in waves, and that's not easy to do with an entire regiment. We'll be tripping over each other."

The group brainstormed how best to make the drop, but without detailed information on the regiment's plan, they couldn't come up with anything solid. Fortis knew they wouldn't, but it wasn't wasted time. He watched how they interacted as ideas were put forward and accepted or rejected. Tempers flared when Vidic pointed out an obvious flaw in one of Stone's ideas, and Litvinenko had to break up the argument, but the discussion was mostly respectful.

After thirty minutes, Fortis called it quits.

"Let's break it up. We're getting nowhere, and we can't do much until we get the word from Regiment. Remember, 1900. Don't be late."

* * *

At 1900, a squat female major with thick glasses perched on a pug nose began the 1st Regiment assault brief.

"Good evening, Colonel Feliz, Colonel Weiss, and fellow officers. For those of you who don't know me, I'm Major Emma Welch, 1st Regiment operations officer. Welcome to the 1st Regiment assault on LAM, code named Operation Grand Slam."

Welch paused as though she expected applause, and when it didn't come, she cleared her throat and continued.

"General Moreno assigned our regiment to assault the spaceport in this area here, known as Sanctuary." The now familiar holo of Sanctuary and the surrounding region appeared. "This spaceport is the center of gravity for the Kuiper Knights on LAM, and it'll be the focal point of our assault." A red X appeared over the spaceport. "This is Drop Zone Firebird." Two more Xs appeared, one northwest of DZ Firebird, and one northeast. "This is DZ Rock Wall," Welch said as she pointed northwest. Her pointer shifted northeast. "And this is DZ Lead Pipe.

"1st Regiment will conduct simultaneous drops on all three drop zones. 1st Battalion will drop on Lead Pipe, 2nd will drop on Rock Wall, and 3rd will drop on Firebird and seize the spaceport.

"Once the spaceport is secured, 3rd Battalion will move north, while 1st and 2nd move toward each other. 3rd will become the hammer and drive the Kuiper Knights ahead of them, while 1st and 2nd will form the anvil. We'll crush the Kuiper Knights between the two forces. Are there any questions so far?"

No one spoke, so Welch continued.

"2nd Division assigned us nine drop ships for the operation. 1st Battalion will get three, 2nd Battalion will get two, and 3rd Battalion will get four."

Fortis stood. "Ma'am, Major Fortis, 2nd Battalion. I have three companies, so I should have three drop ships, right?"

Welch nodded. "Under normal circumstances, you'd be correct, but there are several factors that impact our operation. First and foremost is drop ship pilot availability. Division doesn't have enough pilots to support multiple drops across the area of operations.

"There's also the matter of drop zone size. Rock Wall can accommodate two drop ships simultaneously, while Lead Pipe can fit three.

Speed and surprise are critical elements to mission success, so the decision to assign two drop ships to 2nd Battalion made sense.

"Finally, 2nd Battalion is the smallest of the three battalions. We consulted with the drop ship cargo masters, and they determined that the entire battalion would fit aboard two drop ships."

Ystremski stood up. "Not if they're loaded for assault. If we have to admin load, we'll be packed in all around the mechs, which means they can't roll until the infantry gets clear. We'll have our asses in the breeze waiting for mech support."

A confused look crossed Welch's face. "You're who?"

"This is Gunnery Sergeant Ystremski, my first sergeant," Fortis said as he touched Ystremski's sleeve. "I share his concerns, Major. What's the anticipated level of enemy resistance to our drop?"

Welch stared at Fortis for a long second before a captain seated in the row behind Colonel Feliz stood up.

"Major, I'm Bill Campbell, 1st Regiment Intel. The only signs of activity anywhere near Rock Wall are probable game trails. Therefore, we believe you'll be dropping into a permissive environment. You won't be charging into a hail of enemy pulse rifle fire."

Campbell delivered his last sentence in an almost mocking tone, and several of the other staff officers masked smiles and chuckles behind their hands.

"If it's going to be safe, you're welcome to join us, Captain." The words were out before Fortis could stop them, and it was Ystremski's turn to touch his sleeve.

"Major Fortis, there's no need for that." Colonel Weiss had risen. "The regimental staff has done everything possible to give 2nd Battalion the best chance to succeed. If they say the environment will be permissive and only two drop ships are required, you can be assured that's the situation you'll face. Am I clear?"

Fortis felt a surge of heat in his chest, but he stopped himself before he responded to the colonel. A pissing match with Weiss in front of the regiment commander wouldn't serve him well.

"Crystal clear, sir. I apologize if I came across a little strong, but a combat drop, even into a permissive environment, is a complex operation with a lot of moving parts. My experience has shown that everything can go wrong in a hurry, and when it does, it costs a lot of blood."

Fortis and Ystremski sat down.

Weiss gestured to Welch. "Major, please continue."

The brief continued along a similar vein for the other two battalions. None of the other attendees challenged anything Welch said until the very end, when Major Fitzhugh, CO of 3rd Battalion, spoke up.

"Major Welch, what's the plan for prisoners? Is 3rd Battalion responsible for establishing a collection and holding center at the spaceport?"

Welch looked at Colonel Feliz before she responded.

"We don't anticipate taking prisoners."

"Say again?"

"We're not taking prisoners on this operation," Colonel Feliz said in a loud voice.

"What if they surrender, sir?"

Feliz stood up and faced the crowd.

"There's no interest in affording the terrorists all the rights denied to over a hundred thousand innocent Terrans. They chose their fate when they fired the first rocket, and now they'll regret that decision. Anyone else?"

A heavy silence fell over the briefing room under the weight of Feliz's glare.

"That's it, then. We're due to jump to the Free Sector tomorrow afternoon, so make sure your people are ready."

Everyone jumped to their feet when a staff officer called them to attention.

"Carry on."

Fortis turned for the hatch when Weiss called to him.

"Major Fortis, a word, please."

Here we go.

Fortis locked eyes with Ystremski. "Come on, dickhead," he said in a soft voice. "This is about you."

* * * * *

Chapter Nine

Fortis and Ystremski approached Feliz and Weiss. "Yes, sir."

"This is your new first sergeant?"

"Colonel Feliz, may I introduce Gunnery Sergeant Petr Ystremski."

Feliz eyed Ystremski up and down. "So you're the stowaway?"

"Yes, sir, that's me."

"That's a helluva a story, Gunny."

"Colonel, I apologize for bringing Gunnery Sergeant Ystremski aboard like I did, but—"

Feliz wagged a finger at Fortis. "No apologies are necessary, Major. Any Space Marine that wants to get into the action as badly as Gunny Ystremski does deserves our support, not our apologies."

As veterans often do, Feliz and Ystremski began to trade anecdotes about comrades they had in common. They discovered they'd deployed in different companies with 8th Division when Feliz was an infantry captain and Ystremski was a corporal. All Weiss and Fortis could do was smile and nod as the stories flew. The bad vibes Fortis had sensed from Weiss and Feliz when he'd questioned the assault plan evaporated.

One of staffers saved the pair when he cleared his throat and tapped his wrist.

"Colonel, Division is waiting."

Feliz gave Ystremski a warm smile as the pair shook hands.

"I'm happy to have you, Gunny. If there's anything you need, let me know."

After Feliz and Weiss left the room, Fortis nudged Ystremski.

"You never told me you were best friends with the colonel."

"I didn't know. Are you jealous?"

"A little, maybe. I thought we had something special."

They joined Litvinenko, who'd waited by the hatch. Fortis tilted his head.

"C'mon, you two. Let's go unfuck the drop ship situation."

* * *

They located the lead drop ship commander, a first lieutenant named Bovar, in their assigned drop ship bay. She was sympathetic to their situation, but the issue was out of her hands.

"Major, I thought there was a mistake when I saw the schedule, but the division air boss confirmed it. Two drops ships assigned to 2nd Battalion, 1st Regiment."

"This is fucked," Ystremski said. "We're going to be packed in there nut-to-butt. Begging your pardon, ma'am."

Bovar chuckled. "You're right, Gunny, it is fucked. However, my load master's found a way to make it work. You'll be nut-to-butt on the way down, but it's doable." She winked at Ystremski. "Begging your pardon."

Bovar showed them a diagram of the load arrangement. "Charlie Company isn't a full-strength mech company, so we split the mechs between the drop ships and loaded the infantry around them. It's not a standard load, and we had to play with the deck spots to keep the loads balanced, but I think we got it." She pointed to the diagram. "The one thing we aren't sure about is these trailers. What are they?"

"Two months' worth of food and supplies for the company."

"Two months? The logistics schedule I saw showed drops every two weeks."

"We don't trust anything we read," Ystremski said, "including drop ship load diagrams and logistics schedules."

"Neither do I, Gunny. Major, I analyzed our drop zone, and based on my measurements, we can get both drop ships in at the same time with room to spare. I've been flying with Lieutenant Venn, the other drop ship pilot, for almost two years, and we work well together. I think we can get you down simultaneously."

"Roger that."

Bovar agreed to allow the infantry to train on the drop ships over the next few days, and they parted ways.

"Let's call it a night," Fortis said when the trio reached the battalion office. "Tomorrow morning, after team building, I want full gear checks on every member of 2nd Battalion, including officers. After that, we'll go to the drop ship bay and dress rehearse until everyone knows exactly what to do when the ramp goes down."

Ystremski lingered until Litvinenko was gone, and then closed the door.

"What do you make of that brief, Major?"

"I felt like I was watching a Staff College student present a class project," Fortis said. "Like she'd printed an assault plan template from courseware and filled in the blanks."

"And ignored a lot of blanks, too. Nothing about topography, climate, or any of that other shit the staff geeks love to discuss."

"She can't brief what we don't know, but yeah, she could have acknowledged that we don't know it. I got the impression she was hoping nobody would notice."

"Hammer and anvil is about as basic as it gets," Ystremski said. "We train to it because it works, but I don't like the plan to spread the battalions across three drop zones. Especially without air assets to provide mutual support."

"What about the Kuiper Knights? How many did you see when you were there?"

"I was only there a couple days, but there were a lot. It could have been a couple thousand. They might have moved since then, but we're gonna look stupid if we drop in and find two thousand of the fuckers waiting for us. I don't care what anyone says, a lot of those guys were Space Marines, and they haven't forgotten everything they knew because they took off the uniform."

"Do you think they'll fight?"

"That's hard to say, sir. Most of the guys I met weren't fanatics, and I have a hard time believing they're okay with the Peace Rally attack. They'll definitely *become* fanatics when they find out we're not taking prisoners."

"Colonel or no colonel, we're not killing anyone who surrenders," Fortis said.

* * *

The next morning, Fortis was on his way to the drop ship bay when Weiss caught up with him. The colonel looked askance at his battle armor.

"Major, why are you kitted out?"

"2nd Battalion is training on combat drops, sir. We had to make some adjustments to the drop ship load plans to accommodate all three companies on two drop ships, and I want to make sure everyone knows their role."

"A dress rehearsal? Is that really necessary?"

"Yes, sir, I believe it is. In a few days, I'm leading three hundred and fifty Space Marines I've never operated with before into battle, and our first task is to drop on a strange planet from a non-standard drop ship configuration. I'm sure they're all good Marines, but a drop zone is the wrong time to discover the troops don't know which way to go, especially with mechs involved."

"Hmm. Well, I'm glad you've accepted that you're only getting two drop ships; I was afraid we'd have a conflict about that."

"No conflict, sir. DINLI."

"Make sure you have everything re-stowed by 1600 hours. We'll be at the jump gate at 1630."

"Roger that, sir."

"Carry on, Major."

Fortis found the battalion waiting for him in the drop ship bay.

"We're ready when you are, sir," Ystremski said as he saluted.

"Does everybody know their station?"

"We've been over it a couple times, sir. I think they've got it."

"Let's mount up."

As Fortis expected, the first walkthroughs were rough. Space Marines, both infantry and mech drivers, were trained to race down the ramp and get clear of a drop zone as soon as possible. Mechs went first, with the infantry close behind to provide mutual support. Drop ship engine noise was deafening, and the down blast created stinging clouds of sand and rocks that wiped out visibility. The noise and confusion of a drop demanded that every Marine know their role and stick to it.

Even in practice, the urge to get down the ramp was difficult to suppress. They had to rehearse opening the ramp several times before the infantry waited to let the mechs roll out, and even then, there were Space Marines mixing with the mechs before they were clear of the simulated drop zone.

Ystremski and the company gunnery sergeants watched the training with sharp eyes, and they corrected mistakes and paused the scenarios to drive home training points. It was slow and frustrating at first, and there was a chorus of complaints when Ystremski ordered the troops to reload for the third time.

"There's only one way for this to work, and that's teamwork," Ystremski told them. "We either build it here on the ramp, or in the cargo bay. I have all day, ladies, so you decide."

After an hour, Fortis called a break to hydrate.

"What do you think?" he asked Ystremski when the gunny joined him out of earshot.

"We'll get there. It's not that hard; we just have to keep drilling it."

Captain Williams and Lieutenant Orndorff approached.

"From the mouths of babes," Williams said as he gestured to Orndorff. "Go head, Number Two."

"Sir, why are we in a rush to get clear of the drop zone?" Orndorff asked Fortis. "We're dropping simultaneously, and there are no follow-on waves. The mechs can roll out and stop ten meters away, with the infantry right behind them. Intel said there won't be anyone shooting at us, so we can squat until the drop ships are gone, and we can see and hear. Then we can move out."

Fortis and Ystremski traded looks.

"Why didn't you think of that, Gunny?" Fortis asked with a smile.

"I wanted to try it your way first, sir, so you could see why you were wrong," Ystremski replied without missing a beat.

"Good thinking, Lieutenant," Fortis told Orndorff. "We'll make the change on the next run and see how it works."

While the battalion reloaded aboard the drop ships, Majors Perkins and Fitzhugh entered the drop ship bay. Fortis met them at the hatch.

"Good morning, Abner," Fitzhugh said. "We heard about your rehearsal and figured we'd observe, if that's okay."

"You're welcome to look at anything you want. You can kit up and join the fun on the drop ships if you like."

Perkins chuckled. "I'll pass, thanks. Weiss likes me enough to give me three drop ships, so I'll stick to spectating."

"I have more drop ships than I need," Fitzhugh said. "I'm with Lance. I'm curious to see how you're going to handle the mix of mechs and infantry. Wouldn't it be easier to put all the mechs on one drop ship and cram the infantry into the other?"

"It would, but if the drop goes wrong, I might lose all my mechs or infantry. You've got a full mech company, so you can spread the weight across all four drop ships and get enough firepower on the ground without unloading them all."

Fitzhugh frowned. "Three drop ships. Regiment gets their own drop ship, and Feliz doesn't like riding down with main battle mechs. It's just him, his staff, two command mechs, and a company of my infantry."

Just then, Ystremski called across the hangar.

"Major, we're ready to go."

"Enjoy the show," Fortis said as he trotted to Drop One, his assigned drop ship.

I hope this works.

The ramps dropped, the main battle mechs roared out and stopped, and the infantry filled in around them. When the Space Marines realized they didn't need to clear the drop zone, they were more than happy to allow the mechs to take the lead, which was exactly what Fortis wanted.

"Much better," he told the battalion with a surreptitious glance toward Perkins and Fitzhugh. "Let's do it again."

The next rehearsal went even smoother. Although they were crowded together on the drop ships, the Space Marines accepted the temporary discomfort with good humor because they knew their performance was much improved.

"That's enough for today," Fortis told Ystremski. "Colonel Weiss told me we're jumping through the gate around 1630. Restow the gear and get the lads something to eat before they turn in for the jump."

"Roger that, sir."

* * *

Two Space Marines from Bravo Company had severe adverse reactions to the warp jump and were transported to the infirmary for treatment. Fortis expected it; everyone reacted differently to jumping through a warp gate. Scientists had studied warp jumping for decades, but were unable to predict what symptoms one might encounter, or develop ways to mitigate them. A lucky few were unaffected, while most people felt some degree of nausea and headache. Some unfortunates suffered debilitating symptoms, and in extremely rare cases, death.

"The docs say they should be back on their feet tomorrow. The day after, at the latest," Stone told Fortis. "They'll be missed, but they're both riflemen in 2nd Platoon. If we have to go without them, we can."

"Roger that. They need to be cleared by the medical department before we drop, or they don't go. We can't afford to take anyone who isn't a hundred percent, because there won't be a medevac available."

The mood aboard *Mammoth* that evening was subdued, as was normal aboard ships after a warp jump. Smart planning had arranged the schedule to allow for a slower operational tempo after the jump, so the usual shipboard training and drills were suspended for the evening.

Fortis was in the battalion office, going over the operational plan and burning the details from the imagery into his memory, when Williams stuck his head in the door.

"There you are. I figured you'd be in your rack with a stomachache."

Fortis scoffed. "Nah. Made it through pretty easy this time. I'm just going over our plan, such as it is."

"I feel good about it, but it's pretty thin, isn't it?"

"We could use some more detail, but it'll work."

"Sir, most of the Space Marines I know that were divvied were good guys, and I have a hard time believing they supported the terror attack. I could be wrong, but I think the arrival of four main battle mechs and two companies of infantry is going to make a lot of them decide the Knighthood isn't worth fighting for."

"What do you make of Feliz telling us they don't intend for us to take prisoners?"

"Two of my cousins died in Colorado, so I want revenge as bad as anyone, but I'm not executing prisoners. I don't care who orders it."

Fortis nodded. "I agree. I guess we should hope the fuckers fight to the last man."

* * *

2nd Battalion rehearsed their assault plan twice the next day before Fortis was satisfied. It was critical that the Space Marines perform their individual roles flawlessly, but there was only so much they could accomplish in the confines of the ship. All of them had made training drops, but a training drop was nowhere close to the controlled chaos of a real drop zone, when pulses pounded, palms sweated, and the threat of incoming rounds was an ever-present danger.

It gratified him to learn that 1st and 3rd Battalions were conducting their own rehearsals. If nothing else, that would ensure the rest of the regiment was ready to go, and it would fill the dead time in the schedule as *Mammoth* and her escorts made their way to the Leavitt Peripheral.

Fortis set the company commanders to cleaning and preparing their gear and machines for the drop. Lieutenant Fuller and his logistics people verified that the trailers were full of spare pulse weapon batteries, rations, and a myriad of parts and equipment to keep the battalion fighting at their full potential.

Gunny Porter checked and rechecked the communications circuits between the Space Marines, the mechs, and *Mammoth*. 2nd Division had assigned a temporary comms satellite to the regiment, and Porter spent several hours ensuring the satellite would be in the proper orbit to support their operation.

After Lieutenant Vidic ensured all necessary paperwork was squared away, she took it upon herself to oversee Staff Sergeant Pope and the final preparations of the medical personnel assigned to the battalion. The medical supplies obtained by Ystremski and Dominguez were inventoried and distributed among the company corpsman and the trailers.

At 1600, Colonel Weiss summoned Fortis to his office.

"Division set your drop time for 1400 hours tomorrow. Will your battalion be ready on time?"

"Yes, sir. We worked out how to fit the entire battalion on two drop ships and rehearsed the landing several times. We're as ready as we can be."

"Any last-minute problems or personnel issues?"

"Come to think of it, two of my Marines went to the infirmary after the jump yesterday. The docs didn't think they'd be a problem, but I forgot to ask about them today. I'll check on them right away and report back to you."

"No need. If you have a handle on it, that's good enough. What about you? Are you ready to drop?"

"One hundred percent, sir. I've had a chance to work with the battalion staff and watch the companies in action, and I think we're ready to go."

"Colonel Feliz has a great appreciation for Gunnery Sergeant Ystremski. Although I don't approve of how you brought him aboard, his presence has bolstered our confidence in 2nd Battalion. Please ensure your Space Marines are ready to drop on time tomorrow, and if there are any problems, don't delay in reporting them."

"Yes, sir, will do."

As Fortis returned to the 2nd Battalion office, he struggled not to allow Weiss' words to rankle him. It was clear the colonel was long removed from the field, and it was equally clear that he held a grudge over Ystremski's arrival.

Fuck him.

* * * * *

Chapter Ten

Knight Errant Emil Zerec stood alone in the newly excavated operations center of the bunker and pored over the hand drawn map of Sanctuary and the surrounding mountains. It was rough and lacked the topographical detail Zerec had been accustomed to during his ISMC career, but an experienced infantry officer like Zerec could see the features that would be critical for any operation. He also had the advantage of having walked much of the terrain while scouting locations for the bunker complex, so he'd seen first-hand how steep the gorges were, and how fast and deep the creeks and rivers ran.

When Zerec had returned to Sanctuary from *Colossus,* he'd urged The Master to evacuate Sanctuary and scatter the Knighthood across the Free Sector. The Master had agreed, but the arrival of the Fleet destroyer had interrupted their efforts. The Master had ordered activation of the travelers in response to the destruction of *Colossus,* and Zerec knew what the UNT response would be. When The Master ordered Zerec to organize the defense of Sanctuary, Zerec resisted the order and explained to him that if they tried to defend Sanctuary without anti-air weapons, Fleet could simply stand off and pulverize the colony from space. It took some persuading, but he got The Master's blessing to excavate the bunker, and Zerec put the entire Knighthood to work with picks and shovels. After a few short days, they'd made significant progress.

Zerec had also made organizational changes to the Knighthood. The knights errant were no longer segregated from the regular knights, squires, and pages. Instead, they were put in leadership positions over groups ranging in size from ten to over a hundred. Every brother was assigned to a group and answered to the knight errant appointed over him. This arrangement satisfied Zerec's militaristic instinct to organize into platoons and companies for the war to come.

Knights Errant Eddie Merrill and Dylan Addison entered the operations room and joined Zerec. They were two of Zerec's most trusted lieutenants, and both had combat experience from their service in the ISMC.

"Blessings of The Master upon thee," Zerec said.

"And upon thee," they replied.

"Light of The Master upon thee."

"And upon thee."

"Brothers, I sent for you to discuss our plans to repel an assault by the Space Marines. I wish to draw on your knowledge and experience to ensure that we're prepared when the infidels arrive."

"You're certain they're coming?" Merrill asked.

"The UNT tac police swept up many of our Brothers over the past week, so all we know is 2nd Division deployed two days ago, with the stated mission to destroy us. Our contact on the Freedom Jump Gate didn't respond, and may have been picked up, too.

"The traitor Ystremski was in Sanctuary before he sabotaged *Colossus* and escaped, so they certainly know of this place. It stands to reason that Sanctuary will be one of their targets. I can't say that they'll come here first, but they will come." Zerec gestured to the map. "Please."

Merrill and Addison spent several minutes examining the map. A prominent rocky ridge jutted out of the jungle-covered mountain about ten klicks due north of Sanctuary, and it was under that ridge that the Knights had dug their bunker. Addison had accompanied Zerec on two patrols to the northeast, while Merrill had explored to the west.

"Standard ISMC doctrine for attacking a target like Sanctuary calls for a prolonged bombardment, followed by a direct assault on the spaceport," Zerec said. "If my instincts are correct, they'll assign a regiment to this attack." He pointed to an open area eight klicks east of the ridge. "I expect they'll insert a force in this area here to block a withdrawal from the spaceport. There's also a smaller area to the northwest that could accommodate another, smaller blocking force."

"A regiment?" Addison sounded dubious. "Brother, how will we defend all this against a regiment?"

Zerec smiled. "We won't. It's crucial that we isolate the two forces from each other to fight them separately. Brother Merrill will command a force of two hundred to attack and destroy their aviation element at the spaceport. Once the hovercopters are destroyed, they'll delay and harass the ground force while observing and reporting on enemy movements. Brother Addison, you'll be in command of a similar force here, near the eastern drop zone. Your tasking will be the same; delay, harass, and report. I'll position a company to the west to observe and report on enemy movements in that direction.

"The bulk of our force will stay close to the bunker. After we have confirmation of their strength and intentions, we'll respond with overwhelming force in one direction or the other and destroy them in detail."

Zerec looked up in time to see Merrill and Addison trade looks.

"You have doubts, Brothers? This is the time."

Addison spoke.

"Brother Zerec, if it's the will of The Master that we fight here, then I will fight to my last breath. I don't doubt his blessings and light will guide us in battle, but... the infidels... their numbers."

Zerec nodded. "Their numbers are impressive, but we'll use that against them. Instruct the men you assign to snipe and harass to shoot to wound only. Every wounded Space Marine is a burden to his comrades and will sap their resources. When you attack, that's when you shoot to kill."

"What of their firepower?"

"Their firepower is fearsome, indeed, but our faith is stronger, and our tactics are superior."

Addison and Merrill appeared unconvinced.

"When I was a cadet at Fleet Academy, we studied many battles throughout history. The details of each are lost to me, but something one of the generals said has stayed with me all these years. Now I understand why. His army faced an enemy with advantages like the Space Marines have, and he said, 'We grabbed them by the belt buckle.' His troops got so close to the enemy that they couldn't bring their more powerful weapons to bear. It became a battle of soldier versus soldier. With the blessings of The Master, we'll do the same."

* * *

As usual, Fortis found it almost impossible to sleep the night before an operation. He tossed and turned, but he couldn't silence the thoughts racing through his mind. It didn't help that Bishop snored like a wounded bear in an echo chamber, either. He finally gave up, got dressed in the dark, and went to the battalion office. When he got there, he found Vidic with her feet up on her desk, watching a holo movie. She jumped up when he walked in.

"Good morning, sir."

Fortis waved her back into her seat. "Relax, Vidic. What's wrong, can't sleep?"

"I slept some, sir, but it's a bit hard when one of my bunkmates from 1st Battalion is having an hours-long wet dream."

He burst out laughing.

"She gets a perfect score for creativity," Vidic said. "That girl has an imagination. I can give you her name, if you'd like."

"No, that's okay." Fortis couldn't stop smiling. "It's bad luck to have pre-drop sex."

Vidic's eyes grew wide. "Really?"

"Why, is that a problem?"

Her face flushed bright red. "Well, I uh… well…"

Fortis held up his hands. "I'm just kidding, LT."

Her shoulders slumped in apparent relief. "Why aren't you sleeping, sir?"

"I always have trouble sleeping before an operation. There's a lot to think about, I guess. That, and one of my bunkmates is snoring his head off."

It was Vidic's turn to smile. "It's Bishop, isn't it?"

"How did you know?"

"He was an instructor at Fleet Academy when I went through. One of my classmates hooked up with him on a field exercise during the Advanced Infantry Officer Course. She said he fell asleep, and the tent was shaking so hard, the roving patrol came to investigate. She almost got expelled from the course for it."

They both laughed.

"Is this your cherry drop, Vidic?"

"No, sir. I mean, yes, sir. I made a drop during training, but this is my first real one."

"Real world or training, the rules are the same. Keep your head on a swivel, watch out for your troops, and don't assume the mechs can see you just because you can see them. It's one wave with two drop ships, so there's no rush to clear the drop zone. Just like we rehearsed."

"Yes, sir."

Vidic frowned, and Fortis saw the anxiety in her face, so he changed the topic.

"You did a good job getting everything ready for deployment," he said. "Most Space Marines, officers included, have no idea how much administrivia it takes to deploy a platoon, much less a battalion. I appreciate you riding herd on Doc Pope, too. That's usually a duty for the battalion XO."

Vidic beamed. "Thank you, sir. It's just a paperwork drill, really. Not as much fun as commanding a platoon, but necessary."

"You're infantry?"

"The queen of battle, yes, sir."

"I thought you were an admin type."

"When I reported to the battalion, Seth—Major McNeely—discovered I could read and write, so he stuck me in this job." Her face fell a little. "DINLI."

Fortis grinned. "It's not the end of the world. You'll get your chance."

A short while later, Fortis decided to leave Vidic to her holo and make a tour of the drop ship bay. The massive drop ships assigned to 2nd Battalion squatted side by side, and it made him happy to see the craft gleaming in the dim orange light. Their condition reflected the pride the Fleet crews took in their ships. It was easy to make poor equipment appear top notch, but from his experience with Bovar and her crews during their rehearsals, Fortis was confident that the drop ships were in good working order.

Satisfied with his inspection, he started up the passageway toward his stateroom. As he passed the battalion office, Vidic opened the door, and the aroma of fresh-brewed coffee flooded his nostrils.

"Care for some coffee, Major?"

Fortis followed her inside and accepted a steaming mug. He knew without being told that it was real coffee.

"Courtesy of Lieutenant Orndorff," Vidic said with a smile.

"She has the makings of a general, or at least a good chief of staff."

As they sipped in silence, Fortis could tell from Vidic's body language that there was something on her mind.

"Sir, can I ask you a question?"

"Sure.

"After *Imperio*... I mean... you left us behind, and then 4th Division showed up. Where did you go?"

When Fortis and his team of ISR operatives had discovered the Fleet Academy training ship *Imperio*, he'd been forced to make the gut-wrenching decision to leave the kidnapped cadets and crew, including Vidic, aboard the derelict ship until he could engineer a rescue for all of them. His plan had worked, and ISMC 4th Division was credited with their rescue, and the capture of the slavers and their ship. Vidic was one of very few people who knew the truth about his mission.

"My team and I returned to Terra Earth."

"What about the bastards who kidnapped us, and the slavers who bought the others?"

"I don't know what happened to the slavers aboard *Alharib*. 4th Division captured their ship and took them into custody. I never heard about a trial, so they probably received airlock justice."

"Too good for them."

"Indeed."

"What about the others? Their 'customers.'" Vidic made air quotes. "Will they ever face airlock justice?"

"If it was up to me, we'd hunt down and execute every last one of them."

Vidic gave Fortis a wry smile.

"If you ever run for president, you have my vote."

Fortis drained his mug and stood up.

"First things first. I'm going to try to grab a nap before reveille. I suggest you do the same. Tomorrow's going to be a long day."

"Yes, sir."

Bishop had either suffocated or rolled over by the time Fortis crawled back into his bunk, because the stateroom was quiet. He stared at the darkness as memories of the mission that rescued *Imperio* replayed in his head. He thought about Bender, his team sergeant on that mission, and he fervently hoped the massive Australian wasn't with the Kuiper Knights at Sanctuary anymore. He had a hard time believing his friend would be involved with anything like the terror attack on the Peace Rally, but if he encountered Bender during the attack, and he fought back, Fortis would do his duty. With regrets.

DINLI.

* * * * *

Chapter Eleven

The morning crawled by as the Space Marines waited for the order to board the drop ships. Fortis tried to project positivity and confidence as he moved between the companies, but the fitful nap he'd gotten after his talk with Vidic had left him feeling raw. Finally, Gunny Ystremski pulled him aside.

"You need to leave the lads alone, sir. You're making everyone nervous."

"I have too much to do, Gunny."

"Like what?"

Fortis shook his head.

"Okay, then. Go do some battalion commander stuff. Shuffle papers. Pore over holos. Take a nap. Anything but hovering over the men."

"Am I really that bad?"

Ystremski scoffed. "Yeah, you're that bad. I just overheard you talking to some Alpha Company troops about checking their pulse rifle battery levels. When you do that, the company leaders think you don't trust them, and neither do the Space Marines."

"There are three hundred and fifty Space Marines who'll be risking their lives under my command. What am I supposed to do, let things go wrong?"

"No. You're supposed to trust guys like me, and Williams, and Loren, and all the others, to do our fucking jobs. We've done this before, you know."

Fortis let out a deep sigh.

"You're right, Gunny. I'm down in the weeds, worrying about platoon-level stuff."

"Of course I'm right, sir. I'm a gunnery sergeant. That's what I get paid for. I know you didn't sleep worth a damn last night, so I want you to go up to the battalion office, put your feet up, and grab forty winks. If anything comes up that we can't handle, I'll wake you. Otherwise, I'll poke you at lunch time."

* * *

After lunch, 2nd Battalion mustered in preparation for loading the drop ships. As was his custom, Fortis walked through the ranks and shook hands with each of the Space Marines.

"Remember your training, and I'll see you on the surface," he told them.

When Fortis was halfway through Bravo Company, a regimental messenger reported to him.

"Major, Colonel Weiss wants all battalion commanders to meet him in Bay Three."

The interruption irritated Fortis because he knew he wouldn't have time to finish with the battalion before they had to load up.

"Duty calls," he told the company commanders as he followed the messenger toward the hatch. "Let's get them loaded up."

In Bay Three, Fortis found Weiss, Perkins, and Fitzhugh standing in a loose group. Weiss wore a scowl, and his face was flushed bright red.

"Glad you could join us, Major," he said when Fortis approached.

"Sorry, Colonel. I was inspecting my troops."

"Inspection time is over. We're going to war." Weiss rolled his head on his shoulders as though he had a headache. "I've just been notified that it's nighttime on LAM. Someone forgot to set the ship's clocks to local time after we got through the Freedom Gate, and it's the middle of the night there."

"Is the drop delayed?" Fitzhugh asked.

"Negative. We can't delay the drop until daylight. The division drop schedule is too tight. You all have low light and thermal optics on your helmets. This shouldn't be a problem."

Fortis and the others accepted the news without remark. They knew the blizzard of dirt and rocks created by the drop ship exhaust would blind them anyway.

"The lads will get it done, sir," Perkins said, and they all nodded in agreement. The battalion commanders grinned and traded handshakes.

"Meet you on the surface."

Ystremski met Fortis at the hatch to the drop ship bay.

"Bad news, sir?"

"It's nighttime down there, and we can't delay the drop until daylight."

"I thought it was the middle of the afternoon?"

"Beats me. Their clocks are all fucked up, I guess. Day, night, it doesn't matter. We're going. Now."

"At least it's not raining," Ystremski quipped as he followed Fortis to their assigned drop ship.

"Give it time."

They climbed aboard Drop One, the lead drop ship loaded with Alpha Company and half of Charlie's mechs. It was a tight fit, but they squeezed into their seats. Fortis plugged into the comms panel to brief the battalion on the situation.

"All stations, this is Two Actual. We've just learned that it's nighttime on Sanctuary. There are no changes to the plan. Do your job, watch out for your mates, and we'll be on the surface before you know it."

The command net light blinked. It was First Lieutenant Bovar.

"Two Actual, this is Drop One. Nighttime drops require double the standard distance intervals between drop ships for safety. Is that going to be a problem?"

"This is Two Actual. I don't think so, as long as you can get us down there."

"Not a problem, sir. Stand by for launch."

Fortis surged against his restraints as Drop One released from the artificial gravity of *Mammoth*.

"Commence atmospheric entry."

The drop ship bumped and rattled as it penetrated the atmosphere of Sanctuary. Planetary gravity took over, and Fortis cinched his restraints a little tighter to take up the slack created by low-G. The drop ship engines roared as Bovar guided the craft down to the surface.

Fortis realized he'd forgotten his mouthpiece, which was supposed to protect his teeth when the drop ship slammed down. He leaned over and shouted to Ystremski.

"I forgot my fucking mouthpiece!"

Ystremski fumbled in one of his pouches and produced a tight wrap of gauze, which he passed to the major. Before Fortis could say anything, Ystremski smiled, and Fortis saw he also had a bandage gripped in his teeth.

"Bump and dump in two mikes," Bovar reported.

"This is Two Actual. Bump and dump in two mikes," Fortis repeated over the battalion circuit before he bit down on the bandage.

The final seconds before the operation began were the best moments of Fortis' career. All the administrative noise that stole his time and attention faded away to nothing as his sole focus became the next few minutes and executing his part of the mission.

Wait for the mechs to disembark. Follow them and Alpha Company off the drop zone. Link up with Bravo Company and wait for the rest of the mechs. Easy day.

Drop One slammed onto the surface, and the ramp dropped open. Mech crews scrambled to release the heavy chocks and chains that kept their vehicles secured to the deck while others climbed inside. Engines roared, and the two main battle mechs charged down the ramp, followed by the recon mech and command mech. When the mechs were clear, Alpha Company released their harnesses and raced down the ramp into the maelstrom created by the drop ship engine exhaust.

Fortis switched from low light to infrared, but his visor was whited out. He slapped his helmet a couple times, without success.

Fucking low bidder junk.

Ystremski was at his elbow as Fortis raced across the drop zone. When they reached the mechs, they took cover and waited.

After the drop ships blasted back into the sky, the silence was almost shocking. Fortis listened in as platoon commanders reported to their companies while the rest of Charlie's mechs moved up.

"Two Actual, this is Two Alpha. All Marines in position. We can't see shit, but we're standing by for tasking."

"What do you mean?" Fortis asked.

"The jungle is glowing," Williams replied. *"Some kind of pollen or photoluminescence. We switched to straight visual."*

Bravo and Charlie echoed Captain Williams' report, and Fortis shook his head.

"At least everyone's on the ground with no casualties. That's got to be a first," he told Ystremski.

"We're just getting started, sir."

Fortis chuckled as he switched to the regiment circuit. "Hammer, this is Two Actual. 2nd Battalion drop complete, no casualties. 2nd Battalion moving out."

"This is Hammer. Roger, out."

Fortis slapped Ystremski on the shoulder. "Here we go, old buddy." He keyed his mic. "All stations, this is Two Actual. Let's move out but take it slow until we get some daylight."

Alpha Company took the lead, flanked by one of the recon mechs. The rest of the mechs followed close behind, and Bravo brought up the rear.

"You ought to be in a command mech," Ystremski said.

"Maybe later. Right now, I want to stretch my legs."

When the sky began to lighten, one of the command mechs rolled to a stop next to Fortis, and the mech commander stuck his head out of the forward hatch.

"You want a ride, sir?"

Before Fortis could respond, a pulse rifle bolt flashed out of the jungle, and the mech commander's head exploded. Fortis stared in disbelief for a moment before he dove to the ground.

"*Sniper!*" someone shouted over the circuit. Space Marines fired in all directions, joined by the guns of the mechs. For thirty seconds, they shredded the jungle on full auto until the foliage glowed with bluish white plasma.

"Cease fire! Cease fire!" Ystremski shouted. "Buncha fucking cherries, shooting at ghosts."

The firing stopped, and Fortis jumped up to look inside the command mech. Blood and brains had splashed across the inside of the vehicle. All that remained of the mech commander's head was the lower jaw dangling by a flap of skin, and Fortis choked back the urge to vomit.

Most of the commander's brains had landed in the driver's lap, and she shrieked as she scrambled to get free of the corpse and climb out of the mech. The sensor operator and gunner bailed out the back ramp and dove to the ground.

"What the fuck are you doing?" Ystremski demanded. "Get back in there."

"But the body—"

"Fuck the body. He's dead, and there's nothing we can do for him. That vehicle is out of action right now because you're hiding out here. Go!"

By then, Doc Pope had arrived and climbed inside to bag up the remains. Warrant Loren appeared at Fortis' elbow.

"What happened, sir?"

"Sniper got a head shot on the mech commander," Fortis said. "The crew panicked and abandoned the vehicle."

"I'll fix it, sir."

Several Space Marines lifted the body bag out of the mech and laid it on the ground. Pope climbed out and approached Fortis.

"It's a fucking mess in there, sir, but we got most of it. What do you want to do with him?"

Before Fortis could answer, Captain Williams called.

"Two Actual, this is Two Alpha. We found the spider hole where the sniper was hiding. We searched the whole area, but there's no body."

"Roger that." Fortis looked at Ystremski, who shrugged.

"We gotta move out, sir."

"Okay." Fortis called out to Loren. "Warrant, your people have two minutes to clean up the mech. If they don't want to do it, they can hump with the infantry." He turned back to Pope. "When they're done cleaning, load the body back into the mech. We'll take him with us until we can find a decent place to bury him."

While he waited for the mech crew to finish their task, Fortis dialed up the command circuit.

"Hammer, this is Two Actual. 2nd Battalion took sniper fire. One KIA. Charlie Mike."

"Charlie Mike" was Space Marine lingo for "Continue Mission."

"This is Hammer, Roger, out."

Fortis switched to the battalion circuit. "This is Two Actual. Move 'em out."

Ystremski called Fortis on a direct circuit.

"I wish you'd ride in the command mech, sir."

"Why? What kind of example would I be setting for the battalion?"

"A live *example. That sniper got a head shot kill from distance, which means he's got optics, and he can shoot. We blew the hell out of the jungle and didn't find*

anything, which means he can move. Call me crazy, but seeing as we only have one CO, it might be a good idea to protect him. Him being you."

"Huh. I hadn't thought about it that way."

"You're not supposed to think about things that way, sir. You're an officer, so you're supposed to think about whether you packed enough rose water and bath bombs. Leave the tactical stuff to me."

Fortis laughed at Ystremski's humorous chiding, but he knew his friend meant well. Still, he wasn't going to let the threat of a sniper cause him to hide inside a mech.

"The mech commander wasn't wearing a helmet. That's why the sniper got the kill," Fortis said. "Besides, if the sniper *was* aiming at me, he missed by a lot. Maybe he's not that great a shot."

"Have it your way, sir. I'm trying to keep you in one piece, but if you want to be stubborn and get yourself killed, that's your prerogative."

As the sky grew lighter, Fortis noted that the jungle was devoid of life. No insects skittered away through the leaf litter. No unseen animals rustled the undergrowth, and the sky was clear of birds.

Weird.

* * * * *

Chapter Twelve

High above Drop Zone Lead Pipe, Warrant Officer Anar "Sucky" Sokolov tried to relax as the drop ship she copiloted descended to the surface. This was her tenth drop since she'd earned her wings, but they never got easier.

The status screens on her instrument panel showed all green, and the muted roar of the engines added a comforting background noise. The low light and infrared sensors were ineffective above two thousand meters; until they were activated, there wasn't much for her to do except wait and watch the system status screens.

At two thousand meters, she touched her intercom button as she flipped a switch on her console.

"Activating integrated visual display."

The visual display flickered to life and instantly whited out.

"Fuck."

Sokolov turned the switch off.

"What are you doing, Sucky?" the pilot demanded.

"System malfunction. One of 'em whited out. Let me try one at a time."

"Hurry up. That screen is blinding me."

Sokolov's ears burned at the pilot's rebuke.

"Roger that."

She flipped on the low light sensor, and the display went white. She switched to infrared, and the display remained unchanged, so she turned it off.

"Looks like the display circuits are fried," Sokolov reported.

"Okay, we'll go in on instruments. X marks the spot."

The X was their assigned drop spot on the geographic display; they just needed to drop within the area of uncertainty around the X. The visual references helped, but every drop ship pilot was trained to make instrument landings.

"Fifteen seconds to Drop Zone Lead Pipe," the drop ship pilot advised over the circuit. *"Sensor scan shows the drop zone is clear."*

The engines revved up to slow the drop rate. There was a loud *bang*, and the drop ship tilted to the left. Alarms whooped and control panel lights flashed red.

"Flame out, port side!" the pilot shouted.

Before the pilot could cut the starboard engine, the drop ship touched down, and the port landing gear dug into the surface. The drop ship rolled to the left.

"Emergency! Emer—"

The force of the impact slammed Sokolov against the bulkhead. Stars spangled her vision when her helmet hit, and her restraints dug into her waist and shoulders. She tried to punch the reactor emergency shutdown button, but her arms wouldn't move. A wave of heat swept through the cockpit, and Sokolov knew the ship was on fire.

* * *

Major Perkins flashed a thumbs up to a nervous looking Space Marine seated across from him aboard the lead drop ship for 1st Battalion. The young man gave him a brief smile before he squeezed his eyes shut.

Cherry.

Perkins was a veteran of two combat drops, and he hated the helpless feeling as the drop ship plummeted to the surface. The noise and confusion of a drop zone came as a welcome relief, and he always swore he'd never do it again. Until the next time.

"Fifteen seconds to Drop Zone Lead Pipe," the drop ship pilot advised over the circuit. *"Sensor scan shows the drop zone is clear."*

All around him, Space Marines made final adjustments in preparation for landing. The drop ship engines howled as the pilots slowed the rate of descent. Suddenly, the drop ship pitched over to the left and slammed into the surface.

A loud explosion shook the craft as something in the engine compartment exploded. All around Perkins, Space Marines screamed as a large fireball mushroomed up the centerline of the drop ship. Weapons, gear, and bodies broke loose and tumbled around the compartment as the craft rolled over. The lights went out as the reactor shut down, and a split second after the emergency lights came on, Perkins saw a large shape bearing down on him.

Mech.

* * *

Chaos reigned at the spaceport drop zone codenamed Firebird. As soon as the ramps opened, intense sniper fire disrupted the landing. Dead and wounded Space Marines had to be dragged clear of the ramps so the mechs could disembark, which delayed the deployment of 3rd Battalion. In the confusion, half the force had turned south, away from the buildings that were the initial targets of the assault. Once there, they had to wait until the drop ships were clear of the spaceport before they could cross the spaceport and rejoin their companies.

To complicate the situation, Colonel Weiss had gotten involved in directing the movements of 3rd Battalion. On the console aboard his command mech, he could see the location of every unit down to individual squads, When he grew frustrated with Major Fitzhugh's seeming inability to get control of her battalion, the colonel began to issue orders. Fitzhugh protested on the command net, and he delivered a stinging rebuke on the battalion net for all to hear. After that, she fell silent.

"Colonel! Lead Pipe suffered a drop ship casualty," the tactical communications watch aboard Weiss' command mech reported. *"Button Four."*

"What? What the fuck's going on?"

"I didn't catch the entire transmission, sir. Just the report that one of their drop ships is down."

"You're supposed to be covering that circuit, Sergeant," Weiss spat back. "Do I have to do everything?" He punched Button Four, the 1st Battalion command circuit. "One Actual, this is Hammer. Report your status."

"This is Captain Moore, sir. One Actual was aboard Drop One when it exploded."

"Say again. Drop One exploded? What happened?"

"I'm not sure. I unassed Drop Two in time to see a giant fireball and the jungle on fire. The pilot said Drop One burned in. That's all I know right now, sir."

"Report the status of 1st Battalion, Captain."

"I'm trying to sort it out, sir. The CO, half the headquarters element, two mechs, and all of Alpha Company were aboard Drop One. Bravo and Charlie

have set a perimeter, and we're searching for survivors, but everything is still burning. I don't think we can do much until daylight."

Weiss waited a second before he responded. "You're One Actual now, Captain. I want a full report as soon as possible. Hammer, out."

He broke the connection and dropped his headset on the keyboard.

What else could go wrong?

"Colonel, Top Shot's calling!" the watch shouted from his seat in the compartment forward of Weiss. "Button One."

Colonel Feliz was aboard the regimental command mech fifty meters from Weiss.

Weiss grabbed his headset and stabbed Button One.

"This is Hammer, sir."

"Jo, it sounds like things are off to a rough start," Feliz said.

Weiss winced. He hated when Feliz called him 'Jo.'

"Yes, sir. Fog of war, but we'll get it sorted out."

"Maybe the fog of war here at Firebird, but Lead Pipe is more than confusion."

"No doubt, Colonel."

"What about Rock Wall? Any news?"

"Not since they dropped, sir."

"Hmm. Okay, let's keep 2nd Battalion moving. I'm afraid 1st Battalion's going to need some time to sort themselves out, so I'm delaying the timetable for six hours. That'll give 3rd Battalion more time to secure the spaceport, too."

"Aye, aye, sir." Weiss struggled to keep his emotions in check. In his opinion, this was the time to capitalize on their momentum, not slow things down. The lack of organized resistance told him the Kuiper Knights were in disarray, and every second the Space Marines delayed their assault was a gift to their enemy.

"One more thing, Jo. Stop issuing orders to 3rd Battalion. They have enough problems without staff meddling, too. Top Shot, out."

* * *

Brother Zerec woke with a start and sat up. He somehow knew it was time to be up, and he swung his legs off his bunk and slid his feet into his waiting boots. As he tied them up, there was a soft knock on the door, and a squire poked his head in.

"Brother Zerec, Brother Lyle in the operations room sent me to wake you. The Space Marines have arrived."

Zerec stood and donned his red smock. He didn't care if his clothes became wrinkled when he slept in them, but his smock deserved a higher level of care and attention.

"Lead the way, Squire."

Zerec found Brother Lyle and two other Knights gesturing at carved figures on the map. Squares represented mechs, hovercopters were rectangles, and blue-painted rocks represented company-sized infantry units. They bowed at his approach.

"Blessings of The Master upon thee," Zerec said.

"And upon thee," they replied.

"Light of The Master upon thee."

"And upon thee."

"What's your report?"

Lyle gave him a broad smile.

"The Space Marines have dropped, Brother, but we've received good news from Brother Addison, here to the northeast. One of the drop ships crashed and was destroyed. Two others landed, but their force is disorganized."

"What of the spaceport?"

"Brother Merrill reported four drop ships landed there, but he can't give details about the force until daylight. His force took the Space Marines under fire as they landed."

"How many hovercopters?"

Lyle shook his head. "There was no mention of hovercopters, Brother. I sent runners to both Addison and Merrill to collect more details when it's light enough to see."

Zerec pointed to the northwest. "What about over here? What's this?"

"The Brothers there reported two drop ships with vehicles. Probably an infantry company and mechs. Perhaps a reconnaissance in force. We'll know more when we can see."

Zerec stared at the map and tried to divine the intentions of the Space Marine commander. It was as he suspected; a regiment-sized attack to seize the spaceport, with the secondary drop to trap the Kuiper Knights if they withdrew. If the report from Addison was accurate, they were truly blessed. The loss would improve their chances to destroy that force before turning on the others.

He rubbed his chin as he considered the force to the northwest. Two drop ships meant it wasn't a large force, but why would they drop so far from the others? It didn't make sense that it was a reconnaissance in force because of where it dropped, but what else? Some sort of combat control element? Engineers?

"Send twelve companies to join Addison as soon as possible and order him to attack with everything he has. We must take advantage of their confusion and strike them before they have time to recover. Also, ensure that you send runners to the northwest to collect intelligence there. We must know what we're facing."

* * *

One klick east of Drop Zone Rock Wall, Private Frederick "Ninja" Stauffer took two steps and stopped. All his senses were tuned in to the jungle around him, and he carefully scanned for anything that seemed out of the ordinary.

As if anything on a distant planet is ordinary.

Ninja crouched down and waited for his momentary loss of focus to pass. He'd earned his nickname because he was the best point man in Alpha Company, and he was the best point man in Alpha Company because of his ability to focus.

Satisfied that he was back on task, Ninja stood and took several steps. Somewhere behind him, the rest of the company followed. He paused, listened, and continued. A branch snagged his leg, and Ninja instinctively pulled free. Time slowed to a crawl as he realized his mistake. Before he could warn the others, the world disappeared in an orange flash.

* * *

Fortis heard the *crump-crump-crump* of grenades exploding in quick succession somewhere ahead, followed by the sound of automatic pulse rifle fire. He switched to the Alpha Company circuit to listen in on the action, but all he heard were confused voices and nonsensical orders.

"Stay here. I'm going forward to find out what the fuck's going on," Ystremski said before he ran forward at a crouch. A few minutes later, Williams called Fortis.

"Point man ran into a booby trap, sir. Somebody hung frags in the trees and a couple smokes on the ground. Two KIAs and three WIAs."

"What was the shooting?"

"One of the squad leaders thought he saw something and opened up. We didn't find anything."

"Roger that. Remind your Marines to maintain fire discipline."

Ystremski returned and motioned to the command mech. "Before we move out, there's something you need to see."

Fortis slid into the commander's seat, and Ystremski climbed in next to him.

"Display Alpha Company overlaid on the division map on screen one," Ystremski ordered the system operator.

Blue dots appeared in a staggered line spread across the display.

"That's Alpha Company right now." He pointed to a shaded red area. "That's our objective. Notice anything wrong?"

"Alpha's headed the wrong way. They need to turn and head northeast."

"Correct, except they can't." Ystremski used a stylus to draw a line across the display, from northwest to southeast. "This is a sheer cliff that doesn't appear on the division map. It's about thirty meters high. The infantry can climb down and continue to the ridge, but the mechs can't. The squad on point has been following the cliff, looking for a way down for the mechs."

"Who ordered them to do that?"

"Nobody. They turned northwest to follow the cliff edge, and nobody stopped them, so they kept going."

Fortis shook his head. "Let's go up there and unfuck this mess. We don't have time to waste."

"Negative, sir. You're not going anywhere."

"What?"

"I said, you're not going anywhere." Ystremski stabbed the screen with his finger. "This is the kind of bullshit that happens when nobody's watching the big picture. While you're out there humping like a private and giving orders like a sergeant, Alpha Company's leading us all over the fucking place."

"The company commander—"

"Williams didn't stop them, and neither did Orndorff, because they can't see this. The company NCO, Staff Sergeant Lentz, is too busy keeping his troops from getting lost or shooting each other to worry about the strategic picture. Somebody has to stay above it all, and that somebody is *you*.

"When you're out there, your field of view is limited to what you can see. That's okay when you're commanding a platoon, or even a company, but not a battalion. If you were in here an hour ago, you would've seen Alpha angling in the wrong direction and stopped 'em. You didn't know about the cliff because you didn't ask about it."

Fortis' face grew warm as he stared at the screen and Ystremski's words sank in. He hated to admit it, but his friend was right. Fortis loathed the idea of leading the battalion from a mech console, but it was his job to maintain the big picture over three companies, and he couldn't do it effectively without situational awareness. He nodded.

"Okay, you win. You're right, I should've seen what was happening up front a long time ago. You've been up there; what do you suggest?"

"All three companies are staying put for now. I told Williams to send a squad southeast along the cliff for a few klicks to search for a way down. It'll be light soon, and we'll get this unfucked. In the meantime, I suggest you hop on the horn and tell Regiment what's going on."

"Anything else?"

Ystremski must have detected the resignation in Fortis' voice, because he thumped the major on the shoulder and gave him a big smile. "Look at the bright side, sir. Riding in here means you won't have to change your socks as often."

*****

Chapter Thirteen

Brother Fehoko opened the door to The Master's sleeping quarters and found him sitting on the edge of his bed in the dark.

"Master, the Space Marines have landed."

"Where's Brother Zerec?"

"He's in the operations center. He sent me with the news."

The Knights bowed as The Master entered the room.

"Blessings upon thee," he intoned.

"And upon thee," they replied.

"Light upon thee."

"And upon thee."

"Rise, Brothers."

The Knights straightened up.

"What's the situation?"

Brother Zerec stepped forward and pointed to the map.

"Master, as we expected, elements of the ISMC 2nd Division have dropped on the spaceport at Sanctuary. Our observers reported four drop ships at the spaceport, so I estimate their troop strength at five hundred, with mech support. The lead battalion of a regiment, probably." He pointed to an area northeast of Sanctuary. "Three additional drop ships were reported in this area, and two more here." He indicated an area northwest of Sanctuary.

"How many total, Brother?"

"One company per drop ship means four hundred and fifty here, and three hundred over there," Zerec said. "Added to the force at the spaceport, I estimate fifteen hundred infantry, plus mech and air support. Two thousand, total."

"Why have they dropped there, instead of the spaceport?"

Zerec sneered. "The Space Marines are predictable, Master. The bulk of their attack is meant to seize the spaceport and drive us from Sanctuary. These two smaller drops are intended to serve as blocking forces to hinder our withdrawal. Because we anticipated their tactics, they are grasping at air."

Several of the Knights chuckled.

"Two thousand enemy troops hardly seems like a laughing matter," The Master said.

"This is not the 2nd Division that I and some of the others served in, Master. This 2nd Division is a patchwork of Space Marines left over after the drawdown, thrown together to fill an organizational chart at Manpower. Our sources report that many of their officers are newly reported, and they have not conducted anything larger than company-sized exercises. Individual squads and platoons may be combat effective, but overall it is a weak force. We have them outnumbered. With your blessing, we will be victorious."

"How do you propose to fight them, Brother?" The Master asked.

"I sent some men to harass the smaller force to the west. Another force will engage the force at the spaceport to destroy their hovercopters and slow their advance. Our main force is headed east to destroy the force there. One of their drop ships crashed upon landing, so it appears they're at two-thirds strength. After we've crushed them, we'll turn west and smash that small force."

"You're certain of your plan?"

"As certain as I can be, Master. They made a critical mistake when they divided their force. We'll destroy them piecemeal before they can concentrate their forces. War is, by its nature, uncertain, but with your spiritual guidance and our unshakeable faith, we can hardly fail."

The Master studied the map for a long moment.

"Are we not committing the same mistake by dividing our force?"

It pleased The Master when Zerec blinked.

"Master, we've detached smaller forces to impede their advance. That's hardly the same thing as dividing our force as they have."

The Master nodded. "Brother Zerec, I bless your plan. Make war on the infidels and drive them from our sanctuary." He turned for the door, and the Knights bowed.

"Blessings upon thee."

"And upon thee," they replied.

"Light upon thee."

"And upon thee."

The Master strode back to his sleeping quarters, with Fehoko close behind. He stopped at the door.

"I'm going to pray. Do not disturb me."

As he prostrated himself, The Master's thoughts were on humility, the lesson he hoped Zerec had learned.

* * *

"Hammer, this is Two Actual. Be advised, the divisional map is inaccurate. There's a thirty-meter cliff running northwest to southeast across our intended line of advance. Scouts from Alpha Company are reconnoitering a path for the mechs. I transmitted an updated graphic. 2nd

Battalion has encountered sniper fire and IEDs thus far. Three KIA and three WIA. 2nd Battalion, Charlie Mike, over."

"This is Hammer, Roger. Expedite reconnaissance and get a move on. Hammer, out."

Fortis resisted the temptation to curse aloud. The sensor operator called him over the intercom.

"Don't take it personally, Major. The whole regiment's fucked up."

"What do you mean?"

"I've been eavesdropping on 1st and 3rd Battalion command nets, and they've got big-time trouble. One of the drop ships crashed at Lead Pipe. Killed the CO and a company of infantry. The landing at Firebird got all screwed up, too. They took sniper fire, and half the infantry went the wrong way. I think the colonel relieved the battalion commander, but I'm not sure about that."

"Perkins is dead?"

"Yes, sir. Perkins and Alpha Company, 1st Battalion. Lost a couple mechs, too."

"Damn it." Fortis could see Perkins' smile as they shook hands in the drop ship bay, and his stomach lurched.

A whole company?

"Why did the drop ship crash? Was it hostile fire?"

"They haven't said, but it sounds like it just burned in and flipped. They didn't report taking any fire."

"Okay. Keep listening, and let's see if we can get down off this fucking cliff."

A few minutes later, the sensor operator called again.

"Major, Recon One just launched a tube toy. It's up on video channel three if you want to watch," the sensor operator told Fortis.

A "tube toy" was a shoulder-launched miniature reconnaissance drone designed for infantry use. The drones came packed in individual lightweight tubes and were launched by a blast of compressed air. When launched, the wings automatically unfolded, and the engine activated. Video and infrared imagery was transmitted back to the operator, who could then link it on a standard network.

Fortis pulled up video channel three and watched as the drone flew along the cliff. The ground sloped away several klicks to the southeast and leveled out.

"Looks like there's a way around for the mechs, sir."

"Agreed."

Before Fortis could issue orders to turn Alpha Company, the drone feed disappeared.

"Hey, what happened?"

The Alpha Company circuit exploded to life.

"Contact right!"

"Contact left!"

Fortis listened as Captain Williams directed his company in their response to the ambush. On the tactical display, a squad of blue dots on the left advanced while another on the right moved sideways to outflank their attackers. One of the main battle mechs moved up to support the squad on the left while two others peeled off to the right.

Meanwhile, Bravo Company moved up and formed a perimeter around the rest of the mechs and the command element. Fortis decided it was safe to open the top hatch and look at the troops surrounding the command mech. He strained to hear the ambush, but the jungle absorbed the sound.

"Major, the first sergeant is on the horn," the sensor operator called up to him.

Fortis slid back into his seat, put on his headset, and dialed up direct to Ystremski.

"What's up?"

"I caught up with the squad reconnoitering to the southeast, and I think we found a way around this cliff."

"Affirmative. I was watching a drone feed of the area from Recon One when the ambush kicked off."

"They're mopping up now; you should get a call from Williams any minute."

"Okay. I'll send new waypoints after he does. Hammer wasn't happy to hear about the cliff. He said we're holding up the regiment, and he wants us to move out."

"Fuck him."

Fortis laughed. "I said we were Charlie Mike."

"I'm going to double back and see what's up with the ambush."

"Roger that."

Fortis no sooner got off the circuit with Ystremski than the sensor operator called him again.

"Sir, I replayed the drone feed in slow motion. Right before it cut out, it looks like someone sniped the bird. Channel three again."

Fortis watched as the drone flew along the cliff. He saw a bright flash in the jungle, and the screen went black.

"Did you see it?"

"I did. Can you run back the last few seconds again?"

The recording played again, and Fortis saw the flash. Before he could ask, the sensor operator played it again and froze it at the moment of the flash.

"That looks like a pulse rifle to me, Major."

"Agreed. Can you plot that flash on the tactical screen to see where the shooter was?"

A red X appeared on the screen in the jungle on the far side of the cliff.

"That's a hell of a shot."

Just then, Captain Williams called.

"Two Actual, this is Two Alpha. 2nd Platoon triggered an ambush. We found two enemy KIA and followed a blood trail into the jungle, but it disappeared. I have one friendly KIA and two WIA. Standing by for orders."

"Roger." Fortis moved his cursor over the map display, clicked several times, and hit SEND.

"All stations, this is Two Actual. I just sent new waypoints to follow around the cliff to the southeast. Marching order remains the same; Alpha, Charlie, and Bravo."

The company commanders acknowledged their orders, and Fortis watched as Alpha Company reformed and moved southeast along the cliff.

Ystremski called again.

"Hey, Major, I checked out the ambush site. It was a textbook L-shaped ambush; four shooters, two holes per leg. Nothing fancy, but tactically sound. I can't understand how two of them got away, unless they sprouted wings."

"Yeah, these guys are more than a bunch of religious fanatics playing soldier. Just before the ambush, someone sniped Recon One's tube toy from the jungle beyond the cliff. The sensor operator plotted the position; you should be able to see it on your visor display."

"I see it."

"One more thing. 1st Battalion lost a drop ship. Killed their CO and a whole company. I haven't confirmed that."

"Does Hammer want us to move that way?"

"Negative. He hasn't issued any orders to that effect. He just wants us to get a move on."

"Roger that."

* * *

At DZ Lead Pipe, Captain Elisa Moore sank to the ground beside one of 1st Battalion's recon mechs. 1st Battalion had been on the ground less than two hours, and she was already exhausted. Her head buzzed from the constant barrage of communications as the battalion struggled to deal with the unexpected loss of the CO and a company of infantry. Finally, she gave up and climbed out of the recon mech she'd been using as a command mech.

Two hundred meters away, a thick column of black smoke stained the dawn sky above the fiery wreckage of Drop One. Space Marines had rushed to the crash site to rescue their comrades, and the senior NCOs had to drive the rest away from the wreck at the barrels of their pulse rifles. The company commanders finally got control over their troops and set up a perimeter to wait for full daylight.

Gunnery Sergeant Arridahios "Pappy" Papadopoulos, Bravo Company's gunny, appeared and squatted next to her. He and Moore had formed a tight bond when Moore was Bravo Company's CO, and it had continued after she was promoted to battalion XO.

Moore waved a weary hand. "Hiya, Pappy. How's it going?"

"All this and a paycheck, too," the gunny said.

Moore managed a weak grin. "I'm too tired to laugh."

"Me, too. I came by to fill you in on what's happening. Bravo Company has the perimeter set. It's kind of a kidney bean pointing north. It's not great, but it's the best we can do right now.

"Breaker One, Two, and Four are posted top, middle, and bottom. You've got one of the recon mechs here, and the other is in the southern end. The corpsmen have set up a casualty collection point between you and Breaker Two."

"Casualty collection point?"

"Yes, ma'am. A couple dozen Space Marines got burned when they responded to the crash site. Two of them died, and there are five more the docs can't do anything for but keep them doped up. Captain Nasser is one of 'em."

"Nasser's dead?"

"Not yet, but I don't think he's got much longer."

Moore drew a ragged breath that turned into a sob. "Too many dead."

"Yeah. Too many dead, and there ain't even anybody shooting at us yet."

"What are we going to do, Gunny?"

Pappy stood.

"Captain, we still have over three hundred Space Marines and a handful of mechs. We need to unfuck ourselves, bury our dead, and move out. We have a mission, remember?"

"But the major—"

"Major Perkins is gone, ma'am. So is Alpha Company. There's nothing we can do to change that. Regiment's counting on us to get into our blocking position as soon as possible, and that's what we need to do. Get on your feet and issue the orders, ma'am. This is no time to feel sorry for yourself."

* * *

Brother Sandy Wells led his squad of Kuiper Knights along a slight depression in the jungle floor to a position near the Space Marine perimeter. He waved them down and crept forward to get a better look at their objective.

Brother Addison had entrusted Wells with the critical task of destroying a main battle mech, and he was determined to succeed.

Wells had been a Space Marine until the Corps turned their backs on him. He was angry at the Corps, but he felt a small twinge of guilt at the idea of fighting his former brothers. Still, they had no right to come here and attack his new home.

Wells saw several infantrymen standing sentry along the tree line, but they didn't appear too alert. Inside the perimeter, corpsmen tended to wounded Space Marines who lay in rows in the shelter of a recon mech. He could just make out a main battle mech behind it.

Difficult, but not impossible.

Helenium armor protected main battle mechs from the most powerful battlefield weapons, and attacking one with a handful of troops armed with pulse rifles and grenades should've been a suicide mission. As a former mech commander, Wells knew of two panels located on the underside of the behemoths that gave access to the auxiliary cooling system. If they could get to those panels, two or three frags detonated inside would be enough to disable the mech, His squad wore ISMC lightweight battle armor breastplates stolen from *Colossus*, which should help confuse the Space Marines.

Wells scooted backward until he reached his squad.

"There are a few guards, but nothing we can't handle," he whispered. "When I pop a smoke, shoot the nearest sentries, and then throw frags. After I pop another smoke, we'll move in. Our target is the main battle mech. If we move fast, we can get in and out without too much trouble."

Wells gave the group a few minutes to spread out. He pulled the pin on a smoke grenade and threw it as far as he could.

Headshots dropped the sentries, and frags exploded among the other Space Marines. The suddenness of the attack caused several to freeze, while more scrambled for cover. Those who responded fired wildly into the surrounding jungle.

Wells heaved two more smoke grenades toward the mech. and smoke billowed around the vehicle. His squad jumped to their feet and charged forward into the smoke. Wells dove under the mech and found one of the brothers named Ewing already there with the access panels open. Wells held up two frags.

The other man nodded. Wells pulled the pins and jammed the grenades inside. Ewing slammed the panel shut, and both men scrambled to escape under the cover of the swirling smoke and confusion. A stream of pulse rifle bolts chased them and stitched across Ewing's back. He went down face first, and when Wells paused to help him up, a bolt hit him behind his right knee. His legs flipped out from underneath him, and stars exploded in his head when he landed on his back.

Wells struggled to roll over and crawl to safety, but someone tackled him and knelt on his neck while his arms were yanked behind him, and restraints tightened on his wrists.

"Gotcha, fucker."

* * * * *

Chapter Fourteen

Two Space Marines dragged Wells to a spot next to a command mech and dumped him on the ground. He cried out when he landed on his damaged leg. Someone had bound his wound and tied a tourniquet above his knee, and the pain throbbed throughout his entire body.

"Water," he said in a voice that was barely a croak.

A Space Marine sergeant crouched next to him.

"Water."

The sergeant shook his head. "Not until I get some answers."

Wells shook his head.

"Have it your way."

The Space Marine tapped the bloody bandage. Wells jerked and howled in agony.

"How about now?"

Wells squeezed his eyes shut as a tear leaked from the corner of his eye.

"Sergeant, why don't you stop torturing that terrorist and kill him already?" a female voice demanded from inside the mech.

"No way, Captain. This prick needs to answer some questions, and then he needs to suffer."

"Fine, whatever. At least gag him. I can't fucking think over here."

The sergeant jerked Wells into a seated position. The officer leered at him as he drew his kukri and cut a strip from Wells' ragged trousers.

"You hear that, terrorist? The captain doesn't care what I do to you as long as you're quiet."

Just as the Space Marine stuffed the rag into Wells' mouth, pulse rifle bolts sprayed the area, and Wells heard the sharp *crack* of grenades close by.

"Fuck!"

The sergeant jumped up and tried to move to cover, but he tripped on Wells and landed heavily on his stomach. Wells screamed in pain through the makeshift gag. The Space Marine scrambled toward the mech, but two bolts hit him in the face and destroyed his head. His body jerked, his feet kicked the ground, and then he was still.

Space Marines moved across the clearing while the 20mm pulse cannon on the command mech shredded the jungle in a spray of blue-white energy. The sounds of gunfire moved away and then died out.

Through the red haze of his agony, Wells watched a Space Marine corpsman crouch down to examine the dead sergeant.

"Hey, Captain, they got Sergeant Yarmouth," he called over his shoulder.

"Dead?"

"Yes, ma'am. He's missing his head."

"Dammit. All right, bag him up, Doc."

Wells managed to spit out the gag.

"Corpsman. Water."

The corpsman walked over. He saw the restraints and the shredded remains of Wells' leg.

"What's your story?"

"Water."

"Captain, Yarmouth's prisoner is still alive. What do you want me to do with him?"

"Kill him already, would you?"

"No, ma'am, not my thing. I'm a corpsman, not a killer."

"Fine. I'll get someone else."

The corpsman kneeled next to Wells and put a hydration pack straw to his lips.

"Sorry, pal. At least you won't die thirsty."

Wells gasped with relief as the water eased his parched throat. Another Space Marine joined the corpsman.

"Captain Moore told me to dispatch the terrorist," the newcomer said. "Why are you giving him water?"

"A little mercy never hurt, Jameson."

Jameson?

Wells struggled to focus on Jameson's face. When he did, he blinked in surprise.

"Jameson?" His voice was a croak.

"It's bad luck to know the name of your executioner," Jameson said as he drew his pulse pistol.

"Jameson, it's me, Wells. 3rd Platoon, Echo Company."

"Wells? Holy shit! Hey, Doc, I know this one. Well, I used to know this one. Back in 5th Division." Jameson stared at Wells. "What the fuck are you doing, fighting for the terrorists?"

"I'm not a terrorist," Wells said as he tried to sit up. He grunted as pain shot through his leg, and he slumped back down.

"You bastards killed a hundred thousand people on Terra Earth, and you don't think you're a terrorist?"

Wells shook his head in confusion. "What? No, I didn't. I mean… what are you talking about?"

"You fuckers shot some rockets at a Global Peace Rally full of civilians and killed over a hundred thousand people, including a bunch of kids. Don't tell me you don't know about it."

"I don't know anything about that. I came out here to make a better life for me and my family. The Master said you were here to destroy us."

"Damn right, we're here to destroy you, because you rocketed civilians."

"You gotta believe me. I don't know anything about that."

Jameson leveled his pistol at Wells' head. "You're about to get an education."

* * *

At Drop Zone Firebird, First Sergeant Stefan Webster ducked into the hangar and located Major Selwyn Bishop, squatting on his helmet. He trotted over and shouldered his way through the crowd of staff officers and NCOs gathered around the major.

"Hey, XO, what the hell is going on? I've been all over the place, and nobody knows what they're supposed to be doing. Why aren't we moving?"

Bishop threw up his hands. "How the fuck should I know, Top? Weiss yelled at the CO, so she quit talking. Then the colonel quit talking. The whole battalion is pinned down by a bunch of snipers, and the goddamned CO has her head up her ass."

"Has anyone sent out patrols to engage the snipers?"

"That's what Fitz was trying to do when that jackass Weiss took a very public shit on her. I haven't heard a word from her since."

Webster was incredulous. "We've been sitting here all day because the major's *feelings* are hurt?"

"Nah, it's more than that. The 1st Battalion CO's drop ship burned in and blew up, so they're trying to unscrew that situation. The regimental intel squirrels are confused over the whereabouts of the Kuiper Knights, so they're huffing their own farts in hopes of divine inspiration."

"What about 2nd Battalion?"

"They were lost, the last I heard. They're probably having a circle jerk in the jungle."

Webster laughed. Bishop had risen through the ranks from private to major, and he'd developed a gruff, unapproachable exterior. His profanity was legendary, and when he was under stress, it was on full display. Like now.

"Why don't you go find Major Fitzhugh and ask her what the fuck we're doing?" Bishop asked. "She loves it when sergeants ask questions, and she's not talking to anyone else, including me."

Webster nodded. "Okay, Major. I'll go knock on the CO's mech and kick some ass, see if I can make something happen.

"Be careful when you kick her ass. You don't want to break her neck."

Webster found Fitzhugh's recon mech parked next to one of the biodomes. He trotted over and joined the crowd of officers gathered around the mech.

"Is the CO aboard?" Webster asked one of the Space Marines on security detail.

The Space Marine motioned to the open ramp.

"She's inside, Top."

Webster almost collided with Captain Dina Prior, the 3rd Battalion operations officer, as he mounted the ramp.

"Sorry, ma'am."

Prior gave him a tearful look before she hurried away.

Oh, boy.

He took off his helmet and tucked it under his arm as he ducked into the command mech. Inside, he found Major Fitzhugh hunched over a console. Smeared scrawls in grease pencil covered the screen, and discarded rags covered the deck.

"Excuse me, Major?"

Fitzhugh turned and gave Webster an exasperated look before she pulled off her headset.

"What do you want, Top? I'm kind of busy."

"Why are we sitting here, ma'am?"

"What? Why are you asking me? Ask Regiment."

"I tried, ma'am. I talked to everybody I could find, and nobody knows. Everybody's waiting for someone to tell them what to do. In the meantime, snipers have my Space Marines crawling around on their bellies, and we're not doing anything about them." Webster's voice boomed out of the mech, and all other conversations stopped.

"What do you suggest?"

"I'm going to tell Captain Bouchier to send out patrols from Alpha Company to flush out the snipers. Maybe Regiment will realize it's time to stop fucking around and find the Kuiper Knights."

Fitzhugh scowled. "I don't know, Top. Let me see what Regiment thinks about that."

She reached for the Transmit button on her console, but Webster stopped her.

"Who cares what Regiment thinks, ma'am? Fuck 'em. It's 3rd Battalion's responsibility to secure the spaceport, and right now we aren't securing a fucking thing. Let them command by negation if they don't like what we're doing. We gotta get in the fight, Major."

The major threw up her hands. "Fine, Top. Do whatever you think is right. What's the worst that could happen, Colonel Weiss relieves me?"

Webster smiled and thumped her on the shoulder.

"That's the spirit, Major."

* * *

In the bunker, Lyle handed Zerec a folded piece of paper.

"A report from Brother Merrill."

Zerec read the note and handed it back to Lyle.

"The enemy has deployed patrols into the jungle surrounding the spaceport to chase away our snipers," Zerec said. "I believe this indicates their hovercopters will arrive soon. Perhaps as early as tomorrow morning."

Lyle disagreed, but he knew not to question Zerec, so he stood silent. Finally, Zerec spoke.

"Send two companies to join Merrill at the spaceport. That'll give him four total, which should be enough to hold the enemy and prevent the deployment of their aviation element. It's critical that he hold them in place to give Brother Addison and his force time to destroy the northern force."

* * *

Fortis called a halt after 2nd Battalion navigated their way down the cliff and back up the other side. They were behind schedule, but the Space Marines had been on the move since before daylight, and they had a long night ahead of them. Moving main battle mechs through thick jungle was a slow and difficult process, and two patrols from Charlie Company joined Alpha to trailblaze ahead of the massive vehicles to find the best way forward.

While the battalion set a perimeter, Fortis listened in on the 1st Battalion command net. He didn't know Captain Moore, but it sounded like their situation had stabilized, and she'd gotten control of the battalion.

He dialed up Ystremski.

"When you get a second, come down to the command mech."

"Be right there."

Two minutes later, Ystremski slid into the seat next to Fortis.

"What's up, sir?"

Fortis pointed to the cluster of red around 1st Battalion on his screen. "I told you 1st Battalion's been in the shit all day. Their CO is dead, and they've lost at least one command mech. It sounds like they finally got a handle on things, but they're not moving yet. From what I can gather from the reports, their attackers are wearing battle armor like ours."

"Probably stolen from *Colossus*. What about 3rd Battalion?"

"3rd Battalion secured the spaceport with minimal resistance. Now they're getting sniped at, but that's all they've reported. They're not getting much more attention than we are, but they're not moving."

"Have you heard anything new from Regiment?"

"Nothing. Our orders are still to link up with 1st, but that was based on 3rd Battalion pushing the main enemy force out of

Sanctuary. Since there are no Kuiper Knights to push, it looks to me like the enemy decided to attack 1st Battalion first. I think Regiment will order us to head for 1st Battalion instead of waiting for 3rd.

"With that in mind, I've decided to push past our blocking position and link up with 1st Battalion somewhere east of there."

Ystremski examined the map for a few minutes.

"It looks workable to me, sir. If there aren't any more cliffs or uncharted oceans in the way, I mean. Do you think Regiment will approve?"

"Regiment's sitting on their happy asses at the spaceport, waiting for 1st Battalion to move to their own blocking position. It's obvious to me that won't happen, so we're just going to go.

"Now, I marked a point of no return on the map," Fortis said. "When we get there, I'll call Regiment and tell them what we're doing. By then, Regiment should have some idea what the hell 3rd Battalion is doing."

"Roger that, sir. When do you want to start?"

"After the lads have had a chance to eat and rest up. Say, four hours. I want to move while it's still dark."

"Busting bush in the dark with the Kuiper Knights around is dangerous work."

"It is, but it's dangerous for them, too. We'll take it slow until it gets light, at least. Speed is our friend after that. I want the main battle mechs to take the lead and smash their way through the jungle, with the rest of the battalion right behind them."

"It's a little unconventional, but I'll try anything once."

"DINLI."

Ystremski chuckled. "Indeed."

* * * * *

Chapter Fifteen

During 2nd Battalion's four-hour stop for rest and rehydration, Fortis munched a pig square and listened in as Captain Moore of 1st Battalion reported their status to 1st Regiment.

It had taken her most of the day to compile an accurate status of her battalion. The drop ship crash killed Major Perkins, a handful of battalion staff, and an entire infantry company. The total body count from the crash was 164 KIA and 36 WIA. A main battle mech and the battalion command mech were also destroyed in the crash.

Shortly after dawn, a squad of Kuiper Knights wearing stolen battle armor had penetrated the Space Marine perimeter and destroyed a second main battle mech. Intense sniping throughout the day hindered efforts to deal with the dead and wounded until dark, after which Moore decided to hunker down and wait for daylight to move out. That decision infuriated Colonel Weiss, but there was nothing he could do to prod 1st Battalion into motion.

The cursors on his strategic display that represented 3rd Battalion positions were still clustered at the spaceport. From what he could glean from the command circuit, they'd only encountered sporadic sniper fire, yet they hadn't sent out patrols to suppress the snipers until late afternoon.

Why the delay?

It was obvious to Fortis that 1st Regiment had to revise the scheme of maneuver. Either through good planning or good luck on their part, the Kuiper Knights seemed to have focused their efforts on 1st Battalion. The battalion's combat strength was down almost 40 percent, and they hadn't left their drop zone yet.

2nd Battalion had made progress, despite their misstep at the cliff, but he wasn't sure it meant that much if 1st was stuck. Ystremski's voice in his ear broke his reverie.

"You awake, sir?"

"Yeah, I'm up."

"You didn't sleep, did you?" It was more accusation than question.

"Nah, I'm good. I was listening to the command circuit and thinking about what's going on."

"That's a bad habit, sir. Thinking, I mean."

Fortis chuckled. "It sure is. What's up?"

"It's time to get the lads moving. A glorious new day awaits."

"Roger that. Gimme a minute."

Fortis dug out a stim-pack and chased the pills with a pull from a hydration pack. He stood and groaned as his back protested.

"I'm going out to take a leak," he called to the comms watch forward of his.

"Okay, Major."

Fortis ducked around the side of the mech and relieved himself. When he was finished, he turned around to climb back into the mech and bumped into Lieutenant Vidic, who stood behind him. Her sudden appearance in the dark flustered him.

"Ah, damn. Sorry, Vidic, I was…"

"It's okay, Major. Girls pee, too."

Her amused tone made Fortis' cheeks burn, and he was glad for the darkness.

"What's up, LT?"

"Ops sent me to make sure you were up, sir. Ystremski told him it was time to go."

"I'm up. As soon as I get readiness reports from the company commanders, we're moving out."

2nd Battalion broke their perimeter and formed up to move. Two main battle mechs, Daisy Two and Three, led the way, with Alpha Company in support. Progress was slow, but they didn't encounter any geographic features that hindered their advance.

The Alpha Company circuit exploded.

"Contact right!"

The formation stopped while Captain Williams sent Space Marines to flush out a pair of snipers who'd fired at the convoy from different directions. Fifteen minutes later, he called Fortis.

"Two Actual, this is Two Alpha. We took fire from two different directions, so I ordered patrols out to find them. They were shooting in the dark, and we were searching in the dark, so we had no casualties and no enemy KIA."

"Roger that. Charlie Mike."

The battalion began to move again as the sky lightened.

* * *

Outside the Space Marine perimeter near Drop Zone Lead Pipe, Knight Errant Ameer Deblo crouched in the jungle along with the company of Kuiper Knights Addison had assigned to him.

Even though Addison was a fellow knight errant and a trusted member of Zerec's inner circle, Deblo chafed at taking orders from him. Deblo had come to the Knighthood with JJ Zylstra and the Paladins, and he didn't fully trust anyone who wasn't a Paladin. The Paladins were better trained than most of the other Knights, and in Deblo's opinion, Zerec had waited too long to organize the Knighthood into a military force capable of repelling an invasion by the Space Marines.

Despite his misgivings, Deblo had to admit that Addison's plan made military sense. An assault by the lightly armed Kuiper Knights on the Space Marine position was almost impossible as long as the three main battle mechs were operational. Even though the Knights outnumbered the Marines at the drop zone, they couldn't absorb heavy casualties. As Zylstra had pointed out several days earlier, the Space Marines could call for reinforcements. Every fallen Kuiper Knight was a permanent loss.

To mitigate this advantage, Addison had devised a strategy that depended on sudden strikes aimed at the mechs. An attack the previous day had destroyed one of the mechs, and it was Deblo and his company's job to destroy the remaining two. The snipers on the west side of the perimeter had kept up a steady rate of fire throughout the day and into the night, prompting the Space Marines to shift troops in that direction. Meanwhile, Deblo and his men had spent the night maneuvering around to the eastern side of the Space Marine position in preparation for a dawn assault.

Brothers on the west side would throw smoke grenades and Willie Pete just like they had the previous day to draw the full attention of the Space Marines. With the enemy distracted, Deblo and his company would move in. Two platoons, sixty men total, would target each mech, with orders to destroy it at all costs.

The men around him were barely discernible when Deblo heard a salvo of grenades explode in the distance, followed by a smattering of pulse rifle fire. The firing became a crescendo, and he imagined the jumpy Space Marines were shooting at ghosts in the darkness. He pulled a pin on a Willie Pete and threw it as far as he could. As soon as it exploded, the jungle came alive as Kuiper Knights charged forward.

* * *

In the pre-dawn darkness of DZ Lead Pipe, Pappy Papadopoulos moved among the Space Marine positions to check on his men.

My men.

When the Alpha Company drop ship exploded, it killed most of the 1st Battalion leadership, including the NCOs. After Captain Moore got control of the situation at DZ Lead Pipe, Pappy discovered he was the senior surviving NCO in the entire battalion. He'd challenged Gunny Leif Karlsson, the battalion communications NCO, to a game of Rock-Paper-Scissors, with the loser assuming the duty, but Karlsson had declined the offer.

Pappy had served under Captain Moore before and knew her to be an intelligent, if somewhat indecisive officer. He'd been on two bug hunts under her command, and both were simple nuke jobs. She knew what to do, but when she encountered resistance, indecision took over, and she often did nothing. That's when the NCO had to step in and TACAMO—Take Charge And Move Out.

As Pappy moved from fighting hole to fighting hole, his message was the same. Stay alert, be ready. The Kuiper Knights had taken advantage of the early chaos to destroy one of the battle mechs, and then maintained a steady rate of fire throughout the day and into the night. Captain Moore figured they'd conduct a similar attack in the pre-dawn hours today.

I'll be happy when we get moving.

Pappy crouched next to a fighting hole dug under a fallen tree trunk occupied by three Space Marines from Charlie Company. They were mechanics pressed into service as infantry after Alpha Company was lost, and he knew that even though every Space Marine was trained as an infantryman, they'd need extra attention.

"How's it going? All good?"

"Yeah, Pappy, we're good," one of them drawled in response. "We heard some movement in the tree line but didn't have a visual. You think they're coming?"

"Yeah, I think so. This is their last chance to hit us before we move out."

Pappy started to stand up when he heard the unmistakable *ping* of a grenade spoon.

"Here they come!" he shouted as he jumped into the hole.

Three Willie Petes went off in quick succession, followed by several smoke grenades. Plasma bolts zipped overhead.

Pappy tapped his communicator.

"All stations, this is Pappy. The enemy's attacking from the west."

The Space Marines responded with their own pulse rifle salvos. The mechs joined in, and the thumping of their automatic pulse cannons was comforting.

"Kuiper Knights in the perimeter. East!" an excited voice called over the circuit.

Pappy turned and looked back. He saw the brilliant glow of burning phosphorus and a dense cloud from smoke grenades, and he knew the Space Marines had been fooled.

"Protect the mechs!"

* * *

When the firing started on the west side of the perimeter, Sergeant Malcolm Holmes and PFC Newman Flannery were crouched side by side in their fighting hole, staring at the darkness on the east side of the 1st Battalion perimeter.

"Hey, Flanny, did you hear something?" Holmes whispered.

"Huh? No, I didn't hear anything. What was it?"

"I dunno. Hard to tell over the firing, but it sounded like—"

A brilliant white flash blinded the pair, and they slumped into the mud at the bottom of their hole.

"Fuck!"

Space Marines all around them fired as attackers appeared out of the jungle. Holmes rubbed his eyes and tried to blink away the dots, and he got back up and leveled his pulse rifle. He had some peripheral vision, and he did his best to engage the enemy racing through their positions.

"Get up, Flanny!" he shouted. He punched his transmitter. "Kuiper Knights in the perimeter. East!"

"I can't see! I can't see."

A figure appeared on the rim of their hole. Before Holmes could react, pulse rifle bolts stitched him across the chest. He tumbled backward and saw two bolts hit Flannery in the head before he lost consciousness.

* * *

The Space Marines responded quicker than Deblo expected, and he had to throw himself flat when pulse rifle bolts whizzed past his head. A recon mech fired wildly into the jungle with its automatic pulse cannon, and Deblo knew the Kuiper Knights still had the element of surprise.

"Come on!" he shouted to his men. "It's just ahead."

He fired from the hip as he ran, and his platoons followed. The ground was muddy and churned up by the mechs, and Deblo stumbled several times. He leapt over a row of litters and slid to a stop near his target. The engine wasn't running, but the turret traversed right and left as the crew blasted the jungle.

Heavy clouds hung low over the jungle, but the sky continued to lighten. Deblo knew they were running out of time. The Space Marines would soon discover the direction of the real attack, and the Kuiper Knights had to be back in the jungle when they did or risk annihilation.

A Knight clambered up onto the main battle mech, and another climbed up next to him with a satchel of grenades slung over his shoulder. The first one twisted the locking mechanism on the escape hatch, and the other pulled the pin on a Willie Pete. He let the spoon fly, stuffed the grenade into the satchel, and dropped it into the open hatch. Both Knights jumped clear and scrambled for cover.

The mech engine roared to life, and the massive vehicle lurched into motion just as the grenades exploded. The pressure of the explosion blew the hatch open, and gouts of black smoke belched into the sky. The Kuiper Knights could only stare as the behemoth took off across the Space Marine position, bouncing over living and dead alike, before it disappeared from sight.

A burst of pulse rifle fire reminded Deblo that his men were inside the perimeter, and he jumped to his feet.

"Fall back!"

Several of the Kuiper Knights threw smoke grenades to conceal their withdrawal as they made for the defensive gap they'd entered through. Deblo didn't know if the other two platoons had destroyed the other main battle mech, but now his first priority was to get back into the jungle unscathed. He plunged into the trees without injury and located their rally point fifty meters deep. The remainder of his two platoons soon joined him, and he counted fourteen survivors. Fourteen of the thirty who'd made the attack with him.

Steep, but we destroyed the mech.

* * *

Fortis listened in on the 1st Battalion command circuit during the Kuiper Knights' attack. He overheard a report that the Knights had destroyed another mech before the Space Marines could drive off the attackers. In addition to the mech crew, 1st Battalion had another nine KIA and sixteen WIA. Their strength was dwindling away, and they didn't seem to be doing anything about it.

We need to get there.

Before he could call Ystremski and discuss their options, the 2nd Battalion circuit came to life.

"*Contact left!*"

Snipers fired at Alpha Company from the thick underbrush, and the formation halted again as Williams sent out skirmishers to deal with them. Fifteen minutes later, he called Fortis.

"*Two Actual, this is Two Alpha. We found the spider hole where they fired from, but no bodies or blood. A waste of time.*"

"Roger that. Get your Space Marines back in formation and move out. If there's another sniper, respond with a salvo from a main battle mech. We don't have time to fuck around chasing ghosts."

"This is Two Alpha, Roger, out."

Ystremski called Fortis on a private circuit.

"What's up, sir?"

"1st Battalion got hammered again this morning. They lost another mech, and I'm not certain they're able to move. I think we need to haul ass to link up with them, but we're not going to get to them if we stop every time one of these fuckers takes a potshot at us."

"How far out are we?"

"Ten klicks, give or take."

"What about 3rd Battalion?"

"I don't know what the fuck they're doing. They haven't even left the spaceport yet."

"We're ready to move, sir. We'll get there as soon as we can. Have you looked outside lately?"

"Negative. My mom doesn't let me out of the command mech. What's going on?"

Ystremski snorted. *"Heavy cloud cover this morning. Looks like rain."*

Fortis heard a loud rumble of thunder as the command mech lurched into motion.

* * * * *

Chapter Sixteen

In the bunker later that morning, Brother Zerec pored over the map and rubbed his chin absentmindedly. The Space Marines had done almost exactly what he'd said they would, except they'd divided their forces into three parts instead of two. That came as a pleasant surprise, and he was happy to capitalize on their mistake.

Lyle joined him.

"Greetings, Brother. Good news from Brother Addison. The attack this morning was successful; they destroyed another main battle mech."

"Only one? They were supposed to attack both mechs."

"Their attack was detected by the Space Marines before they could get close to the second mech. The Brothers suffered heavy casualties before they were driven off."

"Hmm. How many Brothers fell?"

"Forty."

Zerec winced. The Kuiper Knights still outnumbered the Space Marines, but they couldn't sustain such losses without substantial reward for the sacrifice.

Lyle continued. "Many Brothers fell, but it appears the Space Marines aren't preparing to move."

Zerec pointed at the Space Marine force to the west.

"What's the status there?"

"We received a report this morning from Brother Campos that indicated those Space Marines were moving again. His company is delaying and distracting them to hinder their progress. The weather's turned, and it should favor us."

"Any news from the spaceport? Have the hovercopters dropped?"

Lyle shook his head.

"All Brother Merrill reported was the Space Marines deployed patrols to suppress our snipers. Nothing about additional drops or hovercopters."

"Strange. They dropped without air support two days ago. The longer they delay, the better, but time won't always be on our side."

Zerec didn't have the communications and intelligence networks his enemies did, but it was obvious what their intentions were. For all their advantages, they were predictable.

"Tell Brother Addison that he must destroy those Space Marines before they can link up with this group approaching from the west. Conduct an all-out attack as soon as possible. He outnumbers them right now, and he must use that to his advantage."

* * *

"*Command, this is Hammer, over.*"

Colonel Feliz sighed as he keyed his mic.

"Colonel Weiss, this is a direct secure circuit. There's no need for callsigns."

"*Sorry, sir. It's getting to be a habit.*"

"Do you have an update, Colonel? The display doesn't show a lot of progress."

"Yes, sir. 1st Battalion lost another main battle mech during a raid this morning, with several KIA/WIA. I ordered Captain Moore to get her Space Marines moving, but so far, she's disregarded those orders."

"What do you suggest, Jo?"

"I think she should be relieved of command, but I'm not certain who to replace her with. I can't get an accurate status of the battalion, so I don't know which officers are still alive."

"It sounds like 1st Battalion has bigger problems than Captain Moore. What are we doing to help? 2nd Battalion is making progress. Why isn't 3rd Battalion moving?

"Sir, the plan called for 1st and 2nd Battalions to get into blocking positions—"

"Colonel Weiss, our plan went to shit as soon as the drop ship crashed at Lead Pipe. For thirty-six hours, we've done little to adjust to the changing situation. What does Ops have to say?"

"Ops? You mean Major Welch? Uh, I haven't spoken to her yet, sir."

"What about Captain Campbell?"

"I haven't spoken to him yet, either."

Feliz's jaw dropped in disbelief, and he was glad they were talking on a circuit and not face-to-face. A commander had to stay in close contact with his staff, especially in a dynamic environment like the one 1st Regiment found themselves in. He took a deep breath to settle his nerves.

"Johann, I've been patient thus far in allowing you to take the lead on this operation, but no more. You haven't consulted with your primary advisors, and the best you can come up with is a recommendation to relieve a beleaguered battalion CO. That's unacceptable.

"Now, I won't relieve you, even though I *do* know who I can replace you with, but from this moment forward, you won't issue any further orders or requests for information that don't come from me. Watch and learn, and perhaps you'll get something out of this. Is that understood?"

There was a long moment of silence, and Feliz wondered if the circuit had dropped.

"Yes, sir. Understood."

"In ten minutes, I want the regiment staff and the 3rd Battalion commander to meet me in the hangar next to my mech. I'll assess our situation and decide what our next steps are. Make it happen, Colonel."

"Aye, aye, sir."

Feliz took off his headset and rubbed his face before he turned his attention back to his screen. A mass of red hostile symbols surrounded 1st Battalion's position. Some were current, while others were twelve or even twenty-four hours old. Old or new, they reflected the determined effort by the Kuiper Knights to destroy 1st Battalion. A tiny flicker of doubt tickled his stomach as he began to see the fatal flaw in the invasion plan.

The concept was simple: attack an enemy force while blocking his escape by positioning forces across his likely avenues of retreat. It was known as the Hammer and Anvil, and Space Marine infantry officers learned about it from their first day at the Advanced Infantry Officer Course.

2nd Division intel estimates had placed the bulk of the Kuiper Knights at the spaceport, which made the Hammer and Anvil the right approach—but the intelligence was wrong. The Knights hadn't resisted the drop, and by the time 3rd Battalion was on the ground, they'd fallen back into the jungle and seemed happy to snipe at careless Space Marines. 1st and 2nd Battalions weren't supposed to meet any resistance at all for the first twelve hours of the operation, but they'd been in contact with the enemy almost since the moment they dropped. The enemy hadn't reacted as the 1st Regiment planners had expected. In fact, it almost seemed as if they had a seat in regimental planning sessions. After the disastrous drop by 1st Battalion, everything had gone sideways.

Feliz recognized he'd made two major mistakes. First, he'd approved a plan that divided his regiment into three pieces without air assets to provide mutual support. 1st Battalion had been engaged by a much larger force, and they'd be forced to hang on until 2nd or 3rd Battalion could reach them.

Second, he'd stubbornly kept his promise to allow Weiss to command the invasion, and it had taken him too long to realize Weiss wasn't capable of dealing with the myriad of problems that faced a battlefield commander.

He stood up and tried to stretch the tightness out of his back and shoulders. He'd been sitting and watching events unfold for too long; it was time to turn this thing around.

Just then, his communicator buzzed. The display read MAJOR ALIYAH AL-SISA, the regimental science officer.

"I'm a little busy, Major. What can I do for you?"

"Sir, I've completed my preliminary analysis of some of the flora samples I collected. I'd like permission to send the data to Division to see what they think."

"Is there anything we should be concerned about? Any hazards?"

"No, sir, I don't think so."

"Then by all means, Major. Send all the data you want."

"Thank you, sir."

* * *

Aboard his command mech, Fortis examined the strategic display. What he saw displeased him.

3rd Battalion had finally deployed patrols into the jungle surrounding the spaceport, only to discover they were opposed by a small force of Kuiper Knights, perhaps less than a company. As a result, Regiment and 3rd Battalion planned to move out first thing the next morning.

Too late for 1st.

1st Battalion hadn't moved since the Kuiper Knights had destroyed another mech earlier that morning. It sounded like Moore had decided to dig in and wait for reinforcements from 2nd or 3rd Battalion. Regiment had alternated between angry orders and desperate pleading, but 1st Battalion wasn't budging.

Most of the 1st Battalion positions in the strategic display hadn't been updated for over twelve hours. Without accurate knowledge of their positions, all Fortis and 2nd Battalion could do was head in that general direction.

Light rain had begun to fall as 2nd Battalion moved out. At first it was just another nuisance, but as it continued to fall, it washed the photoluminescence off the trees and created a slippery, gooey mess on the jungle floor. Their progress had slowed to a crawl, but there'd been no further sniper attacks.

He keyed his mic.

"Two Charlie, this is Two Actual. Take a look at the strategic display and tell me if the full-sized drones can reach 1st Battalion."

"Will do," Warrant Loren replied.

A few minutes later, she called back.

"Two Actual, 1st Battalion is in range with only a few minutes of loiter time, if you want to get the drone back. The weather is shit, too. I don't recommend launching at this time."

"Roger that, thanks."

Two hours later, the battalion halted, and Captain Williams called Fortis.

"Two Actual, this is Two Alpha. We've got a situation with Daisy Two that you need to see. You, too, Charlie One."

The command mech drove forward and stopped near the front of the formation. When Fortis climbed out, he was met by Ystremski.

"This is a fucking mess," Ystremski said as he shook his head.

Williams and Loren joined them.

"Daisy Two slid sideways along this ridge," Loren said as she led the group forward. "The driver tried to get control, but it snagged on some trees and rolled over."

Daisy Two was upside down and half-buried at the bottom of a deep, steep-sided ravine. The trailer it had been towing had broken open and spilled pig squares and hydration packs across the jungle floor.

"Anybody hurt?" Fortis asked.

Williams pointed to a pair of boots that were barely visible sticking out from under the mech. "That's Lieutenant Orndorff. She was walking next to the mech when it rolled over. Her and two others."

Doc Pope tended to two mech crewmen next to the upended vehicle while numerous other Space Marines swarmed around the area.

"Break up the party, ladies!" Ystremski shouted. "Do you want one round to get you all?"

As if to make his point, a sniper fired from the jungle and hit a Space Marine in the leg. The Space Marines responded with a withering barrage, and when they ceased firing, the jungle glowed with blue-white plasma.

Fortis and Loren crouched on the edge of the ravine overlooking Daisy Two.

"Do you think we can get it out?"

Loren nodded. "Sure. We'll have to do some digging and knock down a few of these trees to make room for the other mechs to maneuver. We've got tow chains; when we're ready, we can hook them up and drag it out of there."

"How long?"

"If everything goes right, midday tomorrow."

"Midday tomorrow? Why so long?"

"Major, there's a main battle mech upside down at the bottom of that four-meter hole. The bank collapsed on top of it, so the first thing we have to do is stabilize the area so we don't drop another mech down there on top of it. We don't have dirt-moving blades for the mechs, so we have to do all the digging by hand. Once we get Daisy Two out of there, we'll have to restart the reactor and test the auxiliary systems. I'm sure the main rail is damaged beyond repair, so we'll have to replace it, which is about an eight-hour job. We don't carry spare rails anymore, so we'll have to order the part, and who the fuck knows how long that'll take. Then—"

Fortis cut her off with the wave of his hand.

"Okay, Warrant, I get it. It's a big job, but we don't have time. 1st Battalion doesn't have time."

"What do you want to do, leave it here?"

"It looks like we have to. Strip it of everything you can, police up those rations, and bury the rest. If the Corps wants it back, they can come and get it. We're moving out in fifteen minutes."

"But, Major…"

Fortis turned on his heel and strode away before Loren could argue. Ystremski followed close behind.

"What's she doing?" Fortis asked when they were out of earshot.

"It looks like she's turning, too, sir."

"Good. Warrant Loren is a good officer, but she's lost sight of the big picture. We don't have time to waste trying to dig that thing out of there."

"Roger that."

Fortis stopped when they got to the command mech. He tried to scrape the glowing slime off his boots before he climbed aboard. "I have to call Regiment and let them know what's going on, and then we need to get moving."

* * * * *

Chapter Seventeen

Colonel Feliz stood in front of a holo that displayed 1st Regiment positions and glared at his staff and the leadership of 3rd Battalion.

"We've fucked this up about as bad as we could, ladies and gentlemen," he said in a cold, hard voice.

None of the officers gathered around would meet his gaze, except Major Bishop of 3rd Battalion, who nodded in silent agreement. Feliz pointed a finger at Captain Bill Campbell, the 1st Regiment intelligence officer.

"Bill, your intel squirrels have been wondering where the Kuiper Knights are." With the same finger, he stabbed 1st Battalion's position on the holo. "Let me give you a fucking hint."

Campbell opened his mouth to respond, but Major Emma Welch, the Regiment operations officer, put a hand on his arm as if to say, *This is not the time to argue.*

"We've been spinning our wheels waiting for 1st Battalion to move into their blocking position, but that plan went to hell before we started. We're failing, folks, and Space Marines are dying because of it."

Nobody shifted their feet or cleared their throats, while Bishop continued to nod.

"So here's what we're gonna do," Feliz continued. "First off, we're gonna forget about fixing blame." He shot a look at Weiss. "There'll be time enough for that later." Feliz flashed a sardonic smile. "If we're lucky, we'll all be killed in action and avoid all that."

Nervous chuckles rippled through the group.

"Major Fitzhugh, you have fifteen minutes to get your battalion formed up and ready to move out. We're headed for 1st Battalion's position. Ops, work with the major to figure out our route. Suppo, get with the company supply types and make sure they have all the rations and pulse rifle batteries they need. Does everyone understand? Are there any questions?"

No one spoke up.

"We have to move fast, folks. 1st Battalion's getting hit hard, and we need to get there. Do NOT be the reason we're moving slow, or I'll strap you across the hood of my command mech. Get it done."

As the regiment and battalion staffs scrambled to get started on their tasking, Feliz motioned for Weiss to join him by the holo.

"Colonel, I'm going to call Captain Moore and Major Fortis and inform them about the change to our plan. I want you to ride herd on this group and make sure we're ready to go on time."

"Yes, sir."

Feliz put a hand on Weiss' shoulder. "Jo, it's time to redeem yourself."

* * *

In the bunker, The Master entered the meeting room, followed closely by Brother Fehoko. Zerec, Lyle, and the other Knights bowed.

"Blessings upon thee," The Master intoned.

"And upon thee," they replied.

"Light upon thee."

"And upon thee."

"Rise, Brothers."

After Zerec straightened up, he pointed to the map.

"Master, it appears the Space Marine commander has correctly assessed our intentions and has begun to react accordingly. Their 1st Battalion remains here to the northeast. We attacked them again this morning and destroyed another mech. I believe they're close to collapse." Zerec indicated the Space Marine force to the west. "The rain has been a blessing and a curse. It's slowed the Space Marines to a crawl, but it also washed away the photoluminescence that interferes with their optics. We no longer have the freedom of movement we've enjoyed thus far."

The Master studied the map. "How could the infidels know our intentions? Is there another traitor in our midst?"

His statement was both a question and a rebuke. An enemy agent had recently penetrated the Knights aboard the ex-flagship *Colossus* and almost upset their plans to acquire the massive arsenal of weapons and equipment. Zerec had been responsible overall for the operation, and while the security failure had occurred in recruiting, much of the blame for the subsequent destruction of *Colossus* had landed on his shoulders.

"Their invasion plan was rudimentary, but the Space Marines aren't fools," Zerec said. "After two days of battle, it should be obvious to them that our main effort is aimed at the destruction of their 1st Battalion, not defending the spaceport."

The Master stood silent for a moment as he struggled to form his next sentence. When he spoke, his words were halting. "What of Sanctuary? What do you hear?"

"There's been little activity at the spaceport, Master. After the initial assault, the Space Marines adjusted their positions, but have done nothing since. I initially thought they were awaiting the arrival of air support, but Brother Merrill hasn't reported any drops. After two days, it's beginning to look like they're going to hold the spaceport, even though hovercopters aren't coming."

"Can he defeat the force at Sanctuary?"

Zerec shook his head. "No, Master. Brother Merrill doesn't have sufficient forces to defeat a mechanized battalion. He's done a masterful job of harassing and delaying the Space Marines, but we can't expect much more from him."

The Master leaned on Fehoko's arm for support, and for a moment Zerec thought the older man might collapse.

"I've ordered Brother Addison to attack their 1st Battalion with all his strength as soon as practicable. Even though we outnumber them, the Space Marines have a technological edge, and we can't allow them to concentrate their forces. They're most vulnerable when in motion, so it's critical that we finish 1st Battalion in time to deal with 2nd Battalion before their 3rd Battalion can arrive. If Addison destroys them before they can link up, we stand a very good chance of destroying all of them."

Zerec gestured at the map while he spoke, but when he looked back, he saw The Master standing with his eyes closed.

"Master?"

The Master jerked as if he'd been poked, and he let out a snort.

"Yes, yes, very well, Brother. I don't have a mind for military matters, so we're blessed to have someone of your wisdom and experience, Brother Holcomb. I leave our defenses in your capable hands. Thus it shall be."

Zerec and Fehoko traded puzzled glances as The Master shuffled toward the door. When the door shut behind them, Lyle let out an explosive breath.

"What the fuck was that? The Master's losing it."

Zerec seized Lyle by the smock and slammed him into the wall.

"The Master is The Master," he snarled into the smaller man's face. "He's our father, and no mere Knight will question that. Do you understand?"

Lyle's eyes widened, and his face grew deathly pale. He struggled to form words, but they came out as an unintelligible croak.

"Do you understand?" Zerek punctuated his question by bouncing Lyle off the wall again.

The terrified man nodded. "Yes, Brother," he said with a squeak.

Zerec shoved him away and turned to the rest of the Kuiper Knights in the meeting room.

"That goes for the rest of you, too. The Master has exhausted himself with many hours of prayer seeking guidance for how best to lead the Knighthood through this time of peril. What you saw here today stays in this room, or I'll personally see to your punishment. Is that clear?"

Every head in the room nodded.

"Get out."

As the Knights filed out of the room, a cold finger of doubt poked Zerec in the chest.

Brother Holcomb?

* * *

"Command, this is Two Actual, over."

"This is Command. Go ahead, Major."

"Sir, I'm calling to report the loss of a main battle mech, Daisy Two. It was traversing an unstable hill, and a mudslide carried it to the bottom of a ravine. My mech commander said she can get it out of there in twenty-four hours, but the pulse cannon will require extensive repair with parts we don't carry. Based on that, I ordered her to strip the mech and bury it for recovery later."

"What's the status of your battalion?"

"2nd Battalion has three main battle mechs, two recon mechs, and one command mech operational. We've had eleven KIA and fourteen WIA. Total combat strength is 339, including WIA."

"Roger that. Anything else?"

"Yes, sir. If you look at your strategic display, you'll see our current position is east of our blocking position. I made the decision to push toward 1st Battalion. Based on what I've overheard on the command circuit, they're facing a much larger force. Unless otherwise directed, it's my intention to continue east to reinforce them."

There was a long moment of silence, and Fortis expected Feliz to explode. Instead, the colonel responded in a calm voice.

"This is Command. I concur with your intended movement. I just concluded a strategy session with my staff, and we reached a similar conclusion. 2nd Battalion will continue east at best speed to effect a rendezvous with 1st Battalion. 3rd Battalion will depart the spaceport as soon as possible and link up with 1st and 2nd in two days."

Fortis called his company COs and senior battalion staff on the battalion command net.

"1st Battalion is in a fight with a sizeable enemy force. From what I can tell, they've lost most of their mechs, with about two hundred

KIA, including their CO. They can't move, so we're going to relieve them. 3rd Battalion is still at the spaceport, but they'll be heading out soon."

"We're not headed for our blocking position?" Captain Litvinenko asked.

"There's nothing to block. If the intel estimate on Kuiper Knight troop strength was accurate, then the bulk of the Kuiper Knights are fighting 1st Battalion, and that's where we need to be. Our orders are to close on 1st Battalion as soon as possible, so we'll continue to advance all night.

"We need to move fast, much faster than we have been. I want a couple mechs up front bashing the bush, with strong infantry support. If we take fire, return it with pulse cannons and keep moving. Are there any reasons we can't do what I'm proposing? Alpha Company?"

"The jungle is slippery as hell, but at least we can see now," Williams said. *"We're ready."*

"How about Bravo? Anything to report?"

"Negative, sir. I'll be glad to get into the shit; bringing up the rear sucks."

Fortis chuckled. "Warrant Loren, how's Charlie Company?"

"We're good to go, Major. We got everything we could out of Daisy Two and buried it. Any idea how 1st Battalion lost their mechs?"

"They lost a couple on the drop, and the Kuiper Knights destroyed a couple during their attacks, but I'm not sure how. It sounds like they used a smoke screen to get in close and dropped grenades in the hatches. Which reminds me, I heard a report about some of the Knights wearing battle armor, so caution your Marines to be certain about who's who around them."

"Roger that, sir."

"How about the staff? Any questions or problems?"

All the staff said they had no issues.

"That's it then. I'll transmit new waypoints as soon as we finish here, and then we'll move out. Alpha and Charlie Companies, sort out how we can push through with mechs and infantry support. Bravo Company, sorry, but you're stuck back here with us." Fortis could almost hear Captain Stone cursing. He consulted the time. "We're jumping off in ten minutes."

* * *

A tap on the door interrupted Zerec's ruminations, and he looked up in annoyance when Lyle stuck his head in. "Blessings of The Master upon thee, Brother."

"Blessings of The Master upon thee as well. What is it?"

Lyle entered the room, holding a scorched and bloodied battle armor helmet and sleeve, which he placed on the table in front of Zerec.

"This just arrived from Brother Addison. It was captured from one of the Space Marines of their 1st Battalion."

Zerec examined the helmet and saw the scuffed chevrons of a staff sergeant above the visor.

"Is it functional?"

"Not at present, but one of the brothers who has experience with this equipment says he might be able to restore it to working order."

"Good. Pity it's not from an officer; we might have listened in on their command nets. Still, this might give us insight into their tactical dispositions. Let me know as soon as it's operational."

"Yes, Brother. I'll ensure your orders are carried out."

"Does The Master know?"

"No. The Master retired after evening devotions, and Brother Fehoko said he's not to be disturbed."

"Very well. Please pass on my thanks to Brother Addison for a job well done. The information we gain from that communicator could give us an important advantage in this war against the infidels."

Lyle turned to leave, and Zerec stopped him. "Find Brother Zylstra and send him to me."

"Yes, Brother."

While he waited for Zylstra, Zerec contemplated how to approach the former Space Marine.

He'd first met Zylstra when he and the Paladins had betrayed the ISMC operative Abner Fortis and delivered him to the Kuiper Knights aboard *Colossus*. It was immediately clear that Zylstra was motivated by anger toward the ISMC and UNT, not the religious fervor that had captured so many of the others. Zylstra carried out his orders with prompt attention to detail, so The Master rewarded him with the red smock of a knight errant. Zerec gave him command of a company of the former mercenaries he'd defected with and assigned them to oversee security of the bunker. Thus far, Zylstra's performance had been exemplary.

But is he the right man for what I have in mind?

* * * * *

Chapter Eighteen

At Drop Zone Lead Pipe, Pappy moved around the perimeter, pausing to exchange snatches of conversation with the Space Marines dug in awaiting the next attack. Rain had begun to fall shortly after the attack that morning, alternating between a light drizzle and pelting sheets. The Space Marines were protected from the elements by their lightweight battle armor, but the rain had a palpable negative impact on morale. Something about the effect of rain on the human psyche, he supposed.

From a tactical standpoint, the rain worked in the Space Marines' favor. It washed away the luminescence that whited out their optics so they could see into the surrounding jungle. It also turned the perimeter into a soupy mess, which should make treacherous footing for future attackers.

By mid-afternoon, the entire battalion knew they only had one main battle mech and one recon mech left. Space Marine infantry usually scoffed at the mechanized behemoths, but the automatic pulse cannons were a comforting sight when the enemy attacked in force.

The attack left mangled bodies scattered throughout the perimeter. As the Space Marines went about the ghoulish task of identifying and recovering their dead comrades, the sight of dead enemies armed with Space Marine pulse rifles and clad in Space Marine battle armor shocked them. It made their casualty numbers seem much higher than they were, and Pappy could tell their nerves were stretched to the breaking point. Some had even expressed doubt that they could win this fight.

Anxious to restore morale, Pappy ordered the dead Kuiper Knights stripped of battle armor and their bodies thrown into a pile outside the edge of the perimeter.

"Those thieving fuckers can have their dead guys," he said with a growl, "but we're taking our gear back."

He made a show of exposing himself to sniper fire as he moved about their position, but the snipers never took up the challenge. The Space Marines took heart from his show of bravado, and they became their smiling, swaggering selves again. They weren't going to let a bunch of raggedy-ass divvies beat them, no matter how many of them there were.

* * *

Brother Wulff Hassel watched as the last bit of light fled from the darkness that settled over the forest. His eyes were gritty with fatigue, and his knees and elbows ached from thirty hours of crawling through the jungle to monitor the battle with the infidels, but he grinned with anticipation. In a few minutes, he'd throw a Willie Pete to signal the beginning of the end of the Space Marines' 1st Battalion.

A surge of pride warmed his belly and made his heartbeat pound in his ears. The Knights under Addison were charged with stopping the Space Marines, which they'd done with great skill and valor. Hassel's men had only played a minor role in the fighting thus far, by keeping up a steady barrage of sniper fire, but Addison had given them the honor of leading the next attack. The knight errant hadn't described the assault as the final battle, but Hassel knew if they were successful, the Space Marines were finished.

Brother Zerec's advice to wound, not kill the Space Marines was prophetic. "A wounded Marine is a burden to his comrades," Zerec had advised the Kuiper Knights before they deployed. "They'll dedicate valuable manpower to moving their casualties, which will reduce their fighting strength." Hassel's men had swept the Space Marine positions with constant sniper fire, aimed low to wound and not kill—sometimes at the expense of their own lives—but it worked. The Space Marines hadn't tried to advance under the weight of their own casualties, and they'd dug hasty defensive positions in a kidney bean-shaped perimeter.

The attack plan was as simple as it was audacious. Just after dark, a force of brothers would make a strong demonstration in the southeast, while Hassel and his men would lead the bulk of the Kuiper Knights to breach the defenses at the middle of the kidney bean, along a narrow front from the other direction. Even if the Space Marines suspected a ruse, hundreds of Knights would charge through the gap and split the Space Marine defenses in two, after which they'd destroy each piece in turn.

Victory lay in the hands of the brothers detailed to destroy the remaining mechs. The vehicles gave the Space Marines a decisive advantage over the Kuiper Knights, and every time one was disabled or destroyed, their prospects for victory improved.

The sound of pulse rifle fire from the southeast reached Hassel, and he knew it was time to execute the plan. He pulled the pin on his Willie Pete, let the pin fly free, and lobbed it at the Space Marine position. Almost immediately, more smoke grenades rained down. Thick smoke blanketed the Space Marines, and all along their lines, they fired blindly into the jungle. Blue-white plasma bolts tore through the trees in search of targets.

Hassel imagined the Space Marines searching for targets through the smoke with their infrared visors. He saw his men crawling closer to the defenders to deliver a salvo of Willie Pete grenades. The rain had washed away the photoluminescence that allowed the Kuiper Knights to move undetected, and they hoped the brilliant flash from the phosphorus explosions would white out the Space Marines' optics long enough for them to penetrate the perimeter.

He put a whistle to his lips and blew three long blasts. The signal echoed along the northern and western perimeter, and the jungle around Hassel came alive as Kuiper Knights charged forward to engage the Space Marines.

"Praise to The Master!" Hassel shouted as he climbed to his feet and started forward at a walk. It wasn't cowardice that prompted his caution.

Brother Addison had insisted that his senior leaders hang back and avoid unnecessary risks during their engagements with the Space Marines. Most of the brothers who'd joined the Knighthood after the drawdown were of lower ranks, with a few sergeants and chief petty officers in their number. Only a handful of former junior officers like Hassel became Kuiper Knights, and it was their leadership that had granted the Knights success thus far. The Knighthood could ill afford many losses from that group.

The smoke from the WPs and smoke grenades burned Hassel's lungs and flooded his eyes with tears, but he forced himself to advance with his pulse rifle at the ready. He passed several dead Space Marines in scorched battle armor where a nearby explosion had sprayed them with burning phosphorus. Two Kuiper Knights lay in a tangle of arms and legs, but they were the only casualties among the Knights that Hassel had seen so far.

The pulse rifle fire became more accurate as the air cleared, and Hassel searched for a fighting position. He jumped into a hole with several Kuiper Knights in it and crouched down next to them.

"What's your status?" he asked them.

"There are Space Marines in a row of foxholes over there, about forty meters," one of the brothers responded as he pointed to the northeast. "They've got a group of Knights pinned down behind those fallen trees."

Hassel looked at their faces and smiled. "Let's dig them out. Two of you, follow me. The rest of you, cover us."

Addison's caution was forgotten as Hassel climbed out of the hole, followed by two other Knights. The other four laid down a blanket of covering fire as Hassel ran at a crouch to another covered position. From their new position, the trio poured fire on the Space Marines while the rest of the Knights leapfrogged them. Another group of Space Marines fired from concealment to the right, and one of the Knights went down.

"Stay down, we're in a crossfire," Hassel ordered. He threw a smoke grenade and waited. As soon as smoke began to billow, he jumped up and ran straight at the Space Marine position. He dove behind the wreckage of a main battle mech and threw two incendiary grenades as far as he could. The grenades exploded, and he heard the unmistakable screams of men on fire. Despite his small success, Hassel sensed the attack was losing momentum. He blew his whistle three times and waited.

Hundreds of Kuiper Knights charged out of the smoke, firing blindly from the hip. Blue-white energy bolts flew in all directions as the attackers and defenders intermingled.

Hassel watched a Kuiper Knight race up to the edge of a fighting hole and kill three Space Marines who were engaged from the other direction. A stream of plasma bolts from the far side of the position stitched him across the chest, and he tumbled into the pit atop the dead Space Marines.

A charging Knight paused to fire his pulse rifle, and a wounded Space Marine on the ground next to him rose up and shot him in the armpit. The wounded Knight dropped his rifle and landed on his attacker, and the two grappled on the ground. Blood splashed both men as the Knight bled out, and the fight was over in seconds. Hassel took aim and shot the Space Marine in the head, and he flopped over, dead.

An unseen sniper fired at Hassel, and blue-white plasma splattered off the mech. He scrambled around the damaged vehicle and out of the line of fire. He discovered three Space Marines who'd taken cover on the other side of the mech to pour fire into Knights attacking from the other direction. He pulled the pin of a phosphorous grenade, dropped it between them, and rolled back around the mech. A wave of heat and a choking cloud of white smoke engulfed the mech when the grenade exploded. Incredibly, one of the Space Marines staggered around the mech. Even the helenium in his battle armor couldn't protect him from a point-blank explosion, and his head and hands burned white-hot. Hissing globs of phosphorus and flesh dripped onto the ground like wax melting from a candle as he stumbled toward Hassel.

The Kuiper Knight could only stare, transfixed by the horror of the scene. The burning man fell to his knees, raised his hands skyward as though in supplication, and fell face down.

Hassel crabbed backwards to escape the heat and smoke from the dead man. A plasma bolt ricocheted off the mech just above his head, and he remembered the sniper. Before he could move, another bolt punched him in the back of his battle armor and slammed him into the mech.

Move or die.

Hassel rolled to all fours and scrambled to put the mech between him and the sniper as plasma bolts chased him, but he made it to safety without being hit again. He gasped to catch his breath and took stock of his situation. He'd lost his pulse rifle and a bandolier of grenades, but he was alive. The impact of the plasma bolt on his back had stunned him, but he didn't feel any pain.

Kuiper Knights continued to pour through the gap in the Space Marines' defenses. The thumping of automatic pulse cannon fire from one of the remaining mechs worried Hassel, and he had a moment of doubt. The cannon fire abruptly ceased, and a second later, Hassel heard a loud explosion and watched a fiery mushroom climb into the sky.

He low crawled to the fighting hole where he'd seen the Kuiper Knight shoot three Space Marines. He dug a pulse rifle out from under the bodies and checked the battery charge. Satisfied, Hassel poked his head up to survey the battlefield.

Orange and white light from burning vehicles and Willie Pete grenades danced across the Space Marine position while acrid smoke added a hazy, dream-like quality to the scene. A knot of Space Marines appeared through the mist and crept forward toward an abandoned fighting position to Hassel's left. Before he could take them under fire, two bodies jumped into the hole next to him and startled Hassel. He almost shot them before he saw they were Kuiper Knights.

"How goes the battle, Brother?"

"We're making progress." Hassel pointed to the Space Marines. "I was about to fire on them. Join me."

The trio of Knights readied their weapons and fired in unison. Two of the Space Marines went down hard, and the rest scattered. Two went right, and two went left. Hassel concentrated his fire on the right side and thought he saw another Space Marine go down before they got under cover. The other two took cover, and a three-way firefight developed. A recon mech opened up with a 20mm automatic pulse cannon, and the three Knights huddled in the bottom of the hole.

Hassel pulled out his last smoke grenade. "We have to move, Brothers." He pulled the pin, threw it out in front of their hole, and waited for the smoke. The other two Knights threw theirs, and the air was soon thick with choking smoke. Hassel climbed out of the hole and ran for the mech as he grabbed his last incendiary grenade.

* * * * *

Chapter Nineteen

The sudden ferocity of the Kuiper Knight assault caught 1st Battalion off guard, and it took several minutes for them to organize a response. The Space Marines had grown used to attacks at first light, and since the rain had washed away most of the photoluminescent pollen from the trees, they were overconfident in their ability to see the enemy.

Pappy was on the southeast perimeter when the firing began, and he fought alongside the Space Marines of Charlie Company for the opening minutes of the battle. The situation was confused at first, but things settled down quickly. Then the Kuiper Knights struck from the west, and Pappy realized the first attack was a feint.

Captain Moore issued a stream of confused orders from her position in the recon mech as the attack intensified and some Kuiper Knights breached the Space Marine lines. As the minutes passed, panic was obvious in her voice, and her orders became nonsensical.

Pappy raced to the recon mech and hammered on the hatch with the butt of his pulse rifle.

"Open up! It's me, Pappy."

A plasma bolt splattered on the armored side of the mech as he dropped in and spun the locking device. He found Captain Moore hunched over the tactical console. Some of the lights on the comms panel flashed, others were lit solid, and the rest were dark. Several speakers blared voice traffic from unidentified circuits, and Pappy had to shout to be heard over the bedlam.

"What do you think you're doing, Captain?"

Moore looked up in surprise. "I'm trying to—"

"You stupid bitch, you're going to get us all killed!" Pappy grabbed her arm and yanked her out of the seat. "Get the fuck out of my way."

He snatched her headset and slid in front of the console. He poked the SELECT ALL button on the comms panel, and then DESELECT ALL, and the noise disappeared. He punched buttons for Bravo and Charlie Companies.

"All stations, this is Pappy. Stand fast and listen up. Charlie Company, report your status."

"This is Charlie One. The enemy penetrated our lines in two places. There are some inside the perimeter, but we're holding."

Pappy shot a look at Moore before he responded. "Roger, stand by. Bravo Company, report your status."

"This is Bravo One. Looks like the attack from the south was a feint. Heavy pressure on the north end of our sector near Charlie."

"This is Pappy, Roger. All stations, hold your positions at all costs. It looks like they're making a run at Breaker Four and the recon mechs again. Do not let them through. Bravo, if you can, make an orderly withdrawal to the northwest to shorten the line and reinforce Charlie on the northwest. Make sure you maintain the integrity of your line, and don't lose contact with your flanks."

Pappy tapped the screen with the stylus and hit SEND.

"I just sent new positions to your visors. Watch out for Knights dressed in battle armor. Pappy, out."

He threw the headset on the console and stood up.

"That's how you manage a battle, Captain."

Tears streamed down Moore's face. "Gunny, it happened so fast. Regiment's been calling over and over, and I didn't know what to do."

"Ignore Regiment. They can't do a fucking thing to help us. They can wait for the info to update their displays."

Captain Moore slid back in behind the console. "I'm sorry, Gunny. I'll do better."

"You need to do better than just 'better,' ma'am. We're in serious shit here. Where's 2nd Battalion?"

"The last report had them seven klicks southwest, headed this way."

"They better hurry the fuck up."

Pappy opened the hatch and stopped.

"Stay cool, Captain. We can hold out until 2nd gets here."

Just then, a Willy Pete dropped into the open hatch, bounced off his chest, and landed at his feet.

"Oh, shit."

* * *

Fortis listened with growing concern as the reports from 1st Battalion became more confused. Regiment added to the mayhem with an unending stream of demands for status reports. He wondered if they'd been overrun when Moore went silent. Instead, an unfamiliar voice named Pappy took over the circuit and seemed to get control of the situation. When Pappy signed off, Fortis called his sensor operator.

"Who's Pappy?"

"Gunny Papadopoulos. He's 1st Battalion, Bravo Company's gunny. Sounds like he's the battalion NCO now, too."

"Gotcha."

He turned his attention back to the strategic display, and for the hundredth time that day, shook his head at the situation. 2nd Battalion had been moving as fast as they could, but their progress was slow. The rain had ended just before sundown, and the Space Marines could see their way clearly, but the mechs kept their progress down to a relative crawl. At their current speed, they wouldn't link up with 1st Battalion until sometime the following afternoon.

They can't hold on that long.

Fortis punched the button for the 2nd Battalion leadership circuit.

"This is Two Actual. Let's stop here for a few minutes. Warrant Officer Loren, launch a drone and send it up over 1st Battalion. I need to know what's going on up there. Gunny Ystremski and Captain Stone, join me in the command mech."

Ystremski and Stone climbed aboard the command mech and crowded around Fortis' console.

"The Kuiper Knights are hitting 1st Battalion right now, at sunset. I haven't heard any after action reports on the command net, but it doesn't sound good. The Knights got inside their perimeter again. 1st Battalion is contracting their perimeter, which should make it easier to defend. That's the last I've heard."

"It's a good thing the Kuiper Knights don't have artillery," Stone said.

"Can they hold out until we get there?" Ystremski asked.

"I don't know. At the rate we're moving, we won't be there until late tomorrow afternoon, and that's only if the rain doesn't start again, we don't lose another mech off a cliff, and we don't run into any unmapped rivers."

"What do you want to do, sir?"

"What do you think about detaching Bravo Company to double-time to 1st Battalion's position to help them hold on until we get the mechs there?"

"You want us to run through the jungle? At night?"

Fortis nodded. "Yeah, I do. It's not as crazy as it sounds. We can't get there fast enough with the mechs, and we can't leave them behind, so sending Bravo ahead is the logical choice."

"Sir, you're talking about dividing the battalion in the face of a superior enemy. Haven't we seen enough of that from Regiment on this mission?"

"What superior enemy are you talking about, Gunny? All I've seen is a bunch of snipers, and I'm not convinced the Knights attacking 1st Battalion are actually a superior force. It doesn't take a genius to figure out that we'd seize the spaceport and land a blocking force further inland. Lead Pipe was a pretty obvious spot to drop troops. They got lucky when the drop ship crashed, and they took advantage of the turmoil at the drop zone. If 1st Battalion hadn't lost their CO, an entire company of infantry, and a couple mechs before the battle even began, I think the current situation would be vastly different."

Ystremski and Stone stood silent, but their skepticism was obvious on their faces.

"If you leave right now, and haul ass all night, you can be there just before daylight. Our night vision is working now, so you won't be moving blind. If the Knights stay true to form and attack at first light, they'll get a big fucking surprise when they run into your guns. Then all you have to do is hold them off until we can get the mechs there tomorrow afternoon.

"I've got Loren launching a drone right now to get some idea of what's happening on the ground while you're moving. If the worst has happened, and 1st Battalion is destroyed, I'll call you back."

"Okay, Major. I'll make sure my guys take stim-packs, and we'll move out ASAP." Stone chuckled. "Ace is gonna cry when he hears about this."

"Hold on. I don't want the rest of the battalion to hear about this yet," Fortis said. "Bravo needs to move swiftly and silently, so the Kuiper Knights who've been spying on us don't get wind of this and report back. No catcalls, no joking around. Just get your guys together and go. I'll take care of Alpha and Charlie Companies."

"Roger that, sir. Anything else?"

"One last thing. I'm sending Gunny Ystremski with you."

Ystremski's eyebrows shot up in surprise, and Stone got a puzzled look.

"I've known him my entire career. I mean no offense, Captain, but I've known you less than two weeks. Make no mistake; you're in command. Gunny's there as an advisor; use him as such. He's got socks that have been in the ISMC longer than I have, and I have complete faith in him. And if you don't like it, DINLI."

"Skivvies, sir," Ystremski said.

"What?"

"Skivvies. I have skivvies that've been in the Corps longer than you. I change my socks pretty often."

Fortis chuckled.

"If you don't have any questions, Captain, take this smelly motherfucker and move out."

"Yes, sir."

Fortis dialed up the company commanders and the battalion staff officers and explained his plan to them.

"Make sure your Marines know that I don't want any noise when Bravo leaves. I don't want to give our Kuiper Knight spies a reason to get curious. Just because we're not running with Bravo Company doesn't mean we won't be hustling. We need to get there as soon as possible. Two Actual, out."

* * *

In the jungle near 2nd Battalion, a gentle prod jerked Knight Errant Francisco Campos from his cat nap.

"Brother, the Space Marines are moving again."

Campos shook his head to clear away the fog in his brain. It was still dark, but the rain had mercifully stopped.

"Moving? How long?"

"Just now, Brother. They stopped for fifteen minutes or so, and it sounded like they launched a drone. Now the mechs are moving again."

Campos groaned as he stood up. He'd joined the Kuiper Knights after he retired from the ISMC a decade earlier. After two days shadowing 2nd Battalion through the jungle, scrambling to keep up with their movements, and delaying them with harassing fire, he felt every bit of his 52 years. When the Space Marines stopped, Campos had taken the opportunity to sit down and close his eyes.

"Very well. Let's get the Brothers moving and find a good place to ambush them at first light."

* * *

"Blessings of The Master upon thee, Brother." Zerec turned and saw Zylstra standing in the operations center door.

"Blessings of The Master upon thee, as well." Zerec gestured to a crude stool. "Join me."

Zylstra sat and waited for Zerec to speak.

"How's your company, Brother Zylstra? Are they prepared for action?"

"Very much so, sir. Er, Brother. We're anxious to join the fight."

Zerec nodded. "Excellent. Your time is coming." He considered Zylstra for a moment. "You have combat experience. What do you make of this war?"

"I welcome the opportunity to strike back at the invaders. We must punish them for their arrogance."

"Indeed. We will. This time."

A puzzled look crossed Zylstra's face. "What do you mean, 'This time?'"

"After we destroy this force, do you think they'll meekly accept defeat and stay out of the Free Sector? Or will they return with more powerful forces and attack us again?"

Zerec felt a twinge of uncertainty and decided this wasn't the time to confide in Zylstra. Better to let the former Space Marine think about what he'd said and allow the doubt to percolate. He stood, and Zylstra followed suit.

"Brother, I apologize for burdening you this way. Know that The Master and I have complete confidence in you and your men, and we know you'll bring glory to the Knighthood in due time."

The two men embraced, and Zylstra went to the door. He stopped and turned around.

"Brother Zerec, I remember you from... well, before, and I know you're a man of honor. I'll do whatever you command."

Zylstra pulled the door closed behind him, and Zerec stared after him for a long time.

* * * * *

Chapter Twenty

At DZ Lead Pipe, Sergeant Luigi "Louie" Rizzo, Charlie Company, 1st Battalion, keyed his mic and tried to raise Alpha Actual for the fifth time. For the fifth time, there was no response. He tried Pappy, with the same result.

He'd copied the orders from Pappy to stand fast, but then the net went dead, and uncertainty began to creep in. Were the mechs supposed to move? He didn't think so, but it wasn't clear.

Rizzo and his squad were the maintenance team for Breaker One, the main battle mech that had been destroyed on the first day of battle. Without a mech to work on, they'd joined the infantry element of Charlie Company. He was proud of his squad for the way they'd fought against the Kuiper Knights. They'd defended their fighting holes and no attackers had penetrated their section of the perimeter. Every Space Marine was a rifleman, but his guys were mostly electronics types, with a couple wrench turners thrown in for good measure.

"Louie, what are we doing?" Corporal Cal Simpson, one of Rizzo's squad mates, called from the next hole over. His voice sounded abnormally loud in the silence that followed the attack, and Rizzo winced.

"Keep your voice down, meathead," Rizzo stage-whispered back.

"Louie, what are we doing?" Simpson hissed.

"I don't know. I can't raise Pappy or the captain. Have you seen anybody from Bravo Company yet?"

Just then, a dark shape flopped on the ground next to Rizzo, and he whirled and leveled his pulse rifle.

"Easy, easy. We're friends. Somebody called for Bravo Company to shift positions."

Rizzo forced himself to relax his trigger finger.

"Yeah, Pappy did. We're wondering what's going on back there. Pappy isn't answering."

"Pappy's dead, bro. So is the captain. Fuckers slagged the recon mech with Willie Pete."

"Damn it." Rizzo's mouth dried, and he felt a twinge of panic. "Who's in command?"

"I don't know. We ran into Gunny Karlsson from battalion staff, and he said there were no more officers alive."

"So it's him?"

"Looks that way. Do you need us here?"

"We're okay. Why don't you slide to the left and see if they need help? That's where most of the action has been."

"Okay, thanks, bro."

The figure disappeared, and Rizzo slumped down into his hole.

We're all going to die.

Just then, he heard the buzz of a drone high in the dark sky overhead.

* * *

"*Two Actual, this is Two Charlie. The drone is over 1st Battalion, and all sensors are operational. The feed is on Channel Seven.*"

"Roger that, thanks, Warrant. What's our on-station time?"

"That depends on whether you want the drone back or not, sir. Two hours plus time to recover, or three hours without."

Fortis smiled. "Let's plan on two hours right now. If anything changes, I'll let you know."

He set a countdown timer on the console above his screen and punched up channel seven. The 1st Battalion perimeter was a tight circle centered on a main battle mech and a recon mech. A second recon mech just outside the perimeter was a white blob on infrared, as though it had recently burned. He could make out fighting holes along the perimeter, but the resolution wasn't sharp enough to count individual Space Marines. Luminescence from the surrounding jungle was subdued, but it still threatened to white out the entire display. Fortis dialed up the sensor operator on the command mech intercom.

"Are you looking at the drone feed?"

"Yes, sir."

"Can you count how many Space Marines you see?"

"Sorry, Major, I can't make them out. Do you want me to tell the warrant to put it in a lower orbit?"

"Hmm, no, I don't think so. I don't want to give the Kuiper Knights a chance to shoot it down. They shot down a tube toy two days ago, remember?"

The sensor operator laughed. *"I forgot all about that, sir. It seems like forever."*

"How about manned fighting holes? Can you count them?"

"Sure thing. Gimme a second."

Fortis made his own tally. The movement of the drone and the increasing luminescence complicated the task, but he arrived at a rough count of 62. He counted again, and this time he counted 64.

"I got sixty-seven, Major. Give or take."

"Roger that. I got sixty-four, so let's split the difference and call it sixty-five. Sixty-five holes, with two or three Space Marines per hole. Roughly 160 Space Marines."

"That's not a lot, sir." The sensor operator gave voice to Fortis' thoughts.

"It's not, but they still have mechs, and Bravo Company will be there soon. We're right behind them, too. They'll hold."

* * *

In the jungle near Lead Pipe, Brother Addison fought back the urge to cry out in pain as the medic, a former Fleet corpsman named Ibarra, used a flashlight to examine the charred mess that used to be his left foot. Addison had followed Hassel's attack into the Space Marine perimeter, expecting it to be the last effort they'd need to destroy the invaders. Right after he'd witnessed Hassel's grenade attack on the recon mech, a stray pulse rifle bolt had hit him just above the ankle. The momentum of the attack had been blunted by the quick reaction of the Space Marines, and when the other Knights had seen Addison being carried to the rear, they'd lost heart and retreated.

"Brother, please! You've got to give me something for the pain!" Addison pleaded.

"I have nothing to give you!" Ibarra sobbed, the distress plain in his voice. "We've used all the medical supplies we captured. I'm sorry, Brother."

Addison chewed on the collar of his red smock to smother his screams as the medic splinted and wrapped his leg. When it was over, Addison was soaked with sweat, and his heart thundered in his chest.

"Help me up," he demanded in a weak voice.

"You can't walk," the medic said. "I'll have a couple brothers make a litter and carry you back to the bunker."

"I said, help me up!" Addison grabbed at the medic and pulled himself into a seated position. "Help me."

Ibarra sighed and held out his arm as Addison struggled to his feet. As soon as his left foot touched the ground, searing pain exploded up his leg, and he sank into blessed, agony-free unconsciousness.

* * *

Captain Stone called a halt after several hours of racing through the dark jungle so the Space Marines could catch their breath. Ystremski crouched down next to the captain and passed him a hydration pack.

Ystremski's nerves had been stretched taut when Bravo Company started their dash for 1st Battalion, but his anxiety eased as the distance from 2nd Battalion increased. Running through unfamiliar territory in the dark went against every infantryman instinct Ystremski possessed, but the odds that the Kuiper Knights had foreseen the move and prepared boobytraps or an ambush along their path were almost zero.

"Getting close," he said to Stone.

"Yeah. Another couple hours, and we'll be close enough to try and contact them." Stone took a long pull on the hydration pack and passed it back. "You doing okay, Gunny? We're not moving too fast for you, are we?"

Ystremski chuckled, and Lieutenant Tate, who'd joined them in the dark, snorted.

"I'm good, sir. Just getting warmed up."

"Major Fortis sent an update about thirty minutes ago. He estimates 1st Battalion is down to about a hundred and sixty men, and two mechs."

"Damn. Has he talked to them?"

"He didn't say."

Ystremski drained the hydration pack and tucked the empty back into his pack. "He probably doesn't want to call them and tell them about us until he's sure they're going to hold out. It might give them false hope."

"That's pretty fucking cold, Gunny."

"The major said he'd call us back if they didn't hold. If you were them, would you want to know help wasn't coming, or would you rather know that help could come, but chose not to?"

"Yeah, but…"

"But nothing, sir. There are a hundred ways this plan could fall apart. I don't think he told Regiment what we're doing, and there's no telling what they'll say when they find out. You'd better get comfortable with the idea that they might call this whole thing off, even if we're only a couple klicks away." Ystremski stood and rolled his head on his neck to loosen tight muscles. "Are we ready to move out?"

* * *

2nd Battalion paused to recover the drone and refuel it. While they waited, Fortis' comms panel came to life.

"Two Actual, this is Top Shot, over."

"Major, Regiment's on the circuit," the sensor operator called from the front of the mech. "Colonel Feliz."

"I heard him, thanks," Fortis said. He punched up the command circuit. "This is Two Actual."

"Major, I'm looking at the strategic display, and it looks like your battalion is awfully spread out."

"Yes, sir, we are. I sent an infantry company ahead on foot to reinforce 1st Battalion while we bust our way through the jungle with the mechs."

"An entire company? That leaves you pretty short. Do you think it was wise to divide your force?"

"I took a calculated risk, Colonel. The Kuiper Knights hammered 1st Battalion again at sunset. Based on footage from the surveillance drone I have up over them, they're down to two mechs and about a hundred and sixty men. The soonest we can get there with the mechs is sometime later today, perhaps as late as this evening, and that's if the rain holds off and we don't have any other mishaps."

"I'm not sure that was a sound decision, Major. You should've called for authorization."

Fortis struggled to keep the emotion out of his voice.

"Sir, I can order them to hold up and wait for the rest of the battalion, if that's what you want, but if the Kuiper Knights stick to their pattern, they'll hit 1st Battalion at first light. I'd like my Space Marines to be there for the fight."

There was a long pause, and Fortis wondered if the circuit had dropped synch.

"Carry on, Major, but keep in mind that your battalion is one third of our fighting force, and we can't afford to lose you on an ill-advised adventure."

Fortis stared at the comms panel as the light blinked out and the connection was broken. He tore off his headset and threw it on the console.

"Motherfucker!"

"Everything okay, sir?" the sensor operator asked with barely concealed amusement. He'd heard the entire conversation, and he understood Fortis' ire.

"Just fine," Fortis shot back. He put his headset back on and punched the button for Charlie Company.

"Two Charlie, this is Two Actual. What's the status of the drone relaunch?"

"The bird's refueled and ready to go. There's not much to look at until daylight, but I called for clearance, and the sensor operator said you were talking to Regiment."

Fortis leaned over and looked toward the sensor operator, who shrugged.

"Okay, Warrant. Launch it and let's get moving."

"Roger that, sir."

* * *

Brother Campos crouched in the jungle a klick east of 2nd Battalion along their approximate axis of advance. One of his scouts shone a light on muddy footprints and crushed and broken plants, a sure sign that many troops had recently passed by.

"Here's where they went through, Brother," the scout said. "A sizeable force, perhaps an entire company."

"Why would they send a company so far ahead?" Campos looked at the dark jungle around them. "Are they setting up an ambush for us?"

"I sent two men a half-klick along their trail, and they didn't encounter any Space Marines. I think they're rushing reinforcements to the unit Brother Addison is attacking."

Campos stared at the tracks for a long second as he considered what the scout had told him.

"We must warn Addison. Is there a trail that leads east?"

The scout shook his head. "I'm not aware of any, Brother."

"They'll have to follow this trail until they overtake the Space Marines, and then bypass them. Select two of your best men. Order them to hurry east to find Brother Addison and warn him. I'll bring up our men to slow the rest of this force down. If they've sent an entire company forward, we're close to even strength."

"What of their mechs?"

"In this jungle, their mechs are as much a hindrance as a help. We can move where they can't, and if they continue pushing as hard as they have been, we may find an opportunity to strike them a severe blow."

* * * * *

Chapter Twenty-One

Weiss called up Feliz on a private channel. "Top Shot, this is Hammer, over."

"Go ahead, Jo."

"Yes, sir. I overheard your conversation with Two Actual regarding his force disposition and the decision to divide his battalion. Do you think it would be prudent to hold 3rd Battalion here, or even return to the spaceport? If the Kuiper Knights attack 2nd Battalion with the same force they attacked 1st, we might find ourselves in a tough spot. Maybe even put the entire regiment at risk."

The silence on the line lasted so long that Weiss thought the connection had dropped, but Feliz finally answered.

"Are you suggesting that 3rd Battalion not move in support of 1st and 2nd?"

"Well, not exactly, sir. I'm wondering if it's tactically sound to advance toward an enemy force until we have some idea what we're facing. We haven't received an accurate status report about anything from 1st Battalion since the drop. I don't believe 2nd Battalion has an accurate estimate of enemy troop strength, either. For all we know, Fortis is headed for disaster."

"I've come to trust Fortis' instincts over the past couple days, Jo. I had my doubts when I found out about the stunt with Ystremski, but thus far in this operation, he's been more right than wrong. I'm willing to give him his head and support his advance. As for accurate troop strength, I don't know what the intel

squirrels based their estimates on, but they haven't been right about a damn thing since we dropped.

"For now, we'll continue to advance and monitor the situation as we get closer to Lead Pipe. Fortis mentioned a surveillance drone; do we have access to the feed?"

Weiss winced. "I don't know, sir, but I'll see that we get it."

"Do that, and then let me know when we have it. Anything else?"

"No, sir."

"Thanks, Jo."

The circuit light went out, and Weiss fought the urge to shout in frustration. All the battlefield command and control lessons he'd learned at the Senior Officer War College had gone by the wayside when 1st Regiment landed, and he'd struggled to keep up. This drop was nothing like he'd learned.

It's so... improvised.

* * *

Fortis and 2nd Battalion continued to grind their way east on the trail of Bravo Company. The jungle had begun to bloom with photoluminescent pollen after the rain stopped, and the Space Marines were losing their night vision advantage. The lead scouts managed to follow the trail left by Bravo Company, but their progress was slow, and Fortis chafed at the pace.

"Contact left!"

The Alpha Company circuit crackled to life as invisible attackers fired on the formation from the glowing undergrowth. Fortis listened as the Space Marines returned fire, but continued moving, and soon the Charlie Company rearguard reported all clear.

"Two Actual, this is Two Alpha. One friendly KIA, two WIA. Negative enemy body count. The bastards got up close before they started to fire, but we shot the shit out of them," Williams reported.

"Roger that, Ace." Fortis checked his strategic display. "It looks like Bravo Company has arrived close to 1st Battalion, so we need to catch up as soon as possible."

"Yes, sir. The jungle floor is slimy as hell, and now we can't see anything, but we're pushing as hard as we can. DINLI."

Fortis chuckled. "DINLI."

He dialed up the private circuit to Ystremski and hoped he was in range to make the connection.

"Hey, Gunny, do you copy?"

A few seconds later, Ystremski answered.

"I copy, sir."

"What's your situation?"

"We're about three klicks out, I think. We must be close, because we can hear the drone. We haven't had any enemy contact or heard any firing up ahead."

"Good. Sit tight and tell Stone to come up on the 1st Battalion command circuit. I'm going to let them know you're there, and then you can work out how to bring you in."

"Okay, sir, we'll be standing by."

"Just remember, Regiment's listening in."

"Fuck 'em."

Fortis shook his head as he brought up the 1st Battalion circuit.

"One Actual, this is Two Actual, over."

There was no response.

"One Actual, this is Two Actual, over."

Fortis was about to tell the sensor operator to check the circuit when someone answered.

"Two Actual, this is Gunny Karlsson, comms NCO of 1st Battalion. There is no One Actual. All our officers are dead."

"Are you the senior man?"

"I think so, sir. I've been checking around, but I haven't found anyone else."

"Then you're it, Gunny. I have some good news for you. Bravo Company, 2nd Battalion, is about three klicks to your southwest. They're standing by to reinforce your position."

"Are you shitting me? I mean, seriously, a whole company?"

"Affirmative. They ran through the night, and now they're ready to enter your position."

"Whoo, that's good news. We've been listening to the drone all night, but I didn't realize anyone was that close. What do you want me to do?"

"How's the visibility over there?"

"The jungle's glowing, sir. Infrared is useless right now."

"Okay. Captain Stone, Bravo Company's CO, is listening in. I'm going to turn you over to him, and you can work out the details for them to approach your perimeter without friendly fire incidents."

"Roger that, sir." Fortis heard what he thought was a sob. "Thank you."

"1st Battalion has done a damn fine job, Gunny. You should all be proud. I'm sorry we couldn't get there sooner."

Stone came up on the circuit, and Fortis listened in as the captain and gunny coordinated the arrival of Bravo Company. It pleased him that Regiment didn't come up on the circuit to add their input; it was a surprising show of restraint.

Captain Williams called Fortis on the 2nd Battalion circuit.

"Two Actual, this is Two Alpha. We've got to slow down, Major. We can't see shit anymore, and one of the mechs almost drove into a ravine."

"*This is Two Charlie. I concur with Two Alpha,*" Warrant Loren chimed in. "*Charging through the jungle blind is a good way to lose another mech.*"

Fortis grimaced, but he trusted the judgment of his company commanders. He keyed his mic on the battalion circuit.

"This is Two Actual. Slow it down, but we need to keep moving. I don't know if you overheard, but Bravo Company made it to Lead Pipe, and they're reinforcing 1st Battalion now. The situation there is more stable, but we still need to get there ASAP. When it starts getting light, we need to speed up."

"*Roger that.*"

Fortis heard pulse rifle fire in the background.

"*Contact left!*"

* * *

Stone and Ystremski waited while Bravo Company spread out through the 1st Battalion perimeter. Stone passed the word that he'd taken command of the position and ordered maximum readiness.

"Now we wait," he muttered to Ystremski.

"Fuck that. These guys have been waiting for three days, and it's gotten a lot of them killed for nothing."

"What are you saying, Gunny? You want to attack?" Stone gestured to the dark jungle around them. "Attack who? Where?"

"Mad Minute, sir."

"What?"

"Mad Minute. Just like graduation eve at the Advanced Infantry Officer Course. Full auto spray and pray until we have to change rifle batteries. Those pricks have attacked every day at dawn, so let's hit them before they get a chance to jump off. To hell with fire discipline. Slag the jungle with everything we have and catch them by surprise."

"Reconnaissance by fire. Do you think it'll work?"

"Yeah, I do. If we time it right, we'll catch them moving up into their jump off positions, ready to throw smokes to conceal their attack."

"Should we put out listening posts?"

Ystremski snorted. "Would you go downrange, knowing the entire company is about to light up the jungle over your head?"

"Good point."

"Even if we don't hit them, they'll realize we're here and maybe call off their attack. That'll give the rest of the battalion more time to get here with the mechs."

"What if they still attack?"

"Then we'll make them pay for their mistake with their lives."

* * *

A surprise attack exploded on 2nd Battalion's left flank as a large number of enemy fighters opened up on the Space Marines. The volume of fire was heavy, and it continued unabated even after the Space Marines and the mechs returned fire.

"These fuckers are serious this time," Williams reported. *"They're attacking in company strength at least."*

Fortis stripped off his headset and grabbed his pulse rifle.

"Listen up on the circuits," he called to the sensor operator as he climbed out through the command mech hatch. "I'm going to see what's going on."

What Fortis saw when he exited the command mech was a weird, disjointed firefight between two blind opponents. The Kuiper Knights had no low-light capabilities, and the bioluminescent pollen was in full bloom, which blinded the Space Marines' visors. Fortis crouched next to the command mech and watched the battle unfold.

Pulse rifles fired from the dark jungle, and nearby Space Marines responded with a torrent of plasma bolts. The Kuiper Knights returned fire at the Space Marines, and the cycle of attack and counter-attack continued until one side or the other was silenced. The Charlie Company mechs blazed away with their automatic pulse cannons, and unexpended energy from so many rounds gave the jungle an eerie, blue-white glow. It seemed that there were more attackers than defenders, but the Space Marines managed to establish a crossfire and decimated the Kuiper Knights.

Finally, the firing died down.

"Two Alpha, report."

"This is Lieutenant Tucker of 1st Platoon, Alpha Company. Captain Williams is dead, sir. Took a bolt in the face."

"What's your situation, LT?"

"They tried to hit us on the left flank, but they attacked too far forward and hit the point squad from my platoon instead. I guess they got lost in the dark. Ace—er, Captain Williams—moved up with 1st and 2nd Platoons, and that's when he got hit."

"Casualties?"

"No idea, besides the captain. The point squad isn't answering, and we have guys spread out all over the place. Give me some time, and I'll go find out."

"Negative. Hold what you have." Fortis consulted the time. "I don't want anyone getting shot by mistake. It'll be daylight soon; we'll wait until we can see to move out."

"Roger that, sir."

"Oh, and you're now Two Alpha."

"Yes, sir."

Fortis climbed back into the command mech to plan their next move. He hated the idea of pausing their advance, but after witnessing the confused madness of the firefight in the dark and the resulting confusion, he knew that pushing on before 2nd Battalion could regroup was ill-advised. The urgency to link up with Bravo Company and 1st Battalion grew with every passing minute, but they had to maintain peak combat efficiency.

He put on his headset and dialed up the Bravo Company circuit.

"Two Bravo, this is Two Actual. What's your status?"

After a momentary pause, Stone answered.

"This is Two Bravo. We entered 1st Battalion's perimeter and reinforced them. I'm getting a muster now, but we have a main battle mech, a recon mech, and approximately two hundred and fifty Space Marines."

"Any enemy activity?"

"Negative, but we're expecting an attack at first light. Gunny Ystremski's preparing a surprise for them."

"'Surprise?'"

"Reconnaissance by fire. We're going to slag the jungle in every direction until we find the bastards, and then hit them with everything we have."

Fortis smiled. "You mean 'Mad Minute?'"

"Yes, sir."

"Better than waiting for them to attack."

"That's what Gunny said."

"We just repelled a company-sized attack, and we've been forced to stop until we can see. The jungle is glowing, and it's too dark to see without optics. It should be light enough to move out in an hour or so."

"*We'll be here, sir.*"

"Roger that. Two Actual, out."

* * *

A pair of Kuiper Knights staggered out of the jungle and collapsed near the brothers staging for their next assault on the Space Marines of 1st Battalion. Mud and slime created by the jungle pollen dripped from their clothes, and the Knights almost shot them before they recognized them as friendlies.

"We need to see Brother Addison," one of the newcomers panted. "We have urgent news from Brother Campos."

"I'm Brother Ibarra, a medic. Brother Addison has sustained a grave injury. I'll take you to him."

The two Knights stumbled along behind Ibarra as he walked by the dim glow of a chem light. They heard fighters moving through the dark jungle.

"We must hurry," one of the Knights pleaded.

Ibarra stopped and knelt next to an unconscious man lying propped up against a tree.

"This is Brother Addison," he told the pair. He shook Addison's shoulder, but the knight errant only grunted.

The newcomers squatted next to Addison.

"Brother Addison, please. Brother Campos sends news. You must call off your attack. The Space Marines have been reinforced from the west."

Addison didn't respond.

One of the newcomers stood and looked at Ibarra. "Who's in command?"

Ibarra shook his head. "I don't know. Things are in disarray."

A volley of pulse rifle fire interrupted them, and they threw themselves flat as automatic pulse cannon bolts tore through the jungle.

* * * * *

Chapter Twenty-Two

"Fire!"

As soon as Stone transmitted the order, the Space Marines at Lead Pipe opened fire on the surrounding jungle with everything they had. Ystremski squeezed his trigger and loosed a long stream of plasma bolts that disappeared into the darkness. Fire discipline was forgotten as the Space Marines whooped and hollered while they blasted away at their invisible enemy. The mechs added large caliber automatic pulse cannon fire to the barrage, and the jungle erupted in sprays of blue-white sparks.

Incoming fire from Ystremski's left zipped overhead, and he concentrated his aim where the darkness concealed the shooters. Several other Space Marines aimed at the same spot, and the jungle glowed with the unexpended energy from hundreds of plasma bolts. He lowered his line of fire to target the Kuiper Knights who dove to the ground when the firing started. When his pulse rifle battery died, he threw a look over his shoulder as he grabbed a fresh one. There was little outgoing fire to the east, and no incoming.

He turned back to the west in time to see several brilliant white flashes and the fiery explosions of Willie Pete grenades. Eerie white light illuminated the jungle outside their perimeter, and Ystremski heard screams of agony as super-heated phosphorus found human flesh.

"Fuck 'em," he muttered with grim satisfaction.

"What did you say, Gunny?" Stone asked over the company circuit, and Ystremski realized his transmit button had been depressed.

"Fuck 'em all, sir."

"Damn right."

The lone operational main battle mech abruptly ceased firing, and Ystremski heard cursing over the circuit.

"Two Bravo, this is Sergeant Chester in Breaker Four. The fucking pulse cannon power generator shit the bed, so our main battery's tits up."

"This is Two Bravo, can you fix it?"

"Yes, sir, we can swap the motherfucker out for a ready spare, but it's going to take some time. Fifteen minutes, maybe twenty."

"Any problems with your secondary gun?"

"Negative. She's purring like a bitch in heat."

"Roger that. Keep up the fire and get the main battery up as soon as you can."

"That's my fucking plan, sir."

Ystremski couldn't help but laugh at the exchange between Stone and Chester. The mech commander sounded like an old-school Space Marine, and the gunny made a mental note to seek him out after the battle.

Another salvo of phosphorus grenades detonated in the jungle to the north.

"This is Petrov on the northern perimeter. I can see about a hundred of them in the jungle behind the Willie Pete. We need some supporting fire before they get away."

Space Marines along the perimeter immediately concentrated their fire on the darkness beyond the burning grenades. The recon mech that had been positioned to the south wheeled around and moved to the other end of the perimeter. The combination of the automatic pulse cannon and pulse rifles created a huge smear of glowing plasma in the jungle.

"Cease fire on the north!" Petrov shouted over the circuit. *"They're crispy."*

"This is Two Bravo. All stations, report incoming fire."

There were no responses.

"This is Two Bravo. Cease fire. I say again, cease fire."

The Space Marine perimeter fell silent. As his eyes adjusted, it shocked Ystremski to see the sky had begun to grow lighter.

Now we just gotta hang on until Fortis gets here.

* * *

"Top Shot, this is Eagle, over."

Colonel Feliz scrambled for his headset at the sound of General Moreno's voice over the division command circuit.

"Roger, this is Top Shot."

"Colonel, you must've been born under a lucky star, because your regiment's encountered the only serious opposition from the Kuiper Knights. 2nd and 3rd Regiments have faced minimal resistance at their assigned targets, and we're recovering them back aboard Mammoth *now. What's the timeline to complete your mission?"*

Feliz paused for a moment.

"Three days," Weiss said in his ear over the private command circuit.

"General, I estimate three days to complete major combat operations," Feliz told Moreno.

"Huh. I've been reading your daily reports, and I hoped it would be sooner. What's your current status?"

"1st Battalion's been engaged since they dropped on Lead Pipe, with heavy casualties on both sides. The jungle makes estimating enemy strength difficult, but I'm confident we inflicted many more casualties than we sustained.

"1st and 2nd Battalions are linking up as we speak; I expect that movement to be completed in the next eight hours. I'm moving from the spaceport with 3rd Battalion and will rendezvous in approximately thirty hours."

"That's not three days."

"General, I must reiterate, we're having trouble estimating enemy strength. Be advised that the luminescent pollen from the jungle renders infrared inoperative. If the other regiments have met limited resistance, we could be facing several thousand Kuiper Knights. I simply don't know."

"Okay, Colonel, it's your call. I'll have my staff expedite a surveillance satellite to you to help with your intel picture."

"Thank you.

"As soon as we've completed exfil of 2nd and 3rd Regiments, we'll be on our way. Sixty hours, give or take. Can you hold out that long?"

Feliz's cheeks burned at the implied insult, but he bit back his response.

"Yes, ma'am, we can hold out for sixty hours, and a lot longer if necessary."

"Ensure the spaceport is secure and ready to receive multiple drop ships. Eagle, out."

Feliz squeezed his eyes shut for a long moment as the general's words sank in. He resented her implication that 1st Regiment was somehow *failing*. From her own report, the other regiments hadn't encountered much resistance, while the soldiers of his 1st Battalion were fighting for their lives.

Moreno's parting directions created conflicting priorities for 1st Regiment, as well. He wanted to link up with 1st and 2nd Battalions at Lead Pipe, but he was now charged with securing the spaceport. The biggest problem was enemy troop strength. A company from 3rd Battalion could easily hold the spaceport against a comparable force, but the situation at Lead Pipe told him the Kuiper Knights had a significant advantage in sheer numbers. If a large force outmaneuvered him and engaged the company at the spaceport, he might very well lose both.

Weiss called on the private circuit. *"What are your orders, sir?"*

Feliz heard a mocking tone in Weiss' voice, as if he was saying *I told you so.* He gritted his teeth and fought back the urge to dress down the colonel.

"3rd Battalion will hold here until 1st and 2nd have fully linked up. When I'm confident they're secure, I'll order a retrograde movement to the spaceport to await the arrival of 2nd Division."

"Yes, sir."

"Have you gotten the drone feed from 2nd Battalion yet?"

"Channel five on your console. There's nothing to see on low-light or infrared, but it should be daylight soon."

Feliz dialed up the channel and flipped through the various displays. When he got to the low-light display, his jaw dropped. The glow of pulse weapon fire looked like a major engagement was in progress.

"You might want to check the low-light display again. It appears Lead Pipe is under heavy attack."

"What?"

Feliz smiled with satisfaction at catching Weiss unprepared.

"Unless I'm mistaken, that's a battle."

* * *

The Mad Minute took the Kuiper Knights completely by surprise. The withering fire caught them moving through the jungle from their covered positions for their own planned assault, and many fell dead in the first few seconds. Small knots of fighters rallied and returned fire, but the Space Marines responded with focused salvos that tore through the Kuiper Knights and left behind piles of glowing plasma.

Ibarra tried to render aid to the nearest casualties, but the volume of incoming fire forced him to lay motionless and bury his face in the dirt. Without Addison's steadying presence, the Kuiper Knights recoiled from the attack as panic swept through their ranks. Salvos of phosphorus grenades burned many alive, and their agonized screams unnerved even the most determined attackers. Blinded and disoriented by the brilliant white explosions, clusters of Kuiper Knights stumbled out of the jungle, and the Space Marines mowed them down without mercy.

Survivors of the initial attack scrambled away from the barrage on their stomachs, anxious to escape the murderous fire. The Knights who'd occupied positions back from the perimeter watched in horror as their burned and battered brothers crawled for the safety of the dense jungle. With no leadership to take control and direct otherwise, they joined the withdrawal. Only the discipline instilled in them during their previous service in the ISMC kept the retreat from becoming a rout. As the sky grew lighter, the surviving Kuiper Knights began the long climb back up to the bunker.

* * *

The motion of the command mech made Fortis drowsy, and Stone's voice over the 2nd Battalion circuit startled him.

"Two Actual, this is Two Bravo. Everything's quiet here. It's almost light, and there's no sign of the Kuiper Knights."

Fortis fought the urge to yawn. "This is Two Actual, sit tight and stay ready. We sped up, and there's no sign of the enemy here, either. ETA to Lead Pipe is six hours."

"Roger that. I deployed two patrols to see what the Knights are up to, but the rest of the company is standing fast."

"Okay, Captain. We'll see you in a few hours. Two Actual, out."

Warrant Loren called as soon as Fortis signed off with Stone.

"This is Two Charlie. The drone has about forty minutes of on-station time left before we need to bring it back to refuel. I recommend we stop long enough to recover it and launch another while things are quiet at Lead Pipe."

"That's a good idea, Warrant. Call Stone and let him know you're pulling the drone off-station, but let's not stop until we have to for launch and recovery."

"Yes, sir."

He'd no sooner gotten off the circuit with Loren than the sensor operator called to him.

"Major, Top Shot's on the command circuit."

Fortis sighed as he dialed up the regiment.

"This is Two Actual, go ahead, sir."

"Major, it looks like there was quite a battle at Lead Pipe. What's going on?"

"The firing was mostly outgoing, sir. Bravo Company reinforced 1st Battalion early this morning. The Kuiper Knights have attacked every day at first light, so Captain Stone decided to seize the initiative with a Mad Minute, sir."

"A 'Mad Minute?'"

"Yes, sir. Full auto reconnaissance by fire. Force the enemy to attack before they're ready."

"I haven't heard that term since I was an officer candidate. Did it work?"

"Captain Stone reported that there's no sign of the Kuiper Knights in the jungle around him. He's sent out patrols to investigate."

Feliz chuckled. *"That's the damnedest thing I've ever heard, Major. Well done."*

"Thank you, sir, but that was Stone and Ystremski's idea. I just approved it."

"Well done all the same. Anyway, I'm calling you because there's been a change to our plan. The entire division is due to arrive here in sixty hours, and we've been tasked to secure the spaceport for their drop. With that in mind, I've ordered 3rd Battalion to halt our advance until you arrive at Lead Pipe and assess the situation."

"We'll be there in six hours, sir."

"Good. What I need most from you is a no-shit estimate of enemy strength. We're the only regiment who met any serious resistance; most of the other drops were on dry holes. The intel squirrels really fucked up this time."

"I'm swapping drone coverage at this time, and I'll give you my best estimate as soon as possible."

"Eagle promised dedicated surveillance satellite coverage, but I don't have an ETA on the bird."

"Roger that, sir."

"That's all I have for you right now, Major. Good luck and keep me posted. Top Shot, out."

At some point during his conversation with Feliz, the command mech had stopped. Fortis took off his headset and stood up.

"I'm getting out of here for a few minutes," he told the sensor operator. "I need to stretch my legs and get away from the radio for a while."

* * * * *

Chapter Twenty-Three

Jocko Bender skidded on the slimy jungle trail but managed to catch himself before he sprawled into the underbrush. A knight errant named Bacall had given Bender and the other engineers the daunting task of hauling large stones from the bottom of a steep ravine up to the bunker to reinforce the entrance. It was a big job, but it wasn't bad at first; the stones were heavy, but not unmanageable, and they made good progress.

In the last few days, thousands of boots had beaten down the underbrush and worn a muddy rut down the middle of the trail as the Kuiper Knights headed off into the jungle to confront the Space Marines. The footing had become precarious, and the engineers were forced to carry smaller loads or risk mishap. Progress on the project slowed, and Bacall grew irritated at the pace. When Bender tried to explain, Bacall cut him off with a wave of his hand and a cutting remark. It took several other Kuiper Knights to stop Bender from pummeling the knight errant, and they hadn't seen Bacall since.

After Bender got his feet underneath himself, he looked down the track and saw a handful of Kuiper Knights climbing up toward him. They wore pieces of mud-stained, lightweight battle armor that bore scorch marks from pulse rifle bolts, and one of them had a bloody bandage secured around his chest. Their heads were down, and they leaned into the slope as if struggling against a strong wind.

It stunned Bender to see more men behind them, and many more climbing through the jungle alongside the trail.

"Bloody hell."

He stood aside and watched as Kuiper Knights streamed out of the jungle and disappeared toward the bunker. They were all filthy from several days spent fighting in the jungle. Many needed assistance to walk, and he lost count of the litters bearing wounded men. Most of them had the blank look of defeat on their faces, and several openly sobbed as they staggered along.

One young man with bloody bandages wrapped around his head stumbled and would've fallen if Bender hadn't caught him and lowered him to the ground.

"Water," the wounded man pleaded.

Bender pulled out his last hydration pack and held it to his lips.

"Easy, Brother. You're almost there." He looked around for someone to help, but the column continued upward without a second glance.

The Knight's head lolled to the side, and Bender felt his body relax.

Dead.

He tried to lay the dead man on the trail to get someone to carry him to the bunker, but a knight errant in a torn and bloodied red smock stopped him.

"Get that body out of the way, you fool!"

Bender stared as the knight errant continued toward the bunker. Another Knight wearing scorched lightweight battle armor sank down next to him.

"Let me help you, Brother."

The pair moved the dead man to the side and folded his arms over his chest.

"It's bad out there, yeah?"

The other Knight nodded as he retrieved the hydration pack from where it had fallen on the trail. "We thought we had them, but they were waiting. I've never seen anything like it."

"Where's everyone going? What are your orders?"

"We don't have orders. When the first company broke and ran, the rest followed. I guess we'll regroup at the bunker and find out." He turned to rejoin the line of Knights struggling along the trail. "Blessings of The Master upon thee, Brother."

"And upon thee."

Bender waited until the trail was clear, then descended twenty meters to where it split in two. The left fork led deeper into the jungle toward the battlefield, while the right fork led to the boulder field where he and the others had gathered rocks to reinforce the bunker. He looked around, but he was alone. After a moment's hesitation, he stripped off his mud-stained smock, threw it into the underbrush, and started down the left fork, away from the bunker and the Kuiper Knighthood.

His progress was slow at first, because he stepped back into the jungle when he encountered Kuiper Knights making the long climb to the bunker. He didn't have permission to leave the bunker area, and he didn't want to answer questions from suspicious knights errant. The trail was littered with abandoned weapons and LBA components, so he donned a chest plate and picked up a pulse rifle. The LBA was dented and burned, and the pulse rifle battery was dead, but they gave the impression that Bender had been involved in the fighting. He met knots of survivors with a silent nod, and when he passed knights errant, he averted his eyes.

Bender heard moaning in the jungle, and when he ducked into the underbrush, he saw a young man wearing the blue smock of a squire leaning against a tree with another man cradled in his arms.

"Blessings of The Master upon thee," the squire said.

"Never mind that right now."

"Brother, can you help me?" the squire pleaded. "My knight… he carried me as far as he could."

Bender squatted down to examine the Knight and saw right away that the man was dead. His face was a sick shade of purplish-gray, and the wad of filthy bandages wrapped around his chest had slipped, exposing torn flesh and dried blood.

"He's gone, mate. Let's move him off your lap and get you to your feet," Bender said.

He slid the dead Knight aside and winced when he saw that the squire's legs ended just above his knees. Pinkish fluid-stained bandages under tourniquets tied above the stumps, and the splintered end of a femur poked out through charred flesh.

"Ugh."

Bender was torn. The squire was badly injured, but his wounds didn't appear to be immediately fatal. If Bender got him to the bunker, and he received medical treatment, he might survive. Without proper attention, he'd almost certainly die, but not before he suffered for a long time.

If Bender delivered the squire to the bunker, he might be trapped there along with the rest of the Knighthood. From what he'd seen, it was only a matter of time before the Space Marines pursued the Kuiper Knights back to their lair. He was surprised he hadn't heard hovercopters, but they could be tracking and targeting the retreating Kuiper Knights with space-based platforms.

Zerec's order to relocate the Knighthood to the bunker had surprised Bender. It was a dead end with no escape route, and a senior infantry commander, even a religious zealot, should've seen that. The bunker was the *last* place he wanted to be when the Space Marines showed up.

The squire seemed to sense Bender's indecision, because he cried out as he fumbled at one of his tourniquets.

"My leg. My leg, it hurts so much," he said between deep sobs. "My feet feel like they're on fire!"

Bender threw his hands up in frustration. "I can't help you, mate. I don't have any meds."

"Just… just help me loosen this. Let some blood flow to my foot."

"I can't. Didn't your Knight tell you? I mean, you don't have a foot."

"Please. Just help me."

"Okay. I'll help you. C'mon, I'll carry you."

Bender tried to gather the legless squire in his arms for the long climb up to the bunker, but the injured man pushed his hands away. He'd worked the tourniquet loose, and blood gushed from his stump as he tossed it into the underbrush.

"What are you doing?" Bender scrambled after the discarded strap. "You have to keep that in place, or you'll bleed out, mate."

He located the tourniquet and turned back to the wounded man before it occurred to him that death was what the squire wanted. He waited in silence for several seconds, and then returned to the squire. Bender saw a pool of muddy blood and knew the squire was dead.

Bender set his jaw, slung his pulse rifle, and set off down the trail in search of the Space Marines he knew were somewhere out there.

* * *

In the bunker, Fehoko approached Zerec near the operations center.

"Blessings of The Master upon thee," he said.

"And upon thee," Zerec replied.

"Light of The Master upon thee."

"And upon thee."

"Brother Zerec, I must speak with you in private."

Zerec frowned. As The Master's personal aide, Fehoko occupied a privileged position within the Knighthood, which put him beyond Zerec's authority. He didn't seem to take advantage of his standing, but his constant presence rankled the knight errant.

"Where shall we go?"

The bunker offered little privacy; there were few places to talk without being overheard.

"The Master's quarters." Zerec's eyebrows went up in surprise, and Fehoko put a hand on his forearm. "Please."

When they got to The Master's door, Fehoko entered without knocking. Zerec followed, and Fehoko barred the door. He gestured to the curtain that separated the tiny devotional room from the sleeping quarters.

"He's in there."

Mystified, Zerec pulled the curtain back. By the light of a single dim lamp, he saw The Master curled up in the fetal position on his cot. His face was frozen in a rictus of pain, and his breath came in raspy moans.

"What's wrong with him?" Zerec demanded.

"I don't know, Brother. He said he wanted a nap and instructed me to wake him for devotions. I found him like that. I tried to rouse him, but his eyes are rolled back, and he doesn't respond."

"Who else knows?"

Fehoko shook his head. "Nobody."

"You haven't told anyone?" Zerec's tone was insistent, and Fehoko shrank away from him.

"N-no, Brother. I swear it."

Zerec thought for a second before he nodded his approval. "Good. The Knighthood must not hear of this."

Fehoko's eyes widened. "How will we keep this secret? He's The Master."

Zerec put his hands on Fehoko's shoulders. "Brother, we're engaged in a holy war with the infidels from Terra Earth. We're outnumbered and outgunned, but we have the unshakeable faith of The Master. If we defeat the Terrans here, the entire sector will rally to our banner. If we fail, all our hard work and sacrifices will be in vain."

"But The Master—"

"Do you believe The Master wishes the Knighthood to die with him, or do you believe the Knighthood should live for a thousand years?"

"The Master teaches us that the True Faith is bigger than any man."

"That's true, Brother. If our faith is strong, we'll prevail in this battle. This is a critical moment, and we can't allow anything to shake that faith, not even the death of The Master."

"But he's not dead," Fehoko protested. "He's just... sick."

Zerec fought back the urge to snap at Fehoko. The Master was clearly more than "sick," and there was no hope of getting him medical care. There were no doctors in the Kuiper Knighthood, and he'd deployed all the former Space Marine corpsmen with the Brothers who pressed the attack on the infidels. Instead, he nodded.

"You're right, Brother. The Master's sick, and there's nothing we can do for him but pray. His faith will sustain him. Pray for him, and pray for victory."

Zerec returned to the operations center. He leaned over the map and stared at it without seeing as his mind raced. By all accounts, the battle against the invaders was going well, but he'd known from the beginning that it couldn't last. They'd lost too many brothers when Fleet destroyed *Colossus* to achieve the final victory they needed. Now, if word of The Master's true condition got out, the Knighthood might collapse before Zerec could finalize his escape plans.

He was so deep in thought that he didn't hear Lyle approach, and he jumped when the other Knight touched his arm.

"My apologies, Brother Zerec. You didn't respond, and I—"

"No need to apologize. What is it?"

"Brother Bacall requested your presence outside. Brother Addison's Knights have returned."

* * * * *

Chapter Twenty-Four

Fortis and 2nd Battalion pushed hard toward Lead Pipe throughout the morning. The jungle floor had dried since the recent rains, and even Warrant Loren couldn't complain about the traction for her mechs. Fortis had estimated six hours, but the lead recon mech was three klicks from the drop zone in four and a half. He halted the formation to establish comms with Bravo Company.

"Two Bravo, this is Two Actual."

"This is Two Bravo, Roger."

"This is Two Actual. Be advised, the lead element of 2nd Battalion is three klicks southwest of your position. Standing by for rendezvous."

"Roger, come on in, we'll be waiting for you."

There were many smiles and handshakes when 2nd Battalion emerged from the jungle and rolled into the perimeter. Alpha and Charlie Companies greeted their comrades in Bravo Company like long lost family, even though they'd been apart less than a day. Ystremski and Fortis shook hands and hugged.

"Welcome to Lead Pipe," Ystremski said. "It's not much, but it's home."

Fortis surveyed the jumbled landscape dotted with the hulks of burned-out mechs. "Looks like you've been busy."

Just then, Captain Stone and an unfamiliar gunny approached.

"I'm glad to see you, Major," Stone said. "This is Gunny Karlsson of 1st Battalion."

The two men shook hands, and Fortis saw a mix of relief and gratitude on Karlsson's face.

"Gunny, I'm glad to meet you. It looks like 1st Battalion fought through hell up here."

"We did our best, sir, but if it hadn't been for Bravo Company..." Karlsson shook his head as his voice trailed away.

"What's your status?" Fortis asked Stone.

"1st Battalion has 142 infantry combat effective and eight WIA. They're supported by a main battle mech and a recon mech. Bravo Company has 134 combat effective, with no KIAs or mech support. Total for this position, 276 infantry and two mechs, plus eight WIA."

"Outstanding. What's the enemy situation?"

"I've had patrols out continuously since this morning, but all they've found are dead Kuiper Knights and abandoned weapons and gear. The pulse bolt slag makes it hard to get an accurate body count, but one patrol estimated they found four hundred and fifty enemy dead, and another patrol reported two hundred more. There are tracks all over the jungle heading northwest, but I denied the patrols permission to investigate until you arrived."

The numbers surprised Fortis. "Six hundred and fifty enemy dead? How many did they *have*?"

All eyes went to Karlsson, who shrugged. "No idea, sir. More than we could kill by ourselves."

"What are we getting from the drone?" Ystremski asked. "Any estimates?"

Fortis shook his head. "Not much. The photoluminescence wipes everything out. I'll have Loren send the drones to the northwest and see if we can figure out where they went. Captain Stone, I want listening posts a hundred meters all around this position. I don't want them hitting us without warning in the flanks."

"When will 3rd Battalion be here?" Stone asked.

"Shit. I forgot about them. I talked to Colonel Feliz this morning, and he said the entire division is due here in about two and a half days. If I determine that the situation here is stable, he's going to return to the spaceport with 3rd Battalion to secure it for their arrival."

"Where does that leave us?" Stone responded. "Are we supposed to head for the spaceport, too?"

"I don't know. I don't think the colonel knows, either. Give me a chance to report our status, and I'll find out." Fortis looked around the drop zone. "If I have anything to say about it, we're not staying here."

Before the captain could respond, a call came over the Bravo Company circuit.

"Captain, this is Lieutenant Tate. One of our patrols captured a Kuiper Knight on a trail that leads up into the jungle."

Stone blinked in surprise. "No kidding. Outstanding. Did he tell you where the rest of them went?"

"Not exactly, sir. I mean, he won't say. He said he's with us, and he'll only talk to our CO."

"'With us?' What does that mean?"

"He said he's an agent with the ISR branch, and he has information for the CO."

Tate's report surprised Fortis. He traded puzzled looks with Ystremski.

The ISR branch?

"I thought the ISR branch was closed?" Ystremski asked as the group walked toward Tate's position.

"It was," Fortis said. "Closed by order of Admiral Schein."

"I'll make sure he's searched, and then we'll see what he has to say."

Tate approached them, twenty meters away from the prisoner.

"Major, he's over there," he said and pointed to a man on his knees with a bag over his head and his hands behind his head. Several Space Marines surrounded him with their pulse rifles at low ready.

"Did you search him? Was he carrying any weapons?" Ystremski asked.

"He's clean, Gunny."

Fortis stood in front of the prisoner and nodded at Tate, who whipped the bag off the prisoner's head. Fortis' jaw dropped.

"What the fuck?" Ystremski blurted.

Bender squinted up at Fortis.

"G'day, Lucky."

* * *

Fortis, Ystremski, and Bender sat together near the command mech.

"I was one of the first ones the bastards divvied," Bender said. "Not a surprise, really, given my record. Still, I took it personally. Bit of a shock, yeah? After I spent a week being angry, I looked up a couple mates I knew in the Paladins. They're contractors based in Australia."

Fortis snorted, and Ystremski smiled.

"You know them?"

"Yeah." Fortis unconsciously touched the back of his head. Paladins hired by Fortis to recapture *Colossus* had knocked him unconscious and kidnapped him, taking him into the Free Sector, where they'd turned him over to the Kuiper Knights.

"Buncha wankers, I reckon. I knew the Kuiper Knights were involved in the Free Sector slave trade, so I joined up with them. I figured I might come across some of the bastards who killed my goddaughter."

"What have you been doing? Were you fighting?"

"Nah, mate. I'm bloody slave labor, building walls." He held out his hands, palms up, and Fortis saw thick callouses and ground-in dirt. "I used to have the soft hands of a Space Marine, but now I've got the hands of a helenium miner.

"After you escaped, they took away our communicators and forbade anyone from talking to the outside world. We began to load aboard *Colossus*, but the ship took off before everyone could get aboard. Then Brother Zerec divided us into companies, with knights errant as company commanders. They became bloody paranoid, too. I got put in the bad boy company." Bender chuckled. "They don't trust me because I'm mates with Petr." He grinned at Ystremski. "They're very angry with you, you know?"

"Fuck 'em."

"Indeed, mate." The massive Australian shrugged. "And here we are. Why are you here, anyway? *Colossus* has fucked off to some other part of the sector, I reckon."

Fortis and Ystremski traded glances.

"You don't know anything about what's happened on Terra Earth?"

Bender shook his head. "Nah, mate. I've been too busy digging, and they don't tell us anything, anyway."

"What about the rest of you? Would they know?"

Bender shook his head. "Nah, I don't think so. When they took our communicators away, the rumor mill went into hyperdrive. If anybody knew something, everyone would know it."

Fortis fixed Bender in a steady stare. "You weren't involved in anything on Terra Earth, or why we're here."

The hulking Aussie raised his right hand. "Fair dinkum. On my mum's grave. I have no idea what you're talking about, but it doesn't sound like you're here over a load of stolen weapons."

"A Fleet warship destroyed *Colossus*. In retaliation, the Kuiper Knights attacked a youth global peace rally in North America with rockets and petrol bombs. They murdered over a hundred and ten thousand people, mostly kids. *That's* why we're here."

Bender's eyes widened. "It can't be."

"Fair dinkum," Ystremski said.

Bender squeezed his eyes shut and shook his head. "Why? Why?" he repeated. His shoulders slumped, and he covered his face with his hands.

"We were kind of hoping you could help us out with that one," Fortis said.

Bender looked up; his eyes brimmed with tears. "A hundred and ten thousand?"

The Space Marines nodded.

"At least," Ystremski said.

"I don't know why they did it, but I know where you can find the fuckers who do." He pointed west, up into the jungle-covered mountains. "They're up there, in the bunker."

"What's the bunker?"

"It's a bloody cave complex. The Master and Zerec decided to evacuate Sanctuary, so we dug out the caves, made them big enough for everyone, and reinforced the walls. The Master's up there, and so is Zerec."

"How far?"

"Dunno. Six klicks, I reckon. You can't miss the place. There's a great big ridge, and the cave entrance is dug in just below it."

"How many Kuiper Knights are there?"

Bender shrugged. "Can't say for sure, mate. Before you lot arrived, there were two, maybe three thousand. Half are ex-Space Marines, and the rest are Fleet."

Ystremski tipped his head to the side, and Fortis stood.

"Give us a second, would you?"

The pair walked out of earshot.

"What do you think? Do you believe him?" Fortis asked.

"Yeah, I do, but you've known him longer than me."

"I believe him, too. He could be a plant; he did surrender, but what would he gain from it?"

"Send us on a wild goose chase to this bunker he talked about. Buy time for his Kuiper Knight pals to run. Set us up for an ambush, maybe."

Fortis shook his head. "I can't see it."

"I can't, either, but I had to say it."

"There are a lot of reasons for Bender to be angry with the Corps and the UNT, but he's not a mass murderer."

"So what do we do, sir?"

"I'm going to call Regiment, explain what's happened, and tell Colonel Feliz we're headed for the bunker."

Fortis climbed into his command mech and punched up the direct circuit to Regiment.

"Command, this is Two Actual. Request to speak to Colonel Feliz."

"This is Hammer. Go ahead."

Fortis sighed. It would anger Weiss if he bypassed him, but he needed direction straight from the regimental commander.

"Sir, I'm looking for Colonel Feliz. Is he there?"

"This is Hammer. Send your traffic, and I'll relay if necessary."

"Sorry, Colonel, but I need the commander himself. Is he there?"

A minute later, Feliz answered.

"Go ahead, Major."

"After my last report, a Kuiper Knight surrendered to 2nd Battalion—"

"You were told no prisoners!" Weiss interrupted.

"Jo, it's okay. Major Fortis, as the deputy pointed out, you're not supposed to take prisoners. Did you not understand my direction?"

"I understood perfectly, sir, but there are extenuating circumstances. The man who surrendered is personally known to me. We served in combat together."

"General Moreno gave you the opportunity to opt out of this mission back on Terra Earth before we deployed if you couldn't tolerate fighting former comrades. Do you remember?"

"I remember what the general said, and your instructions, too. Still, I'm not going to kill an unarmed man with his hands over his head, even if he is a Kuiper Knight."

There was a heavy silence on the circuit.

"Major Fortis, it's now clear to me that you have a problem following orders. If—"

"Colonel, please, just listen to me. This man was a master gunnery sergeant before he went AWOL to hunt down the slavers who kidnapped his goddaughter. He returned of his own volition and took a bust down to sergeant to remain on active duty. I served with him during the insurgency on Maltaan. I know him, and I trust him *implicitly*."

"*Why are you telling me all this, Major?*"

"This man gave me two pieces of information you need to know, Colonel. First, he didn't know about the peace rally attack, and he said most of the other Kuiper Knights were unaware, as well. He's furious at the Kuiper Knight leadership, and I think we might be able to use that information to induce others to surrender."

"*What's the second?*"

"He told me about a cave, a bunker, the Kuiper Knights have excavated on a ridge northwest of my current position. That's where they've withdrawn to. He said there were about three thousand Knights before the fighting started, and we've counted about seven hundred enemy KIA so far."

"*That's it?*"

"Yes, sir."

"*Colonel Weiss, what do you think?*"

"*I think it's preposterous, sir. Major Fortis has disobeyed orders and defied authority almost continuously since he reported to the regiment. This is just one more example of his unacceptable behavior. In my opinion, he should be relieved of command and brought up on charges when we return to the flagship.*"

"*Care to respond, Major?*"

"Colonel, my battalion's had no contact with the Kuiper Knights for over six hours now. I have patrols out and drones flying in every direction, and we've found nothing but bodies and abandoned weapons.

"Now, I have information that might lead us to them in that bunker. I'm requesting permission to conduct a reconnaissance in force to investigate this information. We know there are still a lot of Kuiper Knights somewhere around here, and we can't return to *Mammoth* empty-handed. If we locate them, we'll call for 3rd Battalion to join the fight. If the information is false, we'll continue searching until you recall us to the spaceport. Then you can court martial me, and I won't defend myself."

"Just a minute, Major."

Foris smiled as he pictured the conversation between the colonels. Feliz sounded interested in Bender's information, while Weiss sounded furious. He'd slipped in the bit about returning empty-handed as an indirect challenge. Like every colonel, Feliz no doubt imagined himself as a general. With promotion opportunities few and far between, a failure to aggressively pursue the Kuiper Knights would be a career killer.

"Major Fortis, permission granted to conduct a reconnaissance in force in the direction of the cave complex. If you find them, fix them in position and call 3rd Battalion for assistance."

"Aye, aye, sir."

The light on the comm panel blinked and went out as Feliz broke the connection. Fortis climbed out of the command mech and waved Ystremski over.

"Colonel Feliz ordered us to conduct a reconnaissance in force to find the cave complex."

"How much force are we talking about, sir? If Bender's right, there might be a couple thousand Kuiper Knights holed up in there."

"We'll take the whole battalion, and 1st Battalion, too. Without air support, we can't afford to divide our force again."

"What about the mechs and Bender?"

"Charlie Company is going to have to look out for themselves. From what we've seen, and what Bender told us, I don't think the Knights have much interest in another fight right now. As for Bender, we can't let him go, because there's nowhere for him to go. One of our guys will shoot him if they get the chance, and the Knights will probably kill him, too. We can't give him a pulse rifle and let him hump with the infantry for the same reasons. I guess I'll let him ride in the command mech with me."

Ystremski chuckled. "Weiss will lose his *mind* when he hears about that."

"What's the worst that could happen, he sends me to court martial?"

"DINLI."

"Indeed."

* * * * *

Chapter Twenty-Five

Zerec joined Bacall at the entrance to the bunker overlooking the path that led down into the jungle. A ragged line of Kuiper Knights trudged up the path toward the bunker. Defeat was obvious on their faces and in their body language.

"Blessings of The Master upon thee," Zerec said to Bacall.

"And upon thee," Bacall replied.

"Light of The Master upon thee."

"And upon thee."

"What happened, Brother?"

"I don't know. They started to arrive a few minutes ago. A couple at first, and then this." Bacall gestured down the trail.

Zerec scowled as Kuiper Knights continued to stream into the bunker. Many were wounded, and all were filthy from three days of fighting, but he could barely conceal his contempt for them. By his estimate, they had the Space Marines outnumbered four to one, yet they'd allowed themselves to be defeated and panicked. He stopped one of the returning fighters.

"What's your name, Brother?"

"Brother Ibarra. I'm a medic for Brother Addison."

"What happened here, Ibarra? Where's Brother Addison?"

"Addison's dead. He was wounded yesterday and died this morning. I… I couldn't…" Ibarra broke down sobbing, and instinctively, Bacall embraced him.

"What happened?" Zerec demanded again in a tone that indicated there was no right answer to his question. "We had them beaten."

Ibarra straightened up and wiped his face. "I don't know, Brother. Our plan worked perfectly, and the Brothers fought hard. We intended to destroy them with one final assault this morning, but they anticipated our attack. Their mechs decimated our men before we could jump off. It was a slaughter."

"And now you've led them here."

Ibarra's eyes opened wide. "No."

Zerec nodded at the Kuiper Knights who staggered past them and entered the bunker. "Have the Space Marines forgotten how to follow a trail of dead bodies and abandoned equipment?"

"There's been no pursuit, Brother. The ridge is too steep for their mechs. They'd have to leave them behind if they wanted to pursue us."

Zerec willed his ire to subside, and his pragmatic side took over. He couldn't change what had happened, and Ibarra bore no responsibility for the disaster. He put a hand on the medic's shoulder.

"You did your best, Brother," he said in a conciliatory tone. "All of you did, and The Master is thankful he has such skilled and devoted followers. I apologize if I came across too strong; I'm shocked that the Space Marines were able to mount an effective attack after three days of fighting against you and the others. Now, we must all recover from this battle and double our efforts to defeat the infidels. Please, go inside and see to the men, and let no one speak of this further."

Ibarra seized Zerec in a tight hug. The move surprised Zerec, and it took a long second for him to return the gesture. When they separated, Ibarra's eyes brimmed with tears,

"Thank you, Brother," he said in a thick voice. He entered the bunker, and Zerec went back to watching the defeated Kuiper Knights crawl up the track.

* * *

With a great heave, Bender squeezed his bulk into the seat next to Fortis in the command mech.

"Bloody hell, it's a good thing I never wanted to be an officer."

Fortis indicated the zoomed-in topographical map displayed on the screen in front of them.

"The X marks our current position, and the red line shows the main path the Kuiper Knights followed when they retreated this morning. Our recon drones haven't had much luck following them through the jungle, so we don't know where they're going. Use the stylus and tap the screen at the bunker location."

Bender studied the map for a long minute. He reached out to tap the screen with a stylus two times, but pulled back and shook his head.

"Nah, mate. That's not it," he muttered under his breath. He hovered over a third spot halfway down a tall mountain, and after a brief hesitation, tapped the screen.

"Right here, Lucky. That's where the bunker is."

"You're sure?"

Bender shrugged. "As sure as I can be. I think the entrance is here, at the bottom of this cliff face halfway up the mountain. It's a right nasty climb, and your mechs won't make it. Too steep."

Fortis recentered the map to a spot on the back side of the mountain.

"What about circling around? Can they make it through that way?"

"I dunno, mate, I've never been around that way. If it's anything like this side, I'd say no."

"It's settled then." Fortis slipped on his headset. "Two Charlie, this is Two Actual. I just entered a new point in the tactical system that marks the entrance to the bunker. I want one drone to investigate that location, and another to maintain overwatch on our position here."

Loren answered immediately. *"Roger that, sir. The next drone will be ready to launch in ten minutes."*

Fortis doffed his headset and turned to his friend.

"Get comfortable. The drone won't be up there for a while."

"Comfortable? Crikey, I feel like a bloody tinned fish in here."

* * *

The return of Addison's Kuiper Knights created a great deal of confusion in the bunker. The medics placed the wounded men in long rows in the entrance area and tried to give them as much attention as possible. Painkillers and sterile bandages were in short supply, and the medics were forced to leave many of them to suffer, untreated.

Zerec picked his way through the confusion and slipped unnoticed into the passageway that led to The Master's quarters. He paused at the door and looked, but he was alone. Once inside, he went directly to the bedroom.

The Master hadn't moved since Zerec had last seen him. His face muscles had relaxed, and he appeared asleep, but he still moaned with every breath. The stricken man didn't react when Zerec peeled an eyelid open.

He searched through The Master's clothing, but he couldn't locate the communicator he knew the cult leader always carried. The only other furniture in the room was a rickety table that held a lantern, but the communicator wasn't there, either. Just as he returned to the front room, the door opened, and Fehoko entered.

"What are you doing here, Brother?" Fehoko asked, suspicion evident on his face. "Where's The Master?"

"He's on his cot, where we left him."

"Why are you here?"

Zerec hadn't worked out a cover story ahead of time because he hadn't expected to be challenged, so he responded with the truth.

"I'm looking for his communicator."

"The Master doesn't have a communicator."

"I didn't lie to you, Brother. Why do you lie to me?"

Fehoko's face reddened as he struggled to answer Zerec's accusation. He opened his mouth as if to speak, but he stayed silent.

"Where is it?"

"I took it for safekeeping. The Master forbade anyone from having a communicator, and I wanted to spare him the embarrassment if it were accidently discovered."

"A noble courtesy which I now extend to you." Zerec held out his hand. "Give me the communicator."

"But... The Master..."

"The Master has no need for the communicator anymore, Brother. You know it as well as I do. To believe otherwise is foolish."

After a long second, Fehoko reached under his smock and produced the communicator. Zerec turned it on, checked the battery level, and turned it off.

Fehoko's body language told Zerec that The Master's assistant was resigned to defeat. He gave Fehoko a reassuring pat on the shoulder.

"Fear not, Brother. There are still many of the True Faith out there who are willing to help. Once we get organized, I'll summon them."

"What of the Space Marines? Won't they interfere?"

Zerec shook his head. "Not even the mighty International Space Marine Corps would dare interfere with a hospital ship on a mission of mercy, especially here in the Free Sector. Their mission here is illegitimate, and all of humanity will condemn them if they do."

Fehoko nodded, and Zerec shepherded him toward the door.

"Come, and let us not worry over such things, Brother. The Knighthood needs our leadership."

And I need to find Zylstra.

When they were in the passageway, Zerec turned to Fehoko. "Remember, Brother, no one can know of The Master's condition. Their faith in him must remain rock solid if we're to weather this storm."

* * *

"Two Actual, this is Two Charlie. We're getting the first drone images of the bunker area, and it looks like the prisoner was right. Take a look at video channel one."

The video appeared, and Fortis and Bender leaned forward to study it.

"That's it, mate. We were working on that terraced area when you lot showed up."

"Any defenses? Trenches, pillboxes, booby traps?"

"None that I saw. We weren't up there that long, mind you, and there weren't a lot of us engineers. We reinforced the walls around the entrance, but it doesn't look like they've been working on anything else."

"What's it like inside?"

"The bunker is actually a cave system. There's a large chamber at the entrance, and four passages branch off from there. The two on the left lead to the sleeping chambers for knights, squires, and pages. The one straight ahead takes you to the galley and the knights errant quarters. The right-hand passage leads to some meeting rooms. The Master lives down that way, too."

"Is this the only entrance?"

"As far as I know, yeah. I never heard anyone talk about another way out."

Fortis stroked his chin as he thought about what Bender had told him.

"It seems odd that an experienced infantry commander like Zerec would choose a position with few defenses and no back door."

"I reckon the original plan was to spread the Knighthood throughout the Free Sector aboard *Colossus,* but that must have changed when Fleet destroyed her. We didn't know anything about the cave until they decided to move us up there."

"You've seen it; you helped build it. How would you attack it?"

"I'd send somebody up to knock on the door and ask them to surrender."

Fortis chuckled.

"Nah, hear me out, mate. Most of them are like me. They don't know why you're here or what happened back on Terra Earth. I reckon most of them will be quite angry to hear the knights errant committed mass murder on their behalf. They won't be interested in fighting anymore, especially after what I saw this morning."

"What about the fanatics? The knights errant?"

"Bah, they don't have the hold they think they do. They strut around like a bunch of corporals, high on their own rank, but they're paper lions. There aren't enough of them to stop a full-scale mutiny, especially now that everyone has pulse rifles. If the right words land in the right ears, Bob's your uncle."

"What? What does that mean?"

"Bob's your uncle. Fanny's your aunt. You know. Success is assured, and it's a bloodless victory to boot."

"Hmm." Fortis let Bender's words percolate for a moment. "I don't know. It seems like a long shot."

"Ha! You don't have the nickname 'Lucky' for no reason, mate."

"That might be true, but I've never walked up to a cave full of men who want to kill me and asked them to surrender before."

"You don't have to. Send me."

"You? Why would I send you?"

"For starters, you've been shooting it out with them for three days. They may not be in the mood to trust you. I've been with them for a few months now, and I know a lot of them. I can't guarantee they'll listen to me, but I reckon I have a better chance than you."

"What if they don't surrender? What if they open fire instead?"

"Collapse the entrance and bury them alive. Think of me and splash out a bit of DINLI someday. That's the best Mrs. Bender's little boy can expect, I reckon."

"If you're willing to try it, so am I. Let me go talk to Gunny Ystremski and see what he thinks about all this, and then we'll figure out how to get you up there."

Suddenly, the drone video display went blank.

"Two Actual, this is Two Charlie. I think they sniped the drone again."

* * * * *

Chapter Twenty-Six

Zerec stood over the map table in the operations room, but his mind wasn't on tactical dispositions or counter-attack. Instead, he was deep in thought about how to avoid capture or death at the hands of the Space Marines, and how to escape the planet.

The captured Space Marine battle armor helmet and sleeve he'd instructed Lyle to repair had reappeared on the map table. Someone had cleaned it up, and when Zerec pressed the power switch, the unit came to life. He dialed through all the channels, but heard nothing—not surprising, given the range to the nearest Space Marines. He didn't dare attempt a test transmission for fear that someone might identify him as an imposter, and he'd lose an important advantage.

Advantage for what? Certainly not victory. Not now. Escape? To where?

The obvious answer that kept nagging at him was the tunnel. When the Kuiper Knights had first explored the cave system to judge its suitability as a bunker, one of them had discovered a narrow seam in the rock that led from the end of The Master's passageway all the way to the jungle on the far side of the mountain. It ended above a near-vertical drop into a deep ravine, where a thunderous river flowed. It wasn't practical as an entrance and was quickly forgotten in the rush to prepare the bunker, but Zerec remembered it. He tried to picture the far mountainside and decided if trees and large underbrush could grow on it, determined climbers could traverse it, at least by day.

Zerec was loath to attempt such a climb alone unless he had no other option. A lifetime in the ISMC had taught him the value of teamwork, and he thought his chances were better if he had a teammate working with him. He had few trusted subordinates, and no friends in the Knighthood, so his original plan had been to enlist Addison. Now that Addison was dead, he'd set his sights on Zylstra. His introduction to the heavily scarred former mech commander months earlier aboard *Colossus* had been unsatisfactory, but since then, Zylstra had proven to be loyal and reliable.

He's better than nothing, but will he go along with my plan?

"You summoned me, Brother?"

Zylstra stood in the operations center door. His shirt and trousers were muddy and bloodstained, and his face reflected the strain they were all under.

"Yes, I did. How are things going out there?"

"The Brothers fought hard, and their wounds reflect it. If we had more medical supplies, more lives could be saved."

"Indeed, but we're forced to fight with what we have."

Zylstra paled. "I-I didn't mean to criticize, Brother."

"You didn't. You spoke the truth. This battle won't be won by faith alone; it requires more mundane things like bandages and pain meds, too."

Zylstra stood mute.

"The battle is coming here," Zerec said. "Soon, the Space Marines will arrive outside the bunker, with their mechs and their hovercopters. We'll battle with all our might, but our defeat is inevitable. They'll show no mercy, and we'll all die."

"The Master won't allow it. The True Faith will protect us."

"The Master's dying. When he dies, the True Faith dies with him."

Zylstra gaped, and Zerec went to him and put his hands on Zylstra's shoulders.

"It's true. Something happened in his mind, and his condition grows worse as the hours pass. Even now, he lies in a coma from which he won't recover."

Zylstra shook his head as tears leaked down his cheeks. "What do we do?"

Zerec walked back to the map table. "JJ, I've come to think of you as more than just another knight errant. You're loyal, obedient, and reliable, and I consider you my friend. My good friend."

Zylstra blinked in surprise, and the unscarred half of his face flushed a deep red.

"I'm honored, Brother."

Zerec gestured to the battle armor helmet on the table. "What if I told you we don't *all* have to die when the Space Marines attack?"

"You mean surrender?" Zylstra's expression became indignant. "Never!"

"No, not surrender, Brother. Never surrender. What if I told you there's a way for a select group of Brothers to escape and carry on our work elsewhere?"

"Go on."

"At a critical moment in the next few days, I'll tell you it's time to go. At that moment, you must decide for yourself. Stay and die a noble death or come with me and live to carry on our mission elsewhere."

Before Zylstra could respond, Brother Lyle stuck his head in the door.

"Brother Zerec, come quickly. We've shot down a drone!"

The trio joined a throng of Kuiper Knights gathered outside the bunker entrance. From the jungle far downslope, south of their position, a column of oily black smoke climbed up out of the jungle.

Excited brothers congratulated one of their number, who held a pulse rifle over his head.

"What's going on out here?" Zerec demanded.

The crowd fell silent, and many averted their eyes.

"I shot down the Space Marine drone," the shooter said. He pointed to the smoke. "It crashed over there."

Shooting down the drone was a tactical blunder that would reveal their position to the Space Marines, but Zerec forced himself to smile. "Nice shooting, Brother. The Master will be pleased to hear of your marksmanship."

Before he turned to reenter the bunker, he saw Fehoko staring at him from the back of the crowd. At that moment, he realized The Master's aide would never go along with his escape plan.

* * *

"They've got some shooters," Ystremski said when he caught up with Fortis next to the Charlie Company command mech.

"Indeed. I'm surprised they haven't sniped more of us."

"Maybe they don't want to?"

Fortis looked at Ystremski, who shrugged.

"Like Bender said, they're not all fanatics."

Loren poked her head out of the access hatch. "I've got two long range drones, and a couple dozen tube toys," she told Fortis. "One of the long range drones is overhead here, and the other is packed up. Do you want it launched?"

Fortis shook his head. "Not right now. Captain Stone has patrols out and posted LPs, so we'll know if the Kuiper Knights are approaching. Keep a couple tube toys ready to deploy on short notice, just in case.

"When they shot down the drone, they told us where they are, and that they know we know where they are. We need to monitor the bunker. Just do it from a higher altitude."

"Roger that, sir." The warrant disappeared back into her mech.

Several of the 2nd Battalion staff officers had joined the group at the mech, and Fortis pointed to Lieutenant Vidic, and then to Bender.

"Lieutenant Vidic, this is Bender. He's your new best friend. Wherever he goes, you go."

"I don't need a guard, mate."

"She's not guarding you; she's protecting you. We can't afford for anything to happen to you until we get to the bunker."

Bender shook his head before he extended his hand to the lieutenant. "Pleased to meet you, ma'am. Can you show me the way to the rations?"

When they were gone, Fortis outlined Bender's idea to Ystremski.

"He wants to knock on the door and ask them to surrender? *That's* his plan?"

"It sounds a little crazy, but yeah, that's the gist of it. I'll be right behind him with two companies of Space Marines in case they decide to fight."

"With all due respect to your tactical prowess, two companies of Space Marines won't be enough to dig a thousand former Space Marines out of a cave. Not without air support, or mechs."

"I'm not going to dig them out. According to Bender, there's only one entrance, and they haven't had time to build exterior defensive positions. If they won't surrender, we'll collapse the entrance and trap them inside."

Ystremski stared at the major for a long second. "You're a bloodthirsty bastard all of a sudden. You want to bury them alive?"

"No, not bury them. Trap them. A couple days in the dark ought to change some of their minds. When the rest of the division gets here, *they* can go up there and dig them out. Capture them all and declare a big victory."

"It might work. Who do you want to take up there, sir?"

"Bender, of course. You. Alpha and Bravo Companies. I'll leave Stone here to command Charlie Company and 1st Battalion. They'll have all the mechs and plenty of infantry in case the Kuiper Knights try something."

"How soon do you want to jump off? It's going to be dark soon."

"As soon as possible. If we give them time to think, they might start getting ideas."

"Sounds like a plan. Let me go round up the usual suspects, you can brief them, and we'll get moving."

* * *

The photoluminescence was back in full strength, and the Space Marines had lost their night vision, so Colonel Feliz called a halt for 1st Regiment and 3rd Battalion. The Space Marines set up a defensive perimeter, sent out patrols, and settled in for the night.

Weiss leaned back in his seat and tried to get comfortable. Feliz had begun to feel poorly as the day wore on, so he'd asked Weiss to monitor their situation after the medic gave him something to help him sleep.

There wasn't much to monitor. 3rd Battalion hadn't had contact with the Kuiper Knights since they'd left the spaceport, and the whole operation had begun to feel like a lark. It rankled him that even though Feliz had authorized Fortis' movements, in Weiss' view, the requests were made in an approve-or-else manner. That Fortis had bypassed him and gone directly the commander only added to his ire at the major.

On the tactical display, he saw Fortis had once again divided his force. Half the force remained at Lead Pipe, while the other half moved toward the waypoint marking the alleged Kuiper Knight bunker.

A light on his comms panel blinked, indicating a private call from Feliz. He slipped his headset on.

"Yes, sir."

"Colonel Weiss, this is Captain Thoms. I'm sorry to disturb you at this hour, but I'm calling to inform you that Colonel Feliz is dead."

"What? What happened?"

"A medic examined the colonel, and he said it looks like a heart attack."

"Damn it. Okay, I'll be right there."

By the time Weiss picked his way through the darkened perimeter to Feliz's command mech, most of the regimental staff was already there. He boarded the mech and found Thoms and the mech crew gathered around Feliz. One of the medics knelt beside the body, but the colonel was clearly dead; his face was an ashen shade of purple-gray, and the whites of his eyes were visible through half-opened lids.

"What happened?" Weiss demanded of Thoms.

"I don't know, sir." The captain was on the verge of tears. "The colonel asked me to bring some personnel reports to him. It took me fifteen minutes or so to get together what he wanted, and when I got here, I found him like that."

Weiss looked at the mech crew. "What about you? What do you have to say?"

The mech commander spoke. "Sir, Colonel Feliz told us to shut down and get some rest, so that's what we did. I was in my seat the entire evening and didn't see a thing."

The medic stood. "Colonel, I'd like permission to bag him up and send him to *Mammoth* when the division arrives. The jungle's no place to bury a colonel."

Weiss nodded. "Permission granted. I'm going to go out and notify the staff, and then notify the battalion commanders. It would be best if the word didn't get out until I make a formal announcement; we don't need the rumor mill to get ahead of the truth."

He joined the staff outside.

"Colonel Feliz is dead. It appears he died peacefully. As of now, I've assumed command of 1st Regiment. The staff operations officer, Major Welch, will assume duties as deputy commander. All standing orders remain in effect. Unless otherwise directed by higher authority, our tasking remains the same. We'll secure the spaceport and stand by for the arrival of 2nd Division."

* * * * *

Chapter Twenty-Seven

Fortis had just finished briefing his officers and NCOs when the communications watch called.

"Major Fortis, Colone Weiss just came over the command circuit and announced that Colonel Feliz is dead, and he has assumed command of 1st Regiment."

"What? What happened?"

"He said it looked like a heart attack, but they won't know for sure until he's examined aboard the flagship. He instructed all forces to Charlie Mike and acknowledge."

"Roger that. Did you acknowledge?"

"Yes, sir."

"Good, thank you. Let me know if there are any more developments."

"Will do, sir."

Fortis had to suppress a smile. The tone of the comms watch told him it was unnecessary for Fortis to tell him how to do his job. He turned to the group.

"Colonel Feliz is dead, probably from natural causes. Colonel Weiss has taken command of 1st Regiment. Nothing's changed for us; all forces have been instructed to Charlie Mike. We're moving out in ten minutes."

"What about comms, sir? You'll be out of communicator range up there," Loren said.

"Can we use the drone to relay line-of-sight?"

"We can. It doesn't have an electronics pod on it, but it's got a comms channel. It'll be slow, but I guess we can make it work."

"Then let's do it. You've got all the resources of 1st and 2nd Battalions at your disposal."

"I'll try it, but I don't know if it'll work."

"Do your best, Warrant."

After a brief discussion with Stone about the position, Fortis gave the order to move out. Alpha Company, led by Lieutenant Tucker, took the lead. Bender and Vidic accompanied Tucker to show the way. Fortis and Ystremski positioned themselves near the middle of the formation, with Lieutenant Tate and Bravo Company bringing up the rear.

Darkness had fallen by the time they set off, but they had little trouble following the tracks of the retreating Kuiper Knights. It pained Fortis to see bodies littering the jungle alongside the track, because he knew most of them were former comrades who'd become victims of circumstance. Ystremski took to picking up discarded pulse rifles and hurling them deep into the undergrowth.

"Every rifle we find down here is one less we have to face up there," he told Fortis. "Most of them are shit, anyway."

Progress slowed as the trail grew steeper. The Space Marines slipped and slid as their boots churned the mud and photoluminescent pollen into glowing muck. They didn't encounter any resistance, but they discovered a few wounded Kuiper Knights abandoned along the trail. Medics did what they could to relieve their suffering and stabilize them before moving on.

After four hours of non-stop climbing, Fortis called a halt. He dialed up the drone comms relay channel and conducted a comms check with Charlie Company.

"Are we good, sir?" Ystremski asked.

"Yeah. The relay's working fine. Loren's recalling the drone to refuel at first light so it has maximum on-station time when we get to the bunker."

Bender and Vidic made their way back to Fortis and Ystremski.

"We're making good time, mate. We ought to be there shortly after daylight."

"As long as the track doesn't get any worse, you mean," Ystremski said. "This mud sucks."

"It only gets steeper from here, mate."

Fortis gave the order to move out, and the formation continued their climb.

* * *

Zerec sought out Zylstra and found him in the main hall.

"Brother, what's the status of your company?"

"My men are ready to fight," Zylstra replied.

"Excellent. I want you to send a platoon down the track to ambush and delay the Space Marines."

"The Space Marines are on their way?"

"I haven't received any reports, but it's only logical to assume they'd follow up their victory with an advance on our position. There's only two ways up here, and we haven't received any information that they're approaching from the spaceport."

Zylstra gave Zerec a knowing look. "I'll see to it personally, Brother."

"Not you. You're too valuable here. Brother Bacall is assigned to your company; send him."

"Yes, Brother."

Ten minutes later, Bacall led thirty Kuiper Knights into the dark night and began their slippery journey down to meet the invaders.

* * *

Warrant Officer Loren called Fortis.

"Two Actual, this is Two Charlie. We just saw a small force leave the bunker and head down the track toward you before we lost them in the jungle. Probably platoon strength, but the images are too poor for an accurate count."

"This is Two Actual, thanks for the heads up." Fortis switched to a private circuit to call Vidic.

"Hey, Vidic, ask Bender how long it would take a force from the bunker to reach our current position."

"Wait one, sir." Thirty seconds later, she replied. *"Two hours."*

"Two hours? We're more than two hours out."

"Wait one, sir." After another pause, she called back. *"Bender said we're a bunch of wankers who climb too slow, which is why it is taking us so long. He also said they're moving downhill. His words, sir."*

Fortis laughed. "Roger that, thanks." He switched to the battalion channel. "All stations, this is Two Actual. The drone spotted a force leaving the bunker and heading this way. We'll probably encounter them in the next couple hours, so stay alert."

* * *

Brother Scotty McGuire slipped on his ass for the seventh time as the Kuiper Knights descended toward a suitable position to ambush the approaching Space Marines. The man behind him, Caleb Hammond, couldn't stop, and his momentum carried him into McGuire. They wound up in a tangle of arms and legs, covered in mud and slimy pollen.

"Noise discipline!" Bacall hissed from the darkness at the head of the platoon.

"Can you believe this shit, Caleb?" McGuire whispered as they helped each other up.

"I don't know what to believe anymore, except that I didn't sign up for this," came the reply.

A few minutes later, the Kuiper Knights stopped. Bacall moved along the line and instructed them to deploy for an L-shaped ambush. He assigned McGuire and Hammond to the security element on the far side of the track, perpendicular to the line of march. Bacall himself would be at the bend in the L and would initiate the ambush by throwing a Willie Pete. The Kuiper Knights settled into their positions and tried to get comfortable.

"This is bullshit," McGuire whispered to Hammond. "Did you see the guys who came back from the drop zone? A lot of them were fucked up, and there was nothing the medics could do for them."

"Yeah. I saw."

McGuire continued. "A platoon-size ambush isn't going to stop a couple companies of Space Marines. We might slow them down, but we're dead meat. And for what?"

"What do you want to do, Scotty, desert? You want to go hide in the jungle? There's nothing out there, man."

"We never should have followed Zylstra. We should have gone out the door with Herron."

Hammond didn't reply.

When Zylstra led the Paladin mercenary company in a mutiny and turned Fortis over to the Kuiper Knights, most of the Paladins had joined him. The other mercenary leader, Herron, hadn't joined the mutiny.

"Do you like being a slave, Caleb? Because that's what we are. The Master and all his bullshit promises about Sanctuary. Fuck that."

Hammond grabbed McGuire and pulled him close until their noses touched. The jungle had begun to lighten as daylight approached, but Hammond's face was just a dark blob.

"Scotty, I love you like a brother, but I'm tired, and I'm hungry, and I'm feeling a little sorry for myself right now. I don't want to hear your bitching anymore. Either do something about it, or shut the fuck up and go out in a blaze of glory like the rest of us." He shoved McGuire away.

Hammond's reaction shocked McGuire. They'd been privates together in the Corps, the Corps had divvied them together, they'd joined the Paladins at the same time, and they'd gone over to the Kuiper Knights together. In all that time, Hammond had been a steady presence, unflappable under pressure, and stoic in the face of bad news. With his mind made up, McGuire scrambled to his feet.

"Bacall!" he shouted.

"What are you doing?" Hammond asked.

"Bacall!"

"Silence!" Bacall yelled from his ambush position.

McGuire headed in the direction of Bacall's voice. "Where are you, you miserable prick?"

"Shut the fuck up," one of the other Kuiper Knights said as McGuire passed him. When he got to the elbow in the ambush position, Bacall stood up.

"Get back to your post, Brother," he commanded McGuire.

"Fuck you." McGuire raised his pulse rifle and fired. The plasma bolt caught the knight errant high in the chest. His head and one shoulder spun wildly into the underbrush, and the rest of his body flipped over backward.

The shot startled the Knights, and they opened fire as though Bacall had triggered the ambush. Two of them were close enough to see McGuire shoot Bacall, and they fired at him.

McGuire dove for cover as a confused firefight broke out among the Kuiper Knights. The two that engaged McGuire accidentally fired at some other Knights, and they responded with a volley of their own. Unable to distinguish friend from foe in the pre-dawn darkness, the Kuiper Knights fell back on the old adage that there's no such thing as friendly fire, and they returned fire at anyone who fired at them.

As the jungle lightened, the firing dwindled away to individual shots, and then nothing.

"What the hell was that?" someone shouted.

McGuire crawled out from behind the tree he'd hidden behind and looked around. Bacall's body was there, as were the two Knights who'd fired at him. He hadn't fired a shot after killing Bacall, but someone had saved his ass.

He got into a low crouch and clambered along the line until he reached the position where he and Hammond had been posted. Hammond was hiding next to a fallen log.

"Did you see that, Caleb? 'Do something about it,' you said. Well, I did. I shot that prick Bacall. Now, let's get out of here and find the Space Marines."

Hammond didn't answer, so McGuire prodded him with a toe. When he still didn't respond, a dark feeling came over McGuire. He grabbed his friend by the shoulder and rolled him over. He bit back a scream when he saw the scorched hole where Hammond's face used to be, and he rolled the body back over.

"I'm sorry, Caleb."

* * * * *

Chapter Twenty-Eight

Lieutenant Tucker called Fortis from the front of the formation.

"Two Actual, this is Two Alpha. The point man just reported that he heard a firefight somewhere up ahead of us."

"A firefight? Any idea who's shooting?"

"No, sir. He reported shouting, and then a bunch of firing. It's quiet now."

"Okay, well, keep moving, and stay alert. Put a couple flankers out with the point, too."

"Roger that."

"If we're lucky, the Kuiper Knights have started shooting each other," Ystremski said.

"We're not that lucky. They probably triggered an ambush early."

"At least we know where they are."

Thirty minutes later, Tucker called again.

"Two Actual, this is Two Alpha. We found out where the firing came from. The Knights set an ambush, but one of their guys went crazy and shot the platoon leader. There are seven of them here asking to surrender."

"This is Two Actual, Roger. All stations, we'll hold up here for a few minutes. Two Alpha, have Bender talk to them and see what he can find out."

"I told you they were shooting at each other," Ystremski said.

"Yeah, well, I told you they triggered an ambush early, so I guess we're both right." Fortis gestured up the track. "Do you feel like heading up there and talking to these guys?"

"Lead the way, sir. I'll be right behind you."

Fortis and Ystremski exchanged nods and quiet greetings with the Space Marines spread out on both sides of the track as they slogged upward. Fortis was gratified to see many of them munching on pig squares as they maintained their readiness. Experienced infantrymen understood there was no way to know when they'd get another chance to eat or drink. They might plunge into a days-long battle at the top of the track, so it was best to take every opportunity.

They found Tucker and Bender standing over a group of seven muddy, bedraggled Kuiper Knights who were sitting cross-legged with their hands on their heads. They looked exhausted, and two of them wore bloody bandages on their arms.

Tucker approached and stopped them short of the prisoners.

"These guys claim they're all that remains of a thirty-man platoon sent out to ambush us along the track," Tucker said. "One of them, a guy named McGuire, shot the knight errant in charge, and that sparked a firefight among them."

"Why'd he do that?" asked Ystremski.

"He said he'd had enough, and he didn't want to die for the Knighthood. I guess some of the others agreed."

Fortis snorted. "Loyal to the bitter end."

"He says they know you, Major, from when they were with the Paladins. Does that ring any bells?"

Fortis and Ystremski exchanged glances. "Yeah, it does. Let's go meet this guy."

They returned to the prisoners, and Tucker pointed to one of them.

"Stand up, McGuire."

One of the Kuiper Knights stood. His eyes flicked from Fortis to Ystremski and back, and his face betrayed his apprehension.

"What's going on here, McGuire?" Fortis demanded in a stern voice.

"We were sent out to ambush you. I saw what you did to our guys at the drop zone and decided the Kuiper Knights aren't worth dying for. I killed Bacall—he was the knight errant leading the ambush—and some of the others decided to shoot it out."

Fortis looked at Bender, who nodded. "Bacall was a right prick."

"What do you think is going to happen to you?" Fortis asked McGuire.

McGuire shook his head. "I don't know, Major. This whole situation is so fucked up that I can't make sense of it."

"You were a Paladin."

"Yes, sir. We all were. Zylstra and some of the others decided to kidnap you, and we went along with it. We had two choices; follow Zylstra and join the Kuiper Knights, or follow Herron and get airlocked."

"Herron wasn't airlocked. He and the others are back on Terra Earth."

"*What?*"

"That's right," Ystremski said. "After we escaped from *Colossus*, we took him and his men back with us. As far as I know, they're free men."

"Oh, man." McGuire rubbed his face with his hands. "Now what?"

"Are there other ambushes waiting for us?"

"Not that I know of. Brother Zerec held our company back when he deployed the others to resist the… well… you guys. This is our first time out of the bunker since we moved up there."

"How many are still up in the bunker?"

"I don't know. Maybe a thousand?"

"What kind of weapons?"

"Pulse rifles and grenades. Most of it's in pretty rough shape, and there are only about a dozen battery chargers. No crew-served stuff."

"And Zerec is in command?"

"Yes, sir. He's the one issuing orders. I haven't seen the Master for a couple days."

"What's the mood? Do you think they'll surrender?"

"Hmm… no, probably not. The regular Brothers might, but not the knights errant. The Master would have to give his blessing, and I don't see that happening."

Fortis thought for a second before he nodded. "Okay, McGuire. Sit back down and give us a minute to talk about this." He motioned for Ystremski, Bender, and Tucker to follow.

"What do you think?" he asked them when they were out of earshot. "Do you believe him?"

"Yeah, I do," Bender said.

"Me, too," Ystremski added. "He didn't try to bullshit his way around the Paladin situation, and everything he told us jibes with what we already knew. Unless Bender's a plant."

The hulking Australian thumped Ystremski on the shoulder. "Bloody wanker."

"If there are a thousand of them, and they won't surrender, how are we going to get them out?" Tucker asked. "I don't like the five-to-one odds."

"I don't know," Fortis said. "Let's get up there, and then we'll worry about getting them out."

"What do you want to do with McGuire and the others?" Ystremski nodded to Bender. "We can't let them free-range like Bender, but we don't have enough Space Marines to guard them."

"Put McGuire up front in case there's another ambush waiting for us. The rest can take off into the jungle for all I care."

They returned to the prisoners.

"On your feet," Ystremski commanded.

"We're moving out," Fortis told them. "McGuire, you're going first, ahead of our point man. The rest of you can do whatever you want. Follow behind our rearguard, or disappear, I don't care. Let me warn you about one thing. If you pick up a weapon for any reason, we'll engage you with deadly force. No warnings, no second chances." He made eye contact with each of the Kuiper Knights. "Just don't do it."

The former Kuiper Knights took their positions behind the formation, and the Space Marines resumed the climb up to the bunker.

* * *

"*Hammer, this is Eagle, over.*"

General Moreno's voice on the command circuit startled Colonel Weiss, and it took him a second to punch the right button.

"This is Hammer, Roger, over."

"Colonel, I just got your report about Colonel Feliz. Sad news. Eduardo was a good man and a good officer. He'll be missed."

"Yes, ma'am, he was one of the best."

"Are you certain you can handle the regiment until we get there?"

Moreno's question rankled. *Until we get there?* Weiss kept his voice level. "Absolutely, General. Colonel Feliz and I worked very closely together, and we kept things well in hand. I'm confident the change of commanders has been seamless."

"What's the word from 2nd Battalion? The last time I talked to Feliz, he mentioned the reconnaissance in force of a Kuiper Knight position in the mountains."

"Ah, yes, ma'am, that's Major Fortis. 2nd Battalion took a prisoner after they linked up with 1st Battalion—in direct contravention of your orders, I might add. The prisoner told him of a cave system in the mountains that the Kuiper Knights transformed into a bunker, and Colonel Feliz gave him permission to investigate. I don't expect much to come of it, frankly."

"Why not? It seems 1st Battalion has done the bulk of the fighting there, and they'd know best which direction the Kuiper Knights retreated. Whomever came up with the idea of the Mad Minute should be commended. If I understand the situation there, that broke the back of the attack."

"That was the initial report, yes, ma'am."

"Good. We need leaders who think out of the box. Anyway, Colonel, we should arrive in orbit in thirty-six hours, give or take. Have you secured the spaceport?"

"Not yet, ma'am. 3rd Battalion was approaching the drop zone to link up with 1st and 2nd when Colonel Feliz ordered us to double back. I estimate we'll be there between twelve and sixteen hours from now."

"Okay, Colonel. Notify me when you're ready to receive the division. Eagle, out."

Weiss rubbed his chin as he considered the general's call. He thought he'd made a favorable impression on her when they'd interacted back on Terra Earth, but it sounded as if she had doubts about him as a commander. She and Feliz had been personal friends, so his death might've affected her more than another subordinate.

Irritated, he dialed up the 3rd Battalion command circuit.

"Three Actual, this is Hammer. We need to pick up the pace. Division wants us at the spaceport as soon as possible."

* * *

Zerec stood at the entrance to the bunker and looked down over the jungle that covered the track to the drop zone. Sentries stood watch at various points around the bunker, but he was otherwise alone. He felt rather than heard someone approach from behind him, and when he turned, he saw Fehoko. Tears streaked the aide's cheeks, and his face was pale and drawn.

"Blessings of The Master upon thee." Fehoko's voice was a grief-filled croak.

"And upon thee," Zerec replied.

"Light of The Master upon thee."

"And upon thee. What troubles you, Brother?"

"It's The Master. He's..." Fehoko took a big gulp of air. "He's dead. He died in his sleep last night."

Zerec squeezed his eyes shut. Even though his motivation for joining the Kuiper Knights was financial and not spiritual, he'd come to respect and even love The Master during his time at Sanctuary. When he opened them, he fixed Fehoko in a steady gaze.

"The Knighthood mustn't hear of this."

"Brother, please. I agreed to conceal his illness, but his death… we *must* observe the ritual. Brothers must maintain a vigil over his body for three days and nights, and then the pyre—"

Zerec cut him off with a raised hand. "Do you understand the danger we're in from the Space Marines?"

"Yes, but—"

"But nothing. We can't allow anything, including a tragedy like The Master's death, to distract the Brothers from the fight. Even a moment's hesitation at a critical moment could be the difference between victory and defeat."

Fehoko nodded, but Zerec could tell that he was unconvinced. He was in no mood for reconciliation.

"You'll tell no one, Brother Fehoko." He poked the smaller man in the chest. "This must remain between us."

Fehoko's eyes widened, and his face went white. He wasn't a former Space Marine, and he was obviously not accustomed to someone speaking to him in such a direct manner.

"Do I make myself clear?"

Fehoko nodded.

"Then say it. You'll tell no one."

"I'll tell no one."

Zerec smiled as if to reassure him. "Good. Now, let's not speak of this again."

Fehoko turned to reenter the bunker. Zerec called out to him.

"Please send Brother Zylstra to join me."

A few minutes later, Zylstra exited the bunker.

"You called for me, Brother?"

"Yes, JJ. Have you heard anything from the ambush? I haven't seen anyone return."

"No, Brother. I believe they'll fight to the last man."

"Maybe so, but we need to know how close the Space Marines are. Please send some scouts down the track with orders to report back immediately after they make contact."

* * * * *

Chapter Twenty-Nine

Brothers Ted Mellish and John White tried to descend the track in total silence. Zylstra had instructed them to locate the Space Marines, who were presumably advancing toward the bunker, and report back. The track had been a slimy mess the day before, but it had dried overnight to a glue-like consistency, and the going was difficult.

"How far do you want to go?" White whispered over his shoulder.

"Until we find them. Now, be quiet."

Mellish and White had followed Zylstra from the Paladins to the Kuiper Knights, but they hadn't served together until now. Mellish was a former Space Marine with combat experience from the invasion of Maltaan, but White had come to the Paladins after a stint as a weapons technician on a Fleet destroyer. He'd been a weak link during training at the Paladin headquarters in Burketown, Australia, but he'd met the minimum standards to join Zylstra's company. His tactical prowess was low but he had taken to the teachings of The Master much more readily than Mellish. Mellish allowed White to lead the way down the track. He didn't relish the idea of being shot in the back by an incompetent fanatic with a rifle.

"Maybe we should get off the track?"

"Keep it down, White. They'll hear you a hundred meters away."

White stopped and turned around, and the muzzle of his pulse rifle swept across Mellish's chest.

"Mellish, I'm getting tired—"

Mellish jerked the rifle away and shoved White in the chest. The move caught him by surprise, and he stumbled backwards down the trail and fell onto his back.

"Hey!"

Mellish was on him in an instant. He straddled White's chest and put a hand over his mouth.

"Keep your fucking voice down," he hissed into White's face.

"What the hell did you do that for?" White demanded in an angry whisper.

"You won't shut the fuck up, and your muzzle swept my chest."

"Take it easy, Mellish. There's nobody out here."

"Wanna bet?"

Both men jumped at the strange voice from the jungle. White struggled to get up, but Mellish was still on top of him. Three Space Marines emerged from the underbrush with their weapons trained on the pair of Kuiper Knights.

"Drop your weapons and raise your hands nice and slow."

* * *

Bender smiled at the confused looks he and McGuire got from Mellish and White when they joined the Space Marines guarding their newest prisoners. The Knights recognized Bender, but McGuire garnered the most curiosity.

"You're with *them* now?" Mellish asked.

McGuire shook his head. "Not exactly. We're prisoners. The ambush fell apart, and we surrendered."

"And now you're betraying the Knighthood." White spat. "You're betraying The Master."

"Shut the fuck up, mate," Bender said with a snarl. "Nobody wants to hear your bullshit."

Just then, Fortis and Ystremski joined the group.

Tucker gestured. "These are the guys, Major."

"What are your names?" Fortis asked.

"I'm Mellish, and this is White."

"You just came from the bunker?"

White hung his head and averted his eyes, but Mellish nodded.

"Yes, sir. We were sent down to locate the Space Marines and report back."

Bender and Ystremski traded looks and chuckled.

"You found us," the gunny said.

"What's the situation at the bunker? Are they preparing to fight? Have they deployed any troops?"

"They're sitting tight," Mellish said.

White rose up and shoved his companion. "Traitor!"

In one swift motion, Ystremski grabbed White, threw him face-down, and kneeled on his neck. "Go on," he said to Mellish.

"Like I said, they're sitting tight. I didn't see anybody moving out into the jungle. A lot of them don't believe you'll attack because you can't get your mechs up there."

White squirmed under Ystremski's knee, so he leaned more of his body weight atop the prone man.

"Relax, or you're going to hurt yourself."

"These two were Paladins?" Fortis asked McGuire.

"Yeah. Mellish I know from the Corps. The other guy was Fleet."

"How much further to the bunker?"

"Half a klick, maybe less," McGuire said.

Fortis looked at Bender, who nodded.

"We need to get moving," Fortis told them. "If they're sending out scouts, they must think we're getting close."

"What do you want to do with these two?" Ystremski asked as he stood up.

"Same deal as McGuire and his men, I guess." Fortis looked at Mellish. "I can tie you up and leave you here, you can come along quietly with the others, or I can shoot you. Which is it?"

"This fight is over. I'll be quiet."

Ystremski dragged White to his feet.

"How about you, sunshine? Are you gonna be quiet?"

"Blasphemers!" White shouted. "Curses of the Master—"

Mellish stepped forward and drove a fist into White's face. The fanatic was unconscious before he hit the ground.

"I've been wanting to do that for a long time," he told Fortis with a sheepish grin.

"Tie him up and let's get moving."

* * *

Mellish joined the former Paladin climbing ahead of the point man, and they soon arrived at a spot a hundred meters from the bunker.

"Two Actual, this is Two Alpha. The Kuiper Knights say this is about as close as we can get without breaking concealment."

"How's it look to you?"

"I slipped up to have a look, and I agree with them. The jungle thins out as the track gets close to the entrance. The last twenty meters are open ground. I saw one sentry at a post above the bunker, but I'd bet there are more."

"Roger that. I'll call Loren and see if she has anything to report. While I'm doing that, send a couple scouts around to the southwest and see if there's any room for troops to maneuver over there. I don't want to spring the trap shut, only to watch the Kuiper Knights escape in that direction."

"Wilco."

Loren confirmed the presence of at least one sentry on the mountain above the bunker and the possibility of two more on each flank.

"The resolution's poor, and some of these guys must be masters at camouflage, because they're hard to spot," she told Fortis.

"I'm mostly worried about large troop concentrations outside the bunker. You don't see any?"

"No, sir. No troops except yours, and you're mostly just blobs of heat."

"Okay, thanks. We'll be moving shortly, so be ready. Two Actual, out."

Fifteen long minutes later, Tucker called again.

"This is Two Alpha. The scouts report that the southwestern slope is a boulder field among the trees. Somebody could maybe dig in among the rocks, but it's not a good path for an escape."

"Send a squad that way with orders to move in among the boulders when they hear us assault the bunker," Fortis said. "Be ready to block an escape if they try it."

"What do you think, sir?" Ystremski asked.

"Bender said he wanted to knock, so let's send him up there to knock. I'll go up with him and the rest of Alpha Company; you cover us with Tate and Bravo Company. I don't want to sneak; I want their sentries to report that we're there, but I don't want to give them time to come outside to fight."

"Sir, how about if I go up there with Tucker, and you cover us with Tate? Something about sending the battalion commander forward after some of the marksmanship we've seen seems like a *bad* idea to me."

"Don't worry, Gunny. We're just going up to say hi. Besides, I'm the officer, and I want to go up there first."

Ystremski shook his head and sighed. "If that's the way you want it, that's how we'll do it. Please don't make me say 'I told you so.'"

When Fortis got to the head of the formation, McGuire and Mellish were huddled together with Bender and Vidic.

"Major, Bender just told us about the rocket attack," McGuire said. "Is it true?"

"It's true. You guys murdered over a hundred thousand innocent men, women, and children."

"Whoa, hold on, sir. Don't say 'you guys.' I went along with Zylstra because that Fleet ship airlocked some of my former teammates. I had nothing to do with the mass murder of civilians. If I'd known they were planning something like that, I would've shot The Master myself."

Mellish nodded in agreement. "Give me a rifle, and I'll go shoot him right now. Him, Zerec, and the rest of those lunatics."

Fortis explained what he wanted to Bender and Tucker.

"Their sentries will see us as soon as we break out of the jungle. I don't want to snipe them; I want them to report our approach. We need to get up to the cave to stop the Kuiper Knights from coming out, so we're going to be running. Bravo Company will cover us. If everything goes to shit, take positions along the slope and engage them. They probably have us outnumbered, but they can't all come out at once. Anyone have any questions?"

Heads shook around the group.

"All right, then. Let's do the deed."

* * *

"**B**rother Zerec, the Space Marines are here!" Lyle called from the operations center door. "The sentries saw them climbing the track."

Zerec looked up from the map. He could hear excited voices and feet rushing around outside the door. "Where's Brother Zylstra?"

"I-I don't know. Did you hear what I said? The Space Marines are here."

"I heard you, you damned fool," Zerec replied with a snarl. "Now, go find Zylstra and send him here. Go!"

After Lyle left, Zerec retrieved the captured battle armor helmet and sleeve and placed it on the table. He drew the pulse pistol he'd concealed under his knight errant cloak, checked the charge, and tucked back in his waistband. It was time to put Zylstra to the test.

A few minutes later, Zylstra arrived. He had a pulse rifle in a tactical sling across his chest, and Zerec felt a brief stab of fear when it occurred to him that Zylstra might have decided not to join him.

"You summoned me, Brother?"

Relieved, Zerec nodded. "Yes, Brother. The Space Marines have arrived, and the final battle for Sanctuary is at hand. The time has come for you to decide your fate. Will you come with me and live to carry on our work elsewhere, or will you stay here and die for a lost cause?"

Zylstra grimaced. "It pains me to hear you call our accomplishments a lost cause, Brother."

"Don't misunderstand what I said. Sanctuary was a noble idea, and it still is, but not here, not like this." He gestured to the rough-hewn walls of the operations center. "This cave is more suited to a guerilla war, not a holy war. The Terrans have overwhelming advantages right now. We can fight on in futility, or we can survive to take the fight to them at some other time and place."

"What of The Master? He declared there'd be no retreat."

Zerec put his hands on Zylstra's shoulders and looked him in the eye.

"The Master is dead, Brother. He passed last night."

A single tear leaked from Zylstra's eye, but he remained mute.

"I told you there'd be a critical moment when you'd have to decide your future. That moment is now. Will you join me?"

Zerec tensed, ready to draw his pulse pistol if Zylstra made the wrong decision. Instead, Zylstra nodded.

"I'm with you, Brother. What can I do?"

Zerec handed him the helmet and sleeve. "Put this on and try to listen in on their tactical circuits. Go to the end of The Master's passageway and wait for me. I'll join you there, and we'll go."

"There's a way out?"

Zerec nodded. "I'll show you when we meet up. Remember, no matter what, stay there."

After Zylstra left, Zerec took one last look at the map before he joined the throng of Kuiper Knights rushing around the bunker. He found an open case of grenades and stuffed a smoke and two frags under his smock.

Time to go.

* * * * *

Chapter Thirty

Fortis, Bender, and Alpha Company scrambled up the last two hundred meters of the track and raced for the undergrowth around the bunker entrance. As soon as they emerged from the jungle, the Kuiper Knight sentries abandoned their posts and ducked inside. The whole time the Space Marines were charging upward across the open ground, Fortis' infantry instincts screamed in protest with every step, and by the time he took cover behind a large rock outcropping, his pulse pounded in his ears, and his breath came in gasps. Bender dove in next to him, and Fortis chuckled.

"What's so funny, mate?" the Australian said between gulps of air.

"I was just thinking about how many times I've charged across open battlefields. It's becoming a habit."

"Bad habit to have." Just then, Lieutenant Vidic landed between them. Fortis had forgotten about his instructions to remain with Bender, and he shook his head.

"That… was… nuts," she said between pants.

Bender peeked over the top of the boulders at the bunker entrance. "Now what?"

"We'll work our way around to the side while Tucker and the company cover us. When we get close enough, get their attention and explain the situation."

"What do you want me to tell them?"

"Tell them there's a Space Marine division here because the Kuiper Knights committed mass murder on Terra Earth. If they surrender and can prove they had nothing to do with it, we'll ensure they receive fair treatment. Otherwise, we'll assume they intend to fight to the death."

Fortis told Vidic to remain under cover while he and Bender made a wide circle to the right under the watchful pulse rifles of Alpha Company. They made it near the entrance without incident and took cover.

"Time to do your thing," Fortis said.

"You got a hydration pack?" Bender asked. "I'm a bit parched."

After a quick drink, Bender cleared his throat.

"I'm ready."

He crawled to a position right next to the cave and stopped.

"Hello in there, Kuiper Knights!" he shouted. "It's me, Bender."

There was no response, so Bender repeated the hail. Still nothing.

Fortis scrambled up alongside Bender and threw a smoke grenade into the entrance. Red smoke billowed out of the cave.

"The next one is Willie Pete!"

"What do you want?" came a voice from inside.

Fortis pointed to Bender.

"It's me, Bender. Look mate, there's a division of Space Marines out here looking for the bastards who attacked a bunch of innocent civilians on Terra Earth. They murdered a hundred thousand people."

"That's bullshit."

"No, it's fair dinkum. Why do you think the pricks took our communicators and treated us like prisoners? It was to keep their secret from us."

Fortis and Bender ducked away as a burst of pulse rifle fire stitched the bunker entrance.

"Fuck me, I guess they're serious," Bender said.

"Let me try." Fortis stuck his face close to the bunker. "This is Major Abner Fortis, International Space Marine Corps. I'm here to kill or capture the knights errant who were involved in the terror attack on Terra Earth. I'm not interested in the rest of the Knighthood; you're free to exit the bunker right now. Come out empty-handed, and I promise no harm will come to you. If you stay, you'll be killed."

Loud voices argued back and forth for a few seconds before a man in a blue smock burst out of the bunker.

"Don't shoot!" he shouted as he stumbled forward with his hands over his head. "Don't shoot!"

A plasma bolt from inside the bunker hit the man between the shoulders. The force of the close-range impact of the pulse rifle destroyed his upper torso, and his head and arms spun off in different directions as the rest of his body somersaulted down the slope. Fortis heard more shouts and firing inside the bunker, but nobody else emerged.

"What do you think, mate?" Bender asked in a low voice.

"I think we should let them fight it out amongst themselves before we go in there." Fortis keyed up the Alpha Company circuit. "Two Alpha, this is Two Actual. We made contact with the Kuiper Knights, but there's some fighting going on inside. I'll pop a Willie Pete, and then we'll back off and see what happens. Two Actual, out."

"What's the Willie Pete for?" Bender asked as he and Fortis crabbed away from the bunker entrance.

"A reminder of what's waiting for them if they decide to fight." Fortis pulled the pin and made a perfect throw. The grenade bounced in front of the bunker and disappeared inside. Seconds later, there was a bright flash, and white smoke billowed into the sky.

* * *

Two hours later, they returned to the bunker entrance and tried to negotiate with the Kuiper Knights again. This time, Fortis sent Tucker, Bender, McGuire, and Mellish. The former Kuiper Knights insisted on trying to persuade their comrades to surrender, but their appeals were met with angry denunciations followed by stony silence.

They tried two more times, with similar results. Finally, Fortis called a stop to it. He, Tucker, and Bender withdrew down the slope to where Ystremski waited with Tate.

"I don't see them giving up any time soon," he told the group. "I thought we had something going when they were shooting at each other, but nothing's happening now."

"How long do you want to wait, sir?" Tate asked.

"We can wait all night if we have to," Fortis replied. "The problem is, what if they call our bluff? I told them there's an ISMC division out here. If they come out in force, they're going to find out pretty quickly that we're not even a regiment."

"And we don't have mech support, either," Tucker added.

"So let's get some," Ystremski said.

"Mech support? How do we get mech support up here?"

Ystremski looked at Fortis. "Remember how the mech guys shot down those blue bombers? They couldn't elevate their barrels, so what did they do?"

"Blue bombers" was the nickname the Space Marines had given to the Badaax tactical aircraft they'd engaged on Maltaan.

Fortis nodded. "They dug trenches and backed the mechs into them so they could gain the elevation to engage air targets."

"So, tell Loren to do the same thing. Dig a trench for a mech and elevate the barrel. I'm pretty sure the main battery has the range. Then fire a couple pulse cannon rounds this way to pepper the slope. The targeting won't be precise, but the guys in the cave won't know that. All they'll know is the ground is shaking from incoming mech fire."

Fortis thought for a second. "What if the pulse cannon fire drives them out of the cave?"

"Tell her to trench all the mechs and blast the shit out of the mountain with all of them. Between the mech fire and our own infantry, I think we can handle the Kuiper Knights."

The other officers nodded and grinned at Ystremski's suggestion. It was unconventional, but it made a lot of sense to Fortis.

"Okay, that's what we'll do. I'll get on the horn with Stone and Loren and get it set up. The rest of you, make sure your troops are alert. I don't want the Kuiper Knights to short-circuit our plan with a sudden rush."

Bender elbowed Ystremski. "Good idea, mate. You're not just another pretty face."

"Shut up, wanker."

Fortis contacted Captain Stone and Warrant Loren on the drone relay circuit.

"We have the Kuiper Knights bottled up in their cave, but they're not coming out, even after we told them about the terror attack. There was some shooting, and one of them got blasted after he ran outside so nobody else has come out. I don't want to risk a lot of Space Marines to dig them out, but I don't want to sit here for a week waiting on them to get hungry, so here's the plan."

Fortis described what the mechs on Maltaan did.

"Warrant, you've seen the location of the bunker entrance on the tactical display. Do you have the range to hit it with the pulse cannon on a main battle mech?"

"We have plenty of range, especially if we reduce the rate of fire to allow for more energy buildup between salvos. Range isn't the issue; it's elevation. The barrels can't elevate high enough to shoot up a mountain like that. Plasma bolts aren't high explosive, either."

"That's what the trenches are for. If the mechs have the range, the trenches will give them the necessary elevation."

"Sir, that's nuts. We're not artillery. The automatic pulse cannons aren't meant to provide surface fire support, they're meant to support infantry assaults and destroy enemy vehicles."

"That's what I'm asking you to do. Support an infantry assault from long range."

"How will you control the fire, Major? The gunners will be shooting blind. They won't know where the bolts are landing."

"You've got the bunker location in the tactical data system. Once the trenches are dug and the mechs are in place, enter a hostile track symbol over the bunker and fire a test shot. I'll observe from up here and give you corrections; long, short, left, or right."

"I don't think—"

Stone interrupted her. "We'll get it done, sir. I'll call you when we're ready to go. Two Bravo, out."

Ystremski, who'd listened in from Fortis' elbow, snorted and shook his head. "I've never met someone who works so damned hard at not doing her job."

"Don't worry about it, Gunny. She's a technician, not a tactician, and she's worried that we'll break her equipment."

"So what? It's yours to break."

"Let's worry about it later. Stone's on the job, and I think we'll get some results soon." He looked skyward. "I don't want to be out here all night if we don't have to be."

* * *

The scene in the bunker was tense and chaotic. The news of the terror attack raced through the Kuiper Knights and sparked a full gamut of reactions, from outright denial to outrage directed at the knights errant. The knights errant had seized control of as many weapons as they could and took up positions on the right side of the main chamber. About half the remaining Knights joined them, while the rest gravitated to the other side of the chamber and armed themselves with whatever they could find. Shots were fired, but it never became a full engagement. It turned into a strange standoff; they were on the same side against the common enemy outside, but neither party trusted the other.

Zerec moved among the Knights on both sides in an attempt to ease the tension. He denied the stories about the terror attack and otherwise avoided giving direct answers about what the Knighthood's next move was.

"The Master's praying on it," he repeated over and over. "When he receives divine inspiration, he'll tell us. Until then, we must wait with patience."

Many of the knights, squires, and pages on the left side of the chamber pleaded with Zerec to allow them to surrender. He chided them for their lack of faith but told them that he understood their fear.

"Be at ease, Brothers. The Master will give us his answer soon."

Food and water were in short supply, which caused some grumbling in the crowd. To make matters worse, several of the wounded who'd made it back to the bunker after the drop zone fight had died, and their bodies were decomposing. Zerec almost sparked a full-scale riot when he directed that the bodies be moved outside the bunker, so he changed his mind and had them moved into the galley for storage.

Sentries were sent back out to their posts, but there was no reaction from the Space Marines, who were clearly visible on the slope below the bunker. Both sides seemed content to hold their positions and stare at each other with hostile suspicion.

An hour after the last attempt at negotiation, the sentries watched in amazement as a pulse cannon round sizzled over their heads and disappeared behind the mountain.

* * * * *

Chapter Thirty-One

Ystremski and Bender struggled to contain their laughter as the first ranging shot zoomed across the sky and disappeared over the mountain. Fortis scowled at them before he keyed his microphone.

"Two Bravo, this is Two Actual, that first one was a little long. It went all the way over the mountain."

"Roger, adjusting fire. Stand by for shot."

Fortis heard the next shot land in the jungle somewhere behind his position, but he never saw it.

"Too low."

"Roger."

The next round hit the mountain halfway between the bunker entrance and the peak.

"The bearing is good, Two Bravo. Elevation is a bit high."

Another plasma bolt sizzled overhead and hit low and to the left.

"You're off bearing by twenty meters and low by fifty," Fortis said.

"Yes, sir, the mech shifted a bit after the last round. We've got it back in place. Stand by for shot."

The next round hit the mountain just below the bunker entrance and started a mini avalanche of loose rocks and underbrush.

"Perfect, Two Bravo. Five more just like it."

The next five rounds arrived in rapid succession. The first two shook the ground and sent more rocks and dirt plunging down the slope. The third and fourth straddled the bunker entrance, and the fifth impacted less than a meter above it. Nothing moved, and Fortis keyed his mic.

"Two Bravo, this—"

A muted rumble reached Fortis, and he watched, mesmerized, as the entire side of the mountain peeled away in a giant sheet and slid down the slope. The rumble became a roar as the massive slide collected trees and boulders and built up momentum as it raced for the bottom. A dense cloud of choking dust blanketed the side of the mountain.

* * *

The Kuiper Knights gathered on both sides of the main chamber flinched when the first plasma bolt hit the mountain. Trickles of dirt sifted down from the ceiling of the cave.

"The Space Marines have mechs!" one of them shouted.

The impact took Zerec by surprise, but he knew the Space Marines hadn't brought mechs up the track.

"Impossible!" Zerec replied. "The mountain's too steep for mechs."

"Then what was that?"

Before Zerec could answer, the next round shook the mountain. Somehow, the Space Marines had managed to get mech support, which meant the final battle for the bunker would be short and deadly for the Kuiper Knights.

Time to go.

More rounds hit, and one of them sounded like it landed at the bunker entrance.

"Have faith, Brothers!" Zerec shouted as he waded through the knights errant toward The Master's chambers. "Faith will lead us to victory!"

He'd just turned down the passageway when a five-round barrage shook the bunker. Chunks of dirt and rock fell from the roof, and he had to steady himself against the wall. He heard a thunderous *crack*, and the bunker lurched as if a giant had picked it up and shaken it.

When he entered the outer room, Zerec almost collided with Brother Fehoko, who was rushing out with a cloth bag clutched in his hands. Zerec had no legitimate reason to be there, so he decided to brazen his way out and pepper the aide with questions.

"What are you doing here, Brother?"

Fehoko's eyes widened, and Zerec saw fear.

"I, uh, well…" He held up the bag. "The Eyes of Fate. We can't leave them for the Space Marines."

Zerec nodded. "You're right, Brother. The Eyes mustn't fall into their blasphemous hands."

Zerec had completely forgotten about the Eyes of Fate, a collection of stones The Master claimed held mystical powers. They were semi-precious gems, but Zerec doubted they had any special powers. He had a sudden moment of inspiration.

"Wait here," he told Fehoko as he ducked into the sleeping chamber.

The Master was still on his bunk, but the grimace that had contorted his face was gone, and he looked like he was asleep. Rigor mortis had come and gone, and Zerec was able to pull The Master from the bunk and place him face down on the stone floor as though in prayer. He pulled the pin on one of his frags and carefully placed it under the body. When anyone rolled The Master over, the grenade would roll free and detonate.

He found Fehoko waiting for him, and when they went into the passageway, Fehoko turned toward the confusion of the main chamber.

"Wrong way," Zerec said as he grabbed Fehoko by the shoulder. "Our exit is this way."

"I don't understand."

Zerec pushed Fehoko toward the end of the passageway where Zylstra waited.

"We're going out this way, Brother."

Zylstra had the captured helmet on when they met up with him.

"The Space Marines are coming," he told Zerec. "I've only got access to one of their tactical channels, but they just ordered a general advance."

"That's fine, Brother. Fehoko's coming with us."

Zerec felt around the edges of a large boulder at the end of the passageway until he found the handholds. He heaved with all his strength, and the rock shifted enough to reveal a narrow passage.

"Lead the way," Zerec told Zylstra. "It gets tight in several places, but it'll take us out to the far side of the mountain, away from the Space Marines. Fehoko, follow him."

Zerec shoved the rock back in place after they were through, and they started up the passageway. The sounds of chaos faded as they squeezed along the narrow crevice.

"How long has this been here?" Fehoko asked.

"We found it when we first explored the cave," Zerec said. "The Master directed that we conceal it and only use it in an emergency."

The last part was a lie. The Master had been adamant that the Knighthood would never surrender, and sneaking out through a secret passage was anathema to him. Fehoko didn't register the untruth, and they kept moving.

Zerec saw light ahead and knew they'd reached the end of the passage. He drew his pulse pistol and aimed it at Fehoko's back.

"This is where your journey ends, Brother."

The low-power plasma bolt hit Fehoko between the shoulders, and he went down on his face.

"Why did you do that?" Zylstra asked as his hands went to the pulse rifle in the tactical sling across his chest.

"Fehoko was weak," Zerec said as he retrieved the cloth bag containing the Eyes of Fate. "He wasn't speed or strength enhanced, and he would've put us in danger. Better he die here than jeopardize both our lives."

The two men stared at each other for a long second before Zylstra stepped aside and motioned to the entrance.

"After you." He paused for a second. "Brother."

* * *

When the dust cleared, Fortis saw a few people escape the bunker through the huge hole created by the landslide. A few others followed them outside and shot them down as they fled. Still others engaged the first group of shooters, and a confused firefight broke out as the trickle of escapees became a flood.

"Holy shit," Ystremski exclaimed. "The knights errant are shooting the Knights who are trying to escape."

Fortis looked closer and saw Ystremski was right. Men in red smocks fired at anyone who emerged from the cave and tried to make their way down the boulder-strewn slope or into the jungle near the entrance. Other Knights in black and white fired at the red smocks, but there were fewer shooters on their side, and the reds easily suppressed them.

"What should we do?" the gunny asked.

"It's murder! Give me a pulse rifle," Bender pleaded. "Let me go up there and fight for the Knights who are trying to escape."

Fortis and Ystremski exchanged looks.

"Fuck that," Fortis said. "We'll all go." He keyed his microphone. "All stations, this is Two Actual. General assault. Kill the red smocks and take that cave!"

Fortis didn't wait for acknowledgement before he jumped up and began to climb the slope in large strides. He didn't need to look to see if the Space Marines followed him; plasma bolts sizzled as they engaged the knights errant.

Unarmed Kuiper Knights fell to the ground and raised their hands as Fortis climbed past them, but he was focused on the bunker entrance. A red smock fired at him, but the plasma bolt zipped by harmlessly overhead. Fortis fired a double tap from the hip. Both bolts hit the knight errant center mass, and his body disintegrated.

The knights errant finally seemed to realize that the Space Marines were attacking, because they turned and ran back inside. Twenty meters from the cave mouth, someone tackled Fortis from behind. When he rolled over, he saw it was Ystremski.

"What are you doing?" he demanded.

"Let the privates do the privates' job, Major," Ystremski said as Space Marines charged past them up the mountain. "We can't afford to lose our CO because some religious maniac takes a lucky shot."

Fortis' blood was up, and his first instinct was to push Ystremski away and continue the charge. After a moment of thought, he nodded.

"Okay, Gunny, you win. Can you get off me? You weigh a ton."

By then, dozens of Space Marines had gathered around the gaping mouth of the cave. Plasma bolts flashed out of the darkness, and two of them went down.

Bender dove down next to Fortis and Ystremski.

"Fuck me, but you're a bunch of fleet-footed bastards when you want to be," he said between gulps of air. He looked up at the cave. "Now what?"

The Space Marines threw a mix of frags and smoke grenades into the cave. After the frags exploded, three sticks of assaulters disappeared into the smoke, and three more sticks formed up. After a short pause, they entered the cave, and more Space Marines formed up to follow.

"We wait."

A stream of white and black smocks exited the cave and scrambled down the slope. Waiting Space Marines gathered them together at an ad hoc prisoner collection point, searched them, and then sat them down in rows. Medics moved among them to treat the wounded.

Captain Stone called Fortis.

"Two Actual, this is Two Bravo. What's your status? Do you need additional fire support?"

"Negative on the fire support. We've taken the bunker entrance and assaulters have moved in."

"Roger that. Hammer called on the command circuit and wanted to know. Should I tell him?"

"Affirmative. Tell him we've pushed the Kuiper Knights into their cave, and we're digging them out. No casualty figures yet, but they're light." Fortis looked over at the prisoner collection point. "We've got about a hundred prisoners so far."

"I'll pass that on. Two Bravo, out."

"Bloody hell." Bender stood up and pointed at the prisoners. "There's a knight errant in a white smock. Bastard's hiding out as a page."

"We need to segregate 'em," Ystremski said. "We can't let any of those fuckers get away with it."

"Take Bender over there and get him set up with the NCO in charge," Fortis said. "He knows them better than we do. McGuire, too."

Fortis made his way to the side of the bunker, where he joined Tucker and Vidic.

"Any word from inside?"

"Nothing yet, sir. There was a lot of resistance in the main chamber, but the lads suppressed it. I haven't been pinging the assaulters for updates; if they need help, they'll call. Do you want me to ask?"

"No, leave them to their work."

A line of Kuiper Knights exited the cave, guarded by a handful of Space Marines. Two of them helped a Space Marine, who hopped on one foot between them, and several more helped wounded comrades. Most had bewildered looks on their faces, and they filed to the prisoner collection point without resistance.

Lieutenant Tate approached.

"Looks like we missed all the fun, sir," he said. "By the time we got up here, there was nobody left to shoot."

"Have your company relieve Alpha Company at the prisoner collection point so they can finish the job in the cave," Fortis told him. "Bender and McGuire are assisting with culling the knights errant from the group. I want them isolated, and make sure your men search them carefully." By then, the group of Kuiper Knights captured with McGuire had trudged up the track and took their places with the rest of the prisoners.

Ystremski walked over from the prisoner collection point.

"We found one more knight errant hiding out," he told Fortis. "It turns out they're not real popular with the regular Knights."

Twenty minutes later, Tucker reported the bunker was clear. Bravo Company stood guard over almost six hundred Kuiper Knights and twenty-three knights errant at the prisoner collection point. Space Marine medics tended to another three dozen who'd been wounded in the fighting. Lieutenant Tate ordered a platoon to police up and disable all the weapons recovered from the scene. When they were done, the pile was almost three meters high.

"It's a good fucking thing they didn't want to fight," Ystremski said.

Fortis nodded. "Indeed, but that might change if we don't figure out how we're going to feed them."

* * * * *

Chapter Thirty-Two

Colonel Weiss strode along the row of buildings that lined the tarmac and nodded his satisfaction. 3rd Battalion had arrived at the spaceport two hours earlier and set about securing it in preparation for 2nd Division's pending arrival. It was a far easier task this time because there were no snipers harassing the Space Marines. The battalion commander had arranged for constant drone coverage overhead, and thus far, foot patrols in the surrounding jungle had only found old tracks.

The spaceport was a shoddy affair. Dilapidated hangars housed a wrecked shuttle, some rusty vehicles, and a pile of scrap wood. The biodomes that served as living quarters were cramped and dirty, and the biodome that served as a galley smelled of rotting food. Weiss ordered his staff to clean the largest biodome to serve as berthing and workspace for the division staff and 1st Regiment, and an adjacent dome for 2nd and 3rd Regiments.

Just as he got back to his command mech, the communications watch called him.

"Colonel, Eagle is on the horn for you. Button four."

Weiss donned his headset and dialed up button four.

"Eagle, this is Hammer, Roger, over."

"Colonel, what's your status? Have you secured the spaceport?"

"Yes, ma'am, the spaceport is secure, and we're standing by for your arrival. I've arranged for division staff to share berthing and office space with 1st Regiment, with 2nd and 3rd next door. I—"

"I appreciate the effort, but we're not dropping, Colonel. What's the status of the reconnaissance in force by your 2nd Battalion?"

"I received a report that 2nd Battalion has the Kuiper Knights bottled up in a cave system in the mountains, but I'm having difficulty verifying it because we're having to relay our communications through a drone, and it's unreliable. As soon as I can verify, I'll make a report."

"Why aren't you using the surveillance satellite I sent? It's been overhead of your position for at least twelve hours, and it's comms capable."

Weiss couldn't keep the surprise out of his voice. "Satellite? That's the first I've heard of a satellite."

"I told Colonel Feliz I'd send him a dedicated satellite to aid in analyzing enemy troop strength and location. Did he not share that with you?"

"Uh, no ma'am, he didn't. It was just an oversight, I'm sure."

"Get your staff hot and set up on the satellite, Colonel. You've got troops in contact, and I want the no-shit picture of what's going on."

"As soon as possible, General."

"Good."

"Ma'am, before you go, you said you weren't dropping. Did you mean you and the division staff?"

"Negative. There will be no more drops on Sanctuary until we get the mold situation sorted out."

"Mold situation? What mold situation?"

"You said you worked closely with Colonel Feliz. Didn't he tell you anything?"

"Ma'am, I—"

"The shit you and your men have been marching and fighting through for the past few days isn't pollen, it's mold. Bioluminescent mold. Your science officer submitted some data to mine last week, and mine turned it around to the general staff. Fleet Admiral Schein directed that there will be no more drops, and definitely no departures, by Space Marines or Fleet personnel until scientists on Terra Earth finish analyzing it."

"Fuck." The word slipped out before Weiss could stop it.

"'Fuck' is right. As in, 'Fuck, that was a close one.' We almost ended up with the entire division *in quarantine instead of one regiment.*"

"What are your orders, General?"

"Defeat the Kuiper Knights, secure the spaceport, and stand by. As soon as we get word about the mold, we'll proceed from there. Do you have any more questions, Colonel?"

"No, ma'am."

"Good. Get your comms sorted out and get me an accurate status report most rikki-tick. Eagle, out."

Weiss leaned back and massaged his temples with his index fingers.

Quarantine?

He leaned forward and stabbed the intercom button.

"Get Major Welch, Major al-Sisa, and Captain Manella in here ASAP."

* * *

Fortis gathered Ystremski, the company commanders, and Lieutenant Fuller, the battalion logistics officer, for a planning session.

"Thus far, we've accomplished our mission. We took some casualties, but we saved a lot of lives, too. That said, we now face another big challenge." Fortis gestured to the mass of prisoners. "These guys need food and water. Are there any food stores or drinking water in the bunker?"

"Everything in the galley was contaminated by Willie Pete grenades," Tucker said. "There are three storerooms in the back with food in them, but they smell spoiled."

"What the hell were they going to eat?" Ystremski asked.

"I don't know." Fortis looked at Fuller. "How are we fixed for rations?"

"I'm sorry, sir, but we left everything back in the trailers with the mechs. I'm sure the troops are carrying individual pig squares and hydration packs, but I didn't even consider bringing rations with us."

"No apologies are necessary, Lieutenant. Nobody else thought about it, either."

"We can call back to Charlie Company and have them bring some up," Fuller said.

"That's not gonna work, sir," Ystremski replied. "Not for more than a couple days, anyway."

"We could return to the drop zone."

"Same problem, different location." Ystremski looked at Fortis. "We need to get everyone to the spaceport, where Division can make logistics hits."

"They said we had to be ready to wait for two weeks," Fuller protested.

"That was before General Moreno decided to bring the entire division here. In a couple days, we can get all the food we need at the spaceport."

"The gunny's right. Our best move is to head for the spaceport and link up with the rest of the regiment there. We'll let Bender and McGuire lead the way from here."

"What about Charlie Company?" Tate asked.

"3rd Battalion was on their way to Lead Pipe when they turned around and went back to the spaceport, so we know there's a way through. All Charlie Company has to do is head for the spot where 3rd turned around and follow their tracks to the spaceport."

"And the prisoners?"

"As far as I'm concerned, we've only got a couple dozen prisoners, the knights errant. The same rules as before for the rest of them. Come along with us, or take off, I don't care. Just don't pick up a weapon. We'll have chow waiting for anyone who comes to the spaceport. Speaking of prisoners, have we located Zerec or any of the other bigwigs?"

Heads shook all around.

"They might be dead, sir. We'll have to check the KIAs," Tucker said.

"Yeah, grab McGuire and a couple of the other tame guys and start searching. I want to see their bodies."

Gunny Porter, the battalion communications NCO, hailed Fortis.

"Sorry to interrupt, Major, but Colonel Weiss wants you on the satellite circuit."

"Satellite circuit?"

"Yes, sir. Division gave us our own satellite, and we just came up on it. Channel eight."

"Okay, thanks." Fortis tuned his communicator to channel eight. "Hammer, this is Two Actual."

"Ah, it's about time." Weiss sounded furious. *"I've been trying to get an accurate status on your battalion for the last hour."*

"Sorry, Colonel. We've been a little busy fighting the Kuiper Knights. I was just about to call and report that we captured the bunker. We took a few casualties, but we captured six hundred regular Knights and two dozen knights errant."

"Six hundred? Are you serious?"

"Yes, sir. Most of them don't seem too attached to the Knighthood, and when they got the chance to surrender, they jumped on it."

"What do you intend to do with your prisoners?"

"I'm only keeping the knights errant as prisoners. The rest can stay here or follow us to the spaceport; I don't really care."

"Are you mad? You took prisoners in violation of General Moreno's orders, and now you're going to bring them here?"

Fortis smiled at the incredulity in Weiss' voice. "I don't have enough Space Marines to guard them all, and I don't have enough rations to feed them, either. When Division arrives, we'll be able to feed them all."

"Division isn't coming, Major."

"Not coming?"

"Not right away. That glowing pollen is some kind of mold, and until the scientists can figure out if it's a problem, they're not coming."

"Well, sir, my mechs are towing trailers loaded with rations, so we'll have enough until I can work out a logistics hit with Division staff."

"Why don't you leave working things out with Division to me and my staff, Major? Do your job and worry about getting your battalion down here in one piece."

"Roger that, sir."

"Let me know your ETA when you figure it out. Hammer, out."

Fortis laughed aloud after the connection was broken, and Ystremski cocked an eyebrow at him.

"Everything okay with the colonel, sir?"

"Yeah. He lost his cool when I told him we captured so many Kuiper Knights. He got a little upset when I said I'd work out the logistics with Division. Now, I'm supposed to mind my own business, and he'll take care of working with Division."

Ystremski chuckled. "Always a good time with you."

"Don't get too giddy. That photoluminescent pollen is some kind of mold, which means we're stuck here until the medical types decide what to do about it."

"Fuck."

"Indeed."

Fortis called Captain Stone and instructed him to contact Major Fitzhugh of 3rd Battalion to get waypoints for the path they'd taken to the spaceport.

"Recover and stow the drones, and then get moving," Fortis said. "You've got all the rations with you, so I need you to get to the spaceport ASAP. And tell Warrant Loren good work with the mech fire. It won the battle for us."

"Roger that, sir."

* * *

Zerec led Zylstra to the tunnel mouth and stopped. Vines and undergrowth obscured the entrance and blocked much of the light from leaking in.

"Just beyond all this vegetation is a narrow ledge that leads to the left and right, along the face of a cliff. We want to go right. The left side is a dead end." He nodded to Zylstra's pulse rifle as he tucked his pistol and the Eyes of Fate under his smock. "You might want to sling that, because you're going to need both hands."

Zylstra did as Zerec bade and followed him through the green curtain. He fought to suppress his fear of heights, but vertigo caused him to gasp and take a half step backward when he saw the view. The ledge was a half-meter wide, and it dropped off sharply to a wide river that pierced the canopy of trees three hundred meters straight down.

"Bad time to find out you're acrophobic," Zerec quipped as he squeezed his way along the ledge. "Stay up against the rock face and don't look down."

A single word popped into Zylstra's mind, a word he hadn't spoken in a long time.

DINLI.

He forced himself to follow the older man. Fear made his mouth dry and gummy, and he focused on keeping his breath slow and steady. The weight of his pulse rifle felt like a hand pulling him toward the edge and the long fall to certain death.

Zerec's foot slipped on a patch of gravel, and a cascade of small stones disappeared over the edge.

"Oopsie." Zerec smiled at Zylstra's distress. "That was a close one."

Zylstra had a sudden urge to shove the older man off the ledge, but he smiled back instead. "Not close enough."

Zerec finally reached the end of the ledge. He pointed at the rocky wall above them.

"Now we climb up about twenty meters to an area where the slope isn't so steep. Then we'll keep moving horizontally until we circle all the way around the mountain. Can you make it?"

"I was gonna ask you the same thing."

Zerec laughed as he began to climb. There were plenty of hand and footholds, and the former colonel was soon on safer ground.

"Come on," he called to Zylstra. "It's easy. Just keep three points of contact with the wall the whole time, you'll be fine."

Zylstra squeezed the handholds with all his might as he climbed and tried to ignore the invisible force pushing him away from the wall. The battle armor helmet and sleeve felt heavy and clumsy, and he contemplated ditching them, but there was no way to do it safely until he finished climbing.

He came level with Zerec, and the older man grabbed his arm and guided him sideways. When Zylstra was on steadier ground, Zerec clapped him on the back.

"Well done, Brother. That was the hard part."

Zylstra pawed at the battle armor, but Zerec stopped him.

"Keep it. We'll need it when we get around to the other side."

With that, he turned and began to walk along the brush-covered slope. With a shrug, Zylstra followed.

If he was going to kill me, he'd have pushed me off that damned wall.

* * * * *

Chapter Thirty-Three

Fortis climbed atop a large boulder to address the Kuiper Knights gathered at the prisoner collection point.

"I'm Major Abner Fortis, commanding officer of 2nd Battalion, 1st Regiment, 2nd ISMC Division. We were sent here to destroy the Kuiper Knighthood for their attack on innocent civilians at a peace rally on Terra Earth. More specifically, we're here to destroy *them*." He pointed to the knights errant, whom the Space Marines had forced into stress positions in an area away from the main group. "The knights errant perpetrated the crime on your behalf."

Grumbles rippled through the crowd, and many angry looks were directed at the red cloaks.

"I don't believe any of you had anything to do with the attack. After talking to Bender, McGuire, and some others, I believe you were brought here under false pretenses and tricked into fighting for The Master, Zerec, and others." He pointed at the knights errant. "They're the criminals here, and I intend to see that they receive the justice they deserve."

"What about us?" a voice shouted from the crowd.

"You're not prisoners. I don't know what you are, but you're not prisoners. The only prisoners we took are the knights errant."

The Kuiper Knights traded looks as a buzz of voices rose from the crowd. Fortis held up his hands for silence.

"As of now, you're free to go. You can take off into the jungle if you want. After we're gone, you can move back into the bunker and live there. It's up to you. I have one condition, and it's ironclad. Don't pick up a weapon for any reason. If one of my Space Marines sees you holding a weapon, they'll engage you with deadly force. There are no excuses, and there'll be no second chances. Don't do it.

"When we finish clearing the bunker, we're moving out to link up with the rest of 1st Regiment at the spaceport. We have rations waiting there. I can't make any promises about how you'll be received, but if you follow us, I'll do everything in my power to ensure you're treated fairly. You can bury your dead or leave them in the bunker; it's up to you. I won't expend any manpower for that.

"I've been told that the bunker galley was damaged in the assault, and whatever's in the storerooms is rotting. I've asked my men to give up any spare pig squares they have. That's all we can do until we get to the spaceport. If you leave the area or stay behind, you're on your own. Does anyone have any questions?"

"You got any DINLI?" someone shouted from the back, and the crowd roared with laughter. Fortis laughed along with them, relieved that there didn't seem to be much in the way of hard feelings after the recent fighting.

Fortis shook his head. "No, sorry." He shook his head at the chorus of disappointed groans. "What do you expect? I'm just a major."

He stepped down from the boulder and joined Ystremski and Bender.

"Let's go take a look at the bunker."

The sharp, garlicky tang of burnt white phosphorus greeted them in the main chamber, and long rows of bodies bore testimony to the ferocity of the fighting.

"If you were Zerec, where would you be?" Fortis asked Bender.

The massive Aussie pointed to one of the passageways. "That leads to the galley. Just beyond that are the knights errant quarters. Maybe he's down there."

After a fruitless search, the trio returned to the main chamber.

"Maybe the operations center. The Master's quarters are down that way, too. I've never been there. I was just a regular Knight."

Fortis noted a rough, hand-drawn map spread out on the table in the operations center. It surprised him to see how accurately the Space Marine dispositions were depicted despite the Kuiper Knights' lack of modern communications or tactical data systems.

"They had a good idea what they faced from the beginning," he said to Ystremski and Bender. "If 1st Battalion hadn't held on as long as they did, this could've ended very differently for all of us."

A handful of Space Marines slipped past them when the trio reentered the passageway.

"Excuse us, Major. We're still clearing this passageway. Won't be a minute."

They waited as the Space Marines moved from room to room, tracking their progress by the shouts of "Clear!"

Suddenly, there was loud *crack*, the unmistakable sound of a frag exploding. A cloud of gray smoke billowed down the passageway, followed by shouts for a medic.

Fortis took a step toward the explosion, but Ystremski grabbed his arm and pulled him back.

"Stay out of the way, sir. The medics need to get through."

Two Space Marines stumbled down the passageway, their battle armor peppered with shrapnel. Blood leaked from under one's helmet, but he was on his feet and moving. Two medics squeezed past and reappeared a minute later with another Space Marine propped between then.

"Make a hole. Urgent wounded!" one of the medics shouted.

A Space Marine with sergeant stripes on his battle armor found Fortis and the others.

"Fuckin' booby trap," he said. "Somebody stuck a frag under a body on the floor up there, and my guys fell for it. The rest of the passage is clear."

"Thank you, Sergeant," Fortis said as he patted the man on the shoulder. "Go take care of your men."

"This has to be The Master's chambers," Bender said as they entered the small chapel. He stuck his head into a small bedroom behind it. "Yeah, this is it."

Fortis saw blood smeared on the floor and a large scorch mark left behind by an exploding grenade. A mangled body lay heaped in the corner, and Bender squatted down to examine it.

"This is The Master. I'd recognize him anywhere. Somebody booby trapped his body."

"That's half our puzzle solved," Fortis said. "Where's Zerec?"

"Maybe he's dead in the next room."

They inspected all the rooms along the passageway, but found nothing of interest.

"That's it," Bender said as he slapped the boulder at the end of the passageway with a meaty hand. "It was worth a shot."

A large chunk of rock broke free and landed at his feet. The trio exchanged looks.

"Do that again," Fortis said.

Bender hammered the wall, and large cracks appeared. He slammed and kicked, and the outline of a doorway appeared.

"Let me get in there," Ystremski said. He jammed his fingers into the gap and heaved. The boulder moved a few centimeters.

"I'll help you, mate."

Bender and Ystremski strained for a moment, and the massive stone slid free. A cool stream of air blew into the passageway through a narrow fissure concealed by the rock, signaling that the other end was open to the outside.

Fortis leaned in and took a long look.

"Let's go."

* * *

They moved slowly and deliberately, alert to the possibility of more booby traps in the narrow passageway. Bender insisted on going first, even though the rough walls forced him to contort himself to squeeze through the tightest spots. He stopped many times to examine suspicious looking rocks, but discovered nothing.

Fifteen minutes into their exploration, Fortis realized they hadn't told anyone where they were going. He tried various channels on his communicator, but the mountain blocked all signals.

Finally, Bender called back to the Space Marines. "I can see daylight ahead."

"There's no rush," Fortis cautioned. There was a natural urge to speed up at the end of a narrow channel, which would increase the risk of falling prey to a trap. Fortis suspected someone as sly and intelligent as Zerec would know that.

"I found something."

Fortis braced himself for an explosion, but none came.

"It's a body. It looks like The Master's aide."

After a long minute, Bender shouted.

"I need some help up here. He's still alive!"

Fortis barked his shins and banged his elbows as they hustled to join Bender. By the time they got there, Bender had stripped off the man's cloak to expose scorched battle armor.

"Someone shot him in the back, but the plasma bolt didn't penetrate all the way through his battle armor," Bender said.

"You said he was an aide to The Master?" Fortis asked.

"Yeah, his personal assistant. Bloke by the name of Fehoko."

"I guess someone didn't want him to make it out."

"Oh, shit." While Bender and Fortis stopped to examine the wounded Kuiper Knight, Ystremski continued to the entrance of the tunnel and looked out. "Straight down if you slip."

"I don't suppose you see Zerec down there, do you?"

"No such luck." Ystremski came to stand over Fehoko. "The ledge is scuffed up like somebody climbed around the side. Is he gonna make it?"

"If we can get him out of here, he might," Bender said. "His shoulder is torn up, but not bleeding, and it looks like he got this big knot on his forehead when he fell. Whoever shot him in the back knocked him out but didn't kill him."

"We can't go any farther?" Fortis asked Ystremski.

"Not unless you're a mountain goat. It's going to be dark soon, and I wouldn't want to be climbing around out there in the dark."

"Okay. Let's get this guy out of here. Whoever escaped is long gone, even if there's nowhere for them to go. Fuck 'em, we need to get moving for the spaceport."

* * *

Zerec and Zylstra crept through the dark jungle as they made their way around the mountain. They were uncertain how far the Space Marines would patrol or post sentries, and neither wanted to stumble into them in the dark.

"Let's hold up here," Zerec whispered as he sank to the ground and leaned against a tree. "We'll wait until daylight to go further."

Zylstra sat with his back to the same tree, close enough to hold a whispered conversation.

"Where are we going?"

"To the spaceport, eventually," Zerec said. "I have a contact who can arrange transportation if we can get there."

"Won't the Space Marines interfere?"

"There are ways around their interference. The most important thing right now is to remain hidden and be patient. Eventually, they'll leave."

"What are we going to eat?"

Good question.

"The True Faith will sustain us, Brother."

Zylstra scoffed. "Can we stop with the Brother stuff? I watched you murder Fehoko in cold blood. It's become clear to me that you don't have True Faith. Frankly, neither do I."

"Okay, Br—uh, JJ. I'll be honest with you. I've never bought into the mystical side of the Kuiper Knights. The Master had a small following that should have died off like every other cult that left Terra Earth in search of their version of paradise. The Knighthood survived, not because of faith, but because he understood people needed more than faith. He created the rank system, and the martial aspects of the group grew from there. After the drawdown, the Knighthood grew again because men like you and I were seeking a better life."

"Maybe you were. I joined the Paladins, remember? I didn't come to the Kuiper Knights until Fortis allowed Fleet to airlock our comrades."

"Fair point. No matter the path, your journey led you here. Now, we're taking the next steps. When it's light enough, we'll get as close as we can to see what's happening at the bunker and perhaps find something to eat. Then, we'll head to the spaceport."

"If you say so, Br—er, Colonel."

Zerec found Zylstra's shoulder in the dark and gave it a reassuring squeeze.

"Call me Emil."

* * * * *

Chapter Thirty-Four

The jungle had begun to lighten by the time Zerec woke up. The emotional and physical stresses of the past few days had taken their toll, and he'd slept well past his usual pre-dawn internal alarm clock. Zylstra slumbered next to him, leaning against the tree with his pulse rifle cradled on his lap.

The muscles in Zerec's back and legs protested when he tried to stand up, and he let out a soft groan. Zylstra's eyes snapped open, and he looked around in confusion.

"It's just me," Zerec said softly. "It's been a while since I slept on the ground."

Zylstra stood, and both men stretched out their aches and pains. Zylstra's stomach rumbled loudly.

Zerec motioned down the slope. "Let's go see if we can find some food."

They moved at patrol speed; three steps, stop, look and listen, then three more steps. Zerec didn't want to encounter a Space Marine ambush or, unlikely as it would be, a patrol. There were no tracks to follow, so they moved from one clump of underbrush to the next.

When Zerec saw the jungle thinning ahead, he signaled for a halt.

"I think we're close," he whispered in Zylstra's ear. "Stay here, and I'll move up and recon the area."

Zerec moved at a low crouch until he got close to the edge of the jungle and then dropped to his belly and crawled. It surprised him that he didn't encounter any sentries. He stopped when he had a clear view of the massive hole where the bunker entrance had been. The area was empty.

Fearing some sort of trick, he watched the area for ten minutes, but there was no movement. Finally, he scooted backward until he felt it was safe to stand, and he returned to the tree where Zylstra waited.

"There's nobody there," he said in a low voice. "No Space Marines, no Kuiper Knights, nothing. I think they pulled out."

"Where did they go?"

"I don't know. Back to the drop zone, perhaps, or maybe the spaceport. Why don't you crawl up there are have a look in case I missed something?"

Zylstra shrugged and did as Zerec suggested. He returned twenty minutes later.

"It's deserted. Everyone's gone."

"Let's move around to a spot closer to the entrance and see if we can get inside."

The pair slipped through the jungle until they were concealed in a clump of underbrush ten meters from the bunker. After a few more minutes of watching for any human activity, Zerec stood up.

"I think we're alone."

Zerec led the way as they scrambled across the rocky slope to the cave mouth. All the defenses the Kuiper Knights had constructed had disappeared down the slope, leaving behind a gaping hole in the mountain. A tall stack of weapons stood nearby, but a quick glance told Zerec they were disabled. They entered the main chamber and stopped.

Rows of dead Kuiper Knights lined one side of the cavern. Many of them wore the red smocks of the knights errant.

"The fucking Space Marines couldn't be bothered to bury the dead," Zylstra said with a snarl.

"The Space Marines didn't leave them there."

Both men whirled at the unfamiliar voice. Zylstra brought his rifle up, and Zerec drew his pistol.

"Easy." The speaker, a balding man in a black smock with dirty bandages wrapped around his face raised his hands. "We're Brothers."

After a second, they lowered their weapons.

"What happened here?" Zerec asked.

"The Space Marines blew up the mountain," the man said. "Then they came in with guns blazing and shot up the place."

"They're gone now?"

The man nodded. "Yep. They left last night, headed for the spaceport to link up with their regiment. They said there was food down there, so the rest of the Knights followed them."

"Why didn't you go?" Zylstra asked.

"Surrendering isn't my style. I would've kept fighting, but a Willie Pete blinded me, and the others led me outside. As soon as that major said we could leave, I left. When they were gone, I came back."

"Can you see?"

"Well enough to get around in here."

"Is there food here?"

The bandaged man hesitated for a second. "There's food in the galley storerooms, but it's spoiled, I think. I can't see it too well, but I can sure as hell smell it."

Zerec looked at Zylstra and tipped his head toward the galley. "Take a look."

When Zylstra was gone, Zerec turned back to the other man.

"What's your name, Brother?"

"I'm Brother Williamson." He held out his hand, and the two men shook.

"I'm Brother Cole," Zerec said.

Williamson shook his head. "I can see well enough to recognize you, Brother Zerec."

Zerec's face flushed at being caught in his lie, and he hoped Williamson couldn't see it.

Williamson leaned in close. "Your secret is safe with me, Brother." He tilted his head toward the galley. "Does he know?"

"Yes. Brother Zylstra is one of my closest associates."

"You should know that the Space Marines are looking for you. I overhead them talking about searching the bunker." He chuckled. "I guess they thought I was deaf, too."

"What exactly did they say?" Zerec resisted the urge to grab the smaller man. "What was it?"

"I didn't hear anything specific, just your name, and that they had to search the bunker for you. When they couldn't find you, the major ordered everyone to form up and start down the mountain for the spaceport. That's when I left."

"How did you plan to survive up here, alone? You can barely see."

Williamson chuckled. "The Space Marines were kind enough to give me five pig squares before they left. I figure I can stretch them out for two weeks, which should be plenty of time for my eyes to clear up. I'll figure out what to do after that." He pointed to a small sack by the entrance. "I got the pig squares and eight hydration packs, too."

Just then, Zylstra returned. His face had a slight green pallor.

"The food in the storerooms is inedible. I could almost hear it rotting."

"That's okay, JJ. Our new friend Brother Williamson has offered us his pig squares."

"Wait. What?" Williamson looked from Zerec to Zylstra and back. "I did no such thing."

Zerec drew his pulse pistol and pressed the barrel to the blinded man's head. "Yes, you did."

"I-I-I... yes, of course. Please, take them for yourselves," Williamson said, the resignation heavy in his voice.

"That's very generous." Zerec squeezed the trigger, and the plasma bolt tore off the top of Williamson's head and sent his body flopping across the cave floor.

"What the fuck did you do that for?" Zylstra demanded as he raised his pulse rifle.

"The man was practically blind. He wouldn't make it up here alone, and it would be too risky to take him with us. I did him a favor and saved him from a lot of suffering. Besides, he recognized me, so we couldn't afford to leave him behind."

"Are you going to kill everyone who gets in your way?"

Zerec fixed Zylstra in a steady gaze. "I'll kill everyone I have to." He looked at the sack. "Come on, let's break bread."

"I thought we agreed to forget about all the Brother stuff," Zylstra said as he stepped over Williamson's body and followed Zerec.

"You're right. Let's eat."

* * *

After ten hours of slipping and sliding in the dark on the steep, muddy track that led from the bunker to the spaceport, Fortis was happy to see the ground begin to level out as the sky lightened. The medics had run out of stim-packs to keep the Space Marines moving, and those who'd gone without trudged along in sullen exhaustion.

Fortis didn't like the jittery, chemical feel he got from the stimpacks, but he knew he had to keep his wits about him. Even though the possibility of attack by random Kuiper Knights was greatly diminished, he remained alert to the possibility.

"You need to relax, sir," Ystremski told him after he made another round through the formation. "The Kuiper Knights aren't going to attack us. The real enemy is at the spaceport."

Fortis snorted. "You're probably right."

The column of Space Marines and ex-Kuiper Knights encountered their first patrol from 3rd Battalion three klicks from the spaceport. After a brief discussion regarding how best to enter the spaceport, they pressed on and arrived a short while later.

As planned, the Space Marines and their knights errant prisoners headed for the taxiway in front of a long row of hangers and biodomes. 3rd Battalion escorted the other Kuiper Knights to a temporary holding area at the end of the runway.

Fortis found Colonel Weiss in the middle of a discussion with several anonymous staff officers. He drew up to his full height and rendered his best parade ground salute.

"Major Abner Fortis reporting the arrival of Alpha and Bravo Companies from 2nd Battalion, sir."

Weiss looked like he'd swallowed something unpleasant as he returned the salute with a casual wave.

"At ease, Major." He turned to the other officers. "Let me talk with Major Fortis. We'll finish this later." He looked back to Fortis. "Where's Charlie Company?"

"Captain Stone's leading Charlie Company and the remainder of 1st Battalion here from Drop Zone Lead Pipe following the trail blazed by 3rd Battalion, sir. I expect their arrival tomorrow morning."

"What's the status of Alpha and Bravo Companies?"

Fortis enumerated the casualty numbers among the Space Marines. When he got to the prisoners, Weiss stopped him.

"You do understand you violated General Moreno's orders on prisoners, don't you?"

"Yes, sir, but I believe there were extenuating circumstances that gave me—the commander on scene—discretion to interpret those orders as I saw fit."

"What were these extenuating circumstances?"

"They outnumbered us three to one, yet most of them surrendered without much of a fight. Had we started shooting them, they would've continued to fight.

"None of them were aware of the terror attack on the peace rally; their leadership confiscated their communicators and cut off contact with the outside world before the attack occurred. We didn't find any communicators when we searched them, and I consistently heard the same story from too many sources to believe it was a coordinated lie. I haven't been treating them as prisoners, and I strongly urge you to continue that policy.

"We have twenty-four knights errant we took as prisoners. I wouldn't have kept them, but we didn't find Emil Zerec in the bunker or identify him as one of the Knights we killed. We found an escape tunnel out the back of the bunker, and it's probable he evaded capture that way. I think we can get good intelligence from the prisoners that could lead us to Zerec and any others we might have missed."

Weiss stared at Fortis for a long moment, and Fortis could almost hear the wheels turning.

"You think it's wise to allow six hundred of the enemy free run of the spaceport?"

"I don't think of them as the enemy, sir. The knights errant are the enemy. The rest aren't. I told them they were free to do whatever they wanted, but they'd meet deadly force if they picked up a weapon. None did, and almost all of them decided to follow us here. I think they're as anxious to get the hell out of here are we are."

"Hmm. I'll take your report under advisement, but I won't make any promises about your new friends."

Fortis fought back the urge to respond, and Weiss continued.

"Since you brought up the topic of getting the hell out of here, I have some updated information about that. As I'm sure you're aware, mold spores are one of the major reasons for our quarantine protocols. The regimental science officer conducted some tests on the photoluminescent pollen and determined it was mold. Division forwarded those results to Terra Earth, and Admiral Schein directed that there'd be no exfil for 1st Regiment until a thorough analysis was completed. 2nd Division has arrived in orbit aboard *Mammoth*, and they're sending a shuttle down to collect samples for further analysis."

"Any idea how long the analysis will take, sir?"

Weiss threw up his hands. "No idea. Major al-Sisa completed her tests in four hours, so it might be very soon. Any guesses would be pure speculation. The important thing is to maintain discipline within the regiment. Idle hands and all that."

"Gunny Ystremski is a master at keeping Space Marines busy, sir."

"Anything else for me, Major?"

"Yes, sir, one more thing. Captain Tindal Stone is commanding the movement of Charlie Company and the remnants of 1st Battalion to the spaceport. When they arrive, I'm requesting that you assign Captain Stone to permanent command of 1st Battalion. He's demonstrated that he can handle the job, and frankly, he's earned it."

"We'll see when they get here, Major."

As Fortis walked back toward 2nd Battalion, he had a bad feeling about his request. Even though Stone was worthy of battalion command, Weiss was a stickler for the regs, and the regs called for a major to command a battalion.

DINLI.

* * * * *

Chapter Thirty-Five

Six hours after Fortis reported to Weiss, a shuttle from *Mammoth* touched down and taxied to the far end of the runway. A crewmember in a hazmat suit exited and retrieved a small box containing samples of the mold collected by Major al-Sisa. Then the shuttle zoomed down the runway and disappeared into space.

Twelve hours after that, the lead element of 1st Battalion and Charlie Company emerged from the jungle. They traded handshakes and backslaps with the rest of 2nd Battalion, and Fortis greeted Stone and Loren with a big smile.

"I'm glad you made it safely," he said.

"We're happy to be here, sir," Stone replied. "Where do you want us?"

"2nd Battalion is down there at the end, just past the biodomes."

"What do you want me to do with Gunny Karlsson and 1st Battalion?"

"Take 'em with you. There's no area set up for them, and I haven't received any orders from Weiss. We'll take care of them until he says otherwise."

It surprised Stone and the rest to see the former Kuiper Knights wandering freely, but after Fortis explained the situation, they accepted it without complaint. The rations stored in the trailers towed by Charlie Company's mechs were distributed, and a few hours later, Fortis got word that there'd be a logistics drop by 2nd Division. A shuttle landed, pallets of supplies were offloaded at the far end of the runway by crew wearing hazmat suits, and the shuttle took off.

Gunny Ystremski and the NCOs of 2nd Battalion set the example of how to establish a daily routine for their Space Marines. They mustered 2nd Battalion on the runway for morning PT, and the Kuiper Knights joined in. The next day, the rest of the regiment was there, and even Colonel Weiss had to participate to save face.

Ystremski was a sworn enemy of "make-work," so he put the Space Marines of 2nd Battalion to work cleaning and repairing the facilities of the spaceport. They did a creditable job, considering they didn't have a lot of resources to work with, and once again the other battalions were forced to follow their lead.

"Hey, I have something to show you," Ystremski told Fortis one afternoon. "The lads were cleaning up one of the hangars, and they found something very interesting."

Fortis followed the gunny to where someone had piled some wood against the wall. It looked like the remains of a crate, and the piece on top had some smudged words printed on it. Fortis traced the writing as he tried to make it out.

"MK?"

"I agree so far," Ystremski said. "Keep going."

"Okay. 'MK.' Then it's smeared and cracked, and then, 'G-something-M.' Maybe."

"Yeah. I read the same thing."

"So what's it mean?"

"What was the name of the bomb that was on *Colossus*? The big fucker."

"You mean the planet killer?"

In addition to seven divisions worth of weapons and assorted gear, *Colossus* had carried a single Mark-654 High Yield Ground Penetrating Munition (MK-654 HYGPM), colloquially known as the "planet killer" after the first operational test of a MK-654 destroyed the target planet. Fortis and Ystremski had been dispatched on separate missions to find *Colossus*, and either recapture her, or target her for destruction to prevent the planet killer from falling into the wrong hands.

"That's the one."

"You don't think this is a crate from one of those things, do you?"

"I don't know, sir. The Kuiper Knights had possession of *Colossus* for a long time before the Fleet destroyer caught up with her."

"You were on board. What did you hear?"

"Nothing about a planet killer, or I'd have said something."

Fortis picked up the piece of wood and turned it over in his hands.

"What do you think we should do, tell Weiss?"

Ystremski snorted. "Fuck, no. He's already on the edge of a nervous breakdown. If you tell him there's a planet killer loose around here, he's going to have a melt down."

"You're probably right. Maybe I'll send a holo of this thing to Anders and see what he thinks."

Suddenly, they heard the unmistakable roar of drop ship engines.

"What the hell is that?"

When they got outside, they saw five drop ships lined up to land on the runway. The engines shut down, and General Moreno and a group of Space Marines disembarked from one of them. A swarm of Space Marines and Fleet personnel began to offload pallets of cargo down the boarding ramps.

Fortis and Ystremski trotted over to where Weiss greeted Moreno. Most of the other officers from the regiment gathered around as well.

"The mold is non-toxic and not a threat to humans," the general told Weiss. "I've brought along a load of supplies. There are also field showers for your Space Marines to use, just as a precaution.

"The Ministry of Justice is sending a team of interrogators and analysts to process your prisoners. They should arrive in six days. After you hand off with them, you and your regiment will exfil to *Mammoth*, and we'll return to Terra Earth."

"That's excellent news, General, thank you."

Moreno looked at the officers around her. "Which one of you maniacs came up with the idea of a Mad Minute?"

Weiss frowned and gestured at Fortis. "That was 2nd Battalion. Major Fortis."

Fortis smiled and shook his head. "Not me, sir." He nodded to Stone and Ystremski standing next to him. "That was Captain Stone and Gunny Ystremski."

Morene broke into a wide grin and extended her hand to shake, first an awestruck Stone's, followed by an amused Ystremski's. "Before he died, Colonel Feliz sent me a note about it. That's the stuff of fucking *legend*." She put a hand on each of their shoulders and walked toward the biodomes, and they were forced to walk along with her. "Let's go find a quiet place to talk. I want you to tell me all about it."

Weiss glared at Fortis, who could only shrug and follow along with a smile on his face.

"General, the offload is nearly complete, and the drop ship crews are completing their prelaunch checklists," one of her staff officers said.

"Tell them to leave one bird here," Moreno said. "The rest can go back when they're ready. I'll be along later."

Fortis and the rest stood by and watched four of the drop ships fire their engines and claw their way back into the sky.

* * *

Zerec and Zylstra found a position in the heights above the spaceport where they could observe the activity below without risking discovery. They heard no drones, and they were far enough away that the chance of discovery by a patrol were slight.

For three days, they took turns keeping watch over the spaceport during daylight hours and huddled together in a small shelter they'd built in the jungle nearby. At first, they took an intense interest in the happenings in and around the spaceport. The former Kuiper Knights mingled freely with the Space Marines, and they even joined in during morning PT sessions.

"They don't look much like prisoners to me," Zylstra said.

"They're fools," Zerec replied. "The Space Marines are giving them the illusion of freedom to keep them passive. At some point, they'll be betrayed, but by then it'll be too late."

The pair rationed the pig squares Zerec had killed Williamson for, but half a pig square per day was barely enough to replace the calories they burned moving around the jungle.

"Where are your contacts?" Zylstra asked as they munched on the last pig square. "Why haven't they shown up yet?"

"They can't very well land at a spaceport controlled by the Space Marines, can they? They'll get here when they're able."

"Why haven't the Space Marines left yet? There's nothing more for them to do."

"I have no answers for you. We'll have to wait and see. In the meantime, we need more food."

The two crept down to the spaceport after dark, but they quickly discovered the sentries were numerous and alert. They tried three times to get inside the perimeter, and three times they encountered guards. After the third attempt nearly resulted in discovery, they retreated back to their overwatch position.

"There are no sentries during the day, so why post them at night?" Zylstra asked.

"I don't know. We're going to have to find a way in, though."

"What do you want to do, just walk in and ask for rations?"

That's exactly what they did.

Zylstra worked his way around to the end of the spaceport, as far from the former Kuiper Knights as possible, and walked in. The Space Marines barely gave him a second glance, and he nodded and greeted those who did. He got in line at a rations distribution point, asked for and received a case of pig squares, then ducked between some biodomes and into the jungle beyond.

"I can't believe that worked," he said with a breathless smile. "I felt like all eyes were watching me. The whole time, I thought somebody was going to recognize me."

Zerec returned the smile as he dug out a pig square.

"Well done, JJ." He put his pig square down and passed Zylstra his pulse rifle from where he'd left it leaning against the wall of their hut. "Brother."

The two men locked eyes and laughed.

Not long after Zylstra returned with the purloined pig squares, they watched as several drop ships landed at the spaceport and disgorged a group of Space Marines and pallets of supplies. By the way the newcomers were greeted, Zerec knew it had to be the division commander.

"That's the general," he said to Zylstra.

"Maybe they're getting ready to leave," Zylstra said.

"Maybe they're setting up a headquarters," Zerec said, and Zylstra groaned.

* * *

Ystremski found Fortis two hours after he and Stone had disappeared with Moreno into the 2nd Division biodome.

"The general's not a bad sort," Ystremski said. "She's full of shit, like most officers, but not completely."

Fortis laughed. "Careful, Gunny."

"Ha! Gunny Ystremski is no more. Meet Master Sergeant Ystremski."

"What?"

Ystremski nodded. "Battlefield promotions, me and Stone both. When I told her I stowed away to make this deployment, she almost pissed herself laughing. I had to forcefully refuse a position on her staff."

"That's great!"

"The best part was when she told Weiss. I think he aged about five years when he heard the news."

"Unbelievable."

"I hate to go, but I have barter for some DINLI from the 3rd Battalion guys. The general invited me and Stone to join her for a drink tonight."

Fortis groaned. "There'll be no living with you after this."

* * *

On the sixth day, a shuttle arrived with a dozen agents from the Ministry of Justice. The supervisory agent was a sallow-faced woman of indeterminate age named Bellwether who constantly dabbed at her nose with a crumpled handkerchief. She expressed extreme dissatisfaction at the permissive conditions the former Kuiper Knights lived under, but Weiss surprisingly resisted her efforts to take them into closer custody.

Major Fitzhugh seemed to view the arrival of Bellwether and her team as an opportunity to redeem herself after 3rd Battalion's lack of accomplishment during Operation Grand Slam. She became Bellwether's constant companion, and it wasn't long before 3rd Battalion took over as the primary security guards for the knights errant.

"I'm happy about it," Ystremski told Fortis when they heard the news. "Our lads aren't prison guards, and it's nice to see 3rd Battalion with something to do besides preen for Regiment."

Just then, Major Bishop, the XO of 3rd Battalion, stormed up to Fortis. His face was beet red. He was trailed by Major Stone, who wore a wide smile.

"What the fuck, Fortis? Why did you fuck me like that?"

"Hey, take it easy, Selwyn. I didn't fuck anybody. What are you talking about?"

"Your fucking prisoners. You fucked me with your prisoners."

Fortis shook his head and shrugged. "I don't know what you're talking about. What happened?"

"1st Regiment just received orders to exfil to *Mammoth* tomorrow so we can go home. The dipshits from Justice didn't bring nearly enough people to control all the prisoners, so Bellwether requested that Regiment assign a battalion to remain behind and assist. Now that Fitzhugh and Bellwether are butt buddies, guess who she asked for?"

Stone guffawed, and Fortis lost his struggle to stifle his own laughter. Ystremski joined in, and soon even Bishop was smiling.

"Weiss wanted to leave *your* ass here, but Bellwether insisted," Bishop said. "So now I'm stuck here forever."

Fortis clapped Bishop on the shoulder. "I'm sorry, Selwyn. I had no idea."

* * *

Word of their impending departure flashed through the ranks, and Fortis encountered broad smiles everywhere he went. When he and Ystremski caught up with Bender, the Aussie seemed genuinely happy for them.

"Fuck me, I wish I was going with you. Soon enough, I reckon."

"When you get back to Terra Earth, look me up," Fortis told him. "We're re-opening Gunny Pete's, and we can always use a bouncer."

The three men shook hands, and Fortis swallowed the lump that grew in his throat.

"In all seriousness, best of luck to you, and we'll see you again soon."

"Right-o, mate."

* * * * *

Chapter Thirty-Six

Zylstra had grown more impatient by the day as the Space Marine occupation of Sanctuary went on. Zerec was finally forced to allow the younger man to read the messages he'd exchanged with their presumed rescuers.

"When the opportunity presents itself, they'll come," Zerec told him. "The UNT isn't going to leave an entire division here for long."

Zerec's words were more prescient that he could have imagined. The following morning, instead of PT, the regiment formed up and stood easy in ranks along the taxiway. Drop ships touched down, loaded most of the Space Marines and their mechs, and blasted off. When the evolution was complete, Zerec estimated only a battalion remained. Hours later, he received a message that the flagship had departed. He and Zylstra needed to be at the far end of the runway the following night, ready for a short-notice extraction.

The next night, an unidentified shuttle landed at the spaceport, taxied to the end of the runway, and sat with engines running. Zerec and Zylstra ran up the boarding ramp, and the shuttle raced down the runway and climbed into the dark sky as the Space Marines stared in astonishment.

* * *

After 2nd Battalion settled in for the brief trip home, Fortis sat down to catch up on the news from Terra Earth. To his great pleasure, he read that all charges against Generals Boudreaux and Anders had been dropped in exchange for their retirement at the next lowest grade. It wasn't optimal; in Fortis' mind, they shouldn't have been charged, but the deal was better than facing a court martial.

Weiss was surprisingly subdued during the return trip to Terra Earth. Fortis figured he'd be even more overbearing now that he was the acting regimental commander, but it was just the opposite. The colonel left the debarkation to the battalion commanders when *Mammoth* arrived in orbit, and when they were back on the surface, he barely said a word before dismissing the regiment.

"Welcome home, brother," Ystremski said to Fortis when the formation broke up.

"Same to you. Now, let's go find Sam and get a drink. You just got promoted, so you're buying."

"DINLI, dickhead."

"Indeed."

# # # # #

About the Author

Paul A. Piatt was born and raised in western Pennsylvania. After his first attempt at college, he joined the Navy to see the world. He started writing as a hobby when he retired in 2005 and published his first novel in 2018. His published works include the Abner Fortis, International Space Marine mil-sf series, the Walter Bailey Misadventures urban fantasy trilogy, and other full-length thrillers in both science fiction and horror. All his novels and published short stories can be found on Amazon. You can find him on Facebook and MeWe, you can write to him at paulpiattauthor(at)gmail(dot)com, and you can catch him at www(dot)papiattauthor(dot)com.

* * * * *

Get the **free** Four Horsemen prelude story **"Shattered Crucible"**

and discover other titles by Theogony Books at:

http://chriskennedypublishing.com/

* * * * *

Meet the author and other CKP authors on the Factory Floor:

https://www.facebook.com/groups/461794864654198

* * * * *

Did you like this book?
Please write a review!

* * * * *

The following is an
Excerpt from Book One of the The Sol Saga:

Revolution

James Fox

Available from Theogony Books

eBook and Paperback

Excerpt from "Revolution:"

The situation was rapidly degrading. If they couldn't find the enemy in the sea of people, they could be ambushed easily. Every Marine standing here in full battle rattle was a prettily dressed sitting duck. Two well-placed shooters could mow them down like spring grass. Hell, one well-placed IED could kill half of them and maim the rest.

Then he saw him.

"Aegis, please respond! Multiple IED inbound to your position!"

He ignored the intelligence from CENTCOM, instead clicking over to the snipers' and Manu's channel. "Viper Six, Aegis Actual, need confirmation of advancing targets."

There were others, standing still or milling around. Not moving backward.

The solo man, sliding between people, running forward toward the steps.

Don't do it! Don't you do it!

Twenty meters out.

"Aegis, Viper-Six, confirmed Tango on approach."

Brennan switched active channels, then relayed information into the comms, "Tango inbound, fifteen meters at 155 degrees. Hold your fire!"

Weapons pivoted to acquire the target.

Ten meters out.

"Hold!"

He was right on top of them.

"Hold!"

Don't you fucking do it!

The man reached inside his jacket.

The man's chest erupted in a blossom of red Martian blood. The crowd cleared to reveal a little girl right in front of the man dropping limply to his knees. His jacket draped protectively over the girl, staring dumbly at the hole in his chest.

Then, in horrific slow motion, when seconds seemed like hours, all hell erupted around him.

Protectorate automatic rifles were merciless, boasting upward of twelve hundred rounds per minute. Dozens of spooked Marines, *his* Marines, unable to immediately identify a threat despite intelligence from Command, opened fire. Once one fired, they all did.

Screams rose and were cut brutally short by hot rounds slicing through vocal cords, puncturing abdomens. Brennan could hear the impacts. The *thump-squish* of hot metal ripping through cloth, skin, muscle, and back again in rapid succession.

The front of the crowd was so close that blood sprayed up onto the gleaming white marble steps.

Somewhere from far above him, he heard the piercing cry of a woman's scream.

"CEASE FIRE!" Brennan roared over the comms, again and again, for what seemed like hours.

* * * * *

Get "Revolution" here: https://www.amazon.com/dp/B0CRZ6MZTR.

Find out more about James Fox at: https://chriskennedypublishing.com.

* * * * *

The following is an
Excerpt from Book One of Chimera Company:

The Fall of Rho-Torkis

Tim C. Taylor

Now Available from Theogony Books

eBook, Paperback, and Audio

Excerpt from "The Fall of Rho-Torkis:"

"Relax, Sybutu."

Osu didn't fall for the man steepling his fingers behind his desk. When a lieutenant colonel told you to relax, you knew your life had just taken a seriously wrong turn.

"So what if we're ruffling a few feathers?" said Malix. "We have a job to do, and you're going to make it happen. You will take five men with you and travel unobserved to a location in the capital where you will deliver a coded phrase to this contact."

He pushed across a photograph showing a human male dressed in smuggler chic. Even from the static image, the man oozed charm, but he revealed something else too: purple eyes. The man was a mutant.

"His name is Captain Tavistock Fitzwilliam, and he's a free trader of flexible legitimacy. Let's call him a smuggler for simplicity's sake. You deliver the message and then return here without incident, after which no one will speak of this again."

Osu kept his demeanor blank, but the questions were raging inside him. His officers in the 27th gave the appearance of having waved through the colonel's bizarre orders, but the squadron sergeant major would not let this drop easily. He'd be lodged in an ambush point close to the colonel's office where he'd be waiting to pounce on Osu and interrogate him. Vyborg would suspect him of conspiracy in this affront to proper conduct. His sappers as undercover spies? Osu would rather face a crusading army of newts than the sergeant major on the warpath.

"Make sure one of the men you pick is Hines Zy Pel."

Osu's mask must have slipped because Malix added, "If there is a problem, I expect you to speak."

"Is Zy Pel a Special Missions operative, sir?" There. He'd said it.

"You'll have to ask Colonel Lantosh. Even after they bumped up my rank, I still don't have clearance to see Zy Pel's full personnel record. Make of that what you will."

"But you must have put feelers out…"

Malix gave him a cold stare.

You're trying to decide whether to hang me from a whipping post or answer my question. Well, it was your decision to have me lead an undercover team, Colonel. Let's see whether you trust your own judgment.

The colonel seemed to decide on the latter option and softened half a degree. "There was a Hines Zy Pel who died in the Defense of Station 11. Or so the official records tell us. I have reason to think that our Hines Zy Pel is the same man."

"But… Station 11 was twelve years ago. According to the personnel record I've seen, my Zy Pel is in his mid-20s."

Malix put his hands up in surrender. "I know, I know. The other Hines Zy Pel was 42 when he was KIA."

"He's 54? Can't be the same man. Impossible."

"For you and I, Sybutu, that is true. But away from the core worlds, I've encountered mysteries that defy explanation. Don't discount the possibility. Keep an eye on him. For the moment, he is a vital asset, especially given the nature of what I have tasked you with. However, if you ever suspect him of an agenda that undermines his duty to the Legion, then I am ordering you to kill him before he realizes you suspect him."

Kill Zy Pel in cold blood? That wouldn't come easily.

"Acknowledge," the colonel demanded.

"Yes, sir. If Zy Pel appears to be turning, I will kill him."

"Do you remember Colonel Lantosh's words when she was arrested on Irisur?"

Talk about a sucker punch to the gut! Osu remembered everything about the incident when the Militia arrested the CO for standing up to the corruption endemic on that world.

It was Legion philosophy to respond to defeat or reversal with immediate counterattack. Lantosh and Malix's response had been the most un-Legion like possible.

"Yes, sir. She told us not to act. To let the skraggs take her without resistance. Without the Legion retaliating."

"No," snapped Malix. "She did *not*. She ordered us to let her go without retaliating *until the right moment*. This *is* the right moment, Sybutu. This message you will carry. You're doing this for the colonel."

Malix's words set loose a turmoil of emotions in Osu's breast that he didn't fully understand. He wept tears of rage, something he hadn't known was possible.

The colonel stood. "This is the moment when the Legion holds the line. Can I rely upon you, Sergeant?"

Osu saluted. "To the ends of the galaxy, sir. No matter what."

* * * * *

Get "The Fall of Rho-Torkis" now at: https://www.amazon.com/dp/B08VRL8H27.

Find out more about Tim C. Taylor and "The Fall of Rho-Torkis" at: https://chriskennedypublishing.com.

* * * * *

Made in United States
Troutdale, OR
10/09/2024